Abi sat up and nudged Gideon with her foot. "Gid, wake up. Your mother's on the phone." There was no reply, so she shook his shoulder and put her mouth close to his ear. "Gid, your mum's on the phone. Now. Wake up."

This time there was a muffled grunt from the other side of the bed, and Gideon's arm reached up, his hand grasping at the air. Penny leaned forward and put the receiver in his hand, then grinned at Abi and backed out of the room again.

"Mum?" Gideon grunted down the phone. "D'you realise what time it is here? This better be important." He struggled into a sitting position while he listened to Caroline speak, then froze in horror, his face hardening. "She said what?" he bellowed. "No, of course it's not true…Well, I just know it's not…Hang on…" He nudged Abi. "Abs, turn on the TV, quickly. On a news channel."

I0526657

Praise for Rachael Richey

"I loved [*STORM RISING*]…. The characters…are true to life, with a narrative that is authentic. Her descriptions of the 1990's were spot on."

> ~*Whispering Stories (4 Stars)*

~*~

"I didn't want to put it down….I loved the way the story flowed and the way it was written….Richey very cleverly weaves a beautifully crafted piece of work which had me laughing, cringing and crying in all the right places."

> ~*Sharon Adetoro, British Paranormal Romance Author*

~*~

"Was I hooked? I read this book in one sitting, and I LOVED it."

> ~*Anna at A Wondrous Bookshelf (4 Stars)*

~*~

"The author has excelled herself in *RHYTHM OF DECEIT*. The storyline had me gripped throughout."

> ~ *Sarah Hardy, By the Letter Book Reviews (5 Stars)*

~*~

"Her writing flows with the tension of this tale, hits the highpoints and the plummets to the depths of darkness, pacing perfectly through each transition. Brilliant writing that hooks the reader from page one."

> ~ *Tome Tender Book Blog (5 Stars)*

~*~

"I loved *STORM RISING*. …it was brilliant and unique, especially from a début author, but nothing could have prepared me for *RHYTHM OF DECEIT*. This book is truly amazing and I loved every bit of it!"

> ~*Whispering Stories (5 Stars)*

Cobwebs in the Dark

by

Rachael Richey

The NightHawk Series, Book Three

Cobwebs in the Dark

Cover Art by *Tina Lynn Stout*

The Wild Rose Press, Inc.
PO Box 708
Adams Basin, NY 14410-0708
Visit us at www.thewildrosepress.com

Publishing History
First Mainstream Women's Fiction Rose Edition, 2016
Print ISBN 978-1-5092-0483-0
Digital ISBN 978-1-5092-0484-7

The NightHawk Series, Book Three
Published in the United States of America

Dedication

To my great friends, Alison and Jill,
who've gamely read all my books
in their unedited state,
yet apparently still enjoyed them.

Rachael Richey's NightHawk Series
available from The Wild Rose Press, Inc.

Book One: *Storm Rising*
Book Two: *Rhythm of Deceit*
Book Three: *Cobwebs in the Dark*
Book Four: *The Girl in the Painting*
Please note:
The author may add further titles to this series,
so watch for more!

Chapter 1

Saturday 18th April, 2009

Dear Natasha,
Your letter has been passed to me by the son of
Maureen Holmes, who herself sadly passed away some
years ago. I believe my brother is the "Billy the farm
hand" you refer to. I vaguely remember some story
back in my childhood, about twin girls who stayed at
the farm one summer, and my brother made friends
with them. I also remember he was very sad for a time
after they left. I never knew the reason why. It was
fascinating to hear that these twins were your
grandmother and great-aunt. Yes, my brother is still
alive, but unfortunately he emigrated to New Zealand
back in 1955, and I haven't seen him since. Obviously
we still keep in touch with Christmas cards, but that's
all the contact I have with him. He married out there
and had quite a large family. His wife died about two
years ago. Maybe you would care to write to him, so I
have enclosed his address at the end of this letter. It
was lovely to hear from you, my dear, and I hope you
can tell him some more about his old friends…
Natasha lowered the sheet of notepaper, her eyes
shining. She had finally found Billy. She glanced down
at the bottom of the letter to make sure the address had
been included, folded it carefully, replaced it in the

envelope, and laid it on her bedside table. Then, with a little wriggle of excitement, she skipped over to the door and made her way noisily down the polished wooden staircase. At the bottom she turned right into the large bright kitchen, where her mother was sitting at the long pine table sipping tea and chatting to a smiling blonde woman with a scattering of freckles on her nose.

"Judy! I didn't know you'd arrived." Natasha beamed and ran over to give her a hug.

Judy laughed and planted a kiss on Natasha's cheek. "Hello, pet. Yes, I arrived about twenty minutes ago. Abi and I are having a good catch up."

Natasha's mother grinned over at her friend. "A well overdue catch up," she said, nodding to the other side of the room. "Have you looked over there, Tash?"

A Moses basket was lying on the floor in front of the large window, and Natasha gave a little squeak and ran over to peer inside.

"Oh, she's gorgeous!" she breathed as she gazed down on the latest addition to Judy's family, four-week-old Miriam. "Can I hold her?"

Abi laughed. "Not now, Tasha, she's sleeping. Which, according to Judy and Robert, she doesn't do very much. Let's wait until she wakes up."

"Oh, yes, please don't wake her yet." Judy sighed. "This is the longest she's slept since she was born. The Cornish air must be good for her."

"Are Tommy and Sabrina in the conservatory with Ollie?" Natasha asked, standing and moving towards the door.

"No, they decided to go outside and help the men put up the marquee." Judy shook her head. "They might appreciate your help."

Natasha giggled and disappeared through the door, remembering to close it quietly lest she wake the sleeping baby.

Abi grinned over at Judy. "Oh, Judy, this is wonderful. I've missed you so much. It's been far too long. I'm so glad you could make it for the party."

Judy reached across the table and gave her hand a squeeze. "I wouldn't have missed it for the world," she said firmly. "It's not every day your best friend turns thirty." She glanced over at the window. "And it looks like you might be lucky with the weather, too. It only needs to hold off raining until midnight…"

"One thirty, actually," interjected Abi with a grin. "I was born at one thirty in the morning, so technically I won't be thirty until then."

Judy tutted. "You can't put off the evil moment," she said with a laugh. "You'll still get the bumps at midnight."

Abi squeaked in horror. "No way," she stated. "I am not having the bumps. No one's done that to me since I was twelve."

Judy shook her head knowingly. "Well, you'd better take that up with Gideon—I believe he has plans."

Abi's husband Gideon was the lead singer of the grunge band NightHawk, who were just about to start their comeback tour. In a couple of weeks they would be heading off to Australia and New Zealand and had managed to fit Abi's birthday party into a break in the rehearsing. She sighed and sat back in her chair.

"I can't believe I'm this old," she moaned, pushing her long, dark auburn hair back over her shoulders. "Do I look it?"

"You still look fifteen to me," Judy pronounced with a whimsical smile, "and if you're anything like me, you probably still feel it."

Abi grinned. "I think I've grown up a bit since then," she objected. "At least I hope so. Just hope Tasha doesn't make my mistakes. I hate the fact that she's a teenager now."

Judy looked serious for a moment. "Abi, Tasha is nothing like you in that way," she said earnestly. "You have nothing to worry about there. She might look like you, but she's got more common sense in her little finger than you ever had in your whole body. She suffered because of your mistakes just like you did; she's not going to repeat them."

Abi frowned. "Steady on. You make me sound completely dreadful. I was just a bit high maintenance and…" She tailed off as Judy finished the sentence.

"And cocky and strong-willed and a complete nightmare." Judy laughed. "But don't worry; you've matured nicely."

Abi picked up a tea towel and threw it at her. "Hey, you're supposed to be my best friend," she objected, trying not to laugh. "I'm lovely now. A paragon of virtue."

Judy chuckled and threw the tea towel back. "Hope not. That sounds far too boring," she retorted, getting to her feet and stretching. "Shall we go and see how the guys are doing with the marquee? I need to make the most of the time Miriam's asleep."

The large garden overlooking the long sweep of Sennen Cove was a hive of activity, and Abi and Judy stood in the doorway of the conservatory watching in amusement. A huge marquee was being erected in the centre of the garden under the direction of both Gideon and Judy's husband Robert, who were beginning to appear slightly harassed by the unsolicited help supplied by the younger generation. Abi's two-year-old son Oliver was holding tightly to his father's leg and attempting to climb onto his foot, and Judy's older two children, six-year-old Tommy and four-year-old Sabrina, were swinging around one of the supporting poles, singing lustily. Natasha had just joined them and was almost doubled up with laughter at the sight of her father's face.

Abi grinned and leaned towards Judy. "Shall we rescue them, or leave them to their fate?" she asked pensively.

Judy chuckled. "Leave them to their fate," she said at once. "It's your birthday—or nearly. You shouldn't have to help. Let's go and open the wine."

****

"Caroline, if we don't leave right now, we're not going to arrive in time for the party!" Roger Hawk called to his wife and drummed his fingers impatiently on the roof of the Volvo. "What on earth are you doing anyway?" He stared as his wife appeared at the front door, several large tins balanced precariously in her arms. With a sigh he darted forward and relieved her of the top one just before it toppled onto the driveway. "Really?" he muttered, frowning at her. "More cakes? Surely they'll have enough?"

Caroline bustled past him and deposited her armful on the back seat. "You can never have too many cakes," she replied, opening the front door and sliding gracefully into the passenger seat. "Now come on, let's get going. We don't want to miss the start."

With an incredulous glance at his wife, Roger pulled the front door shut and climbed into the car. Caroline had made herself comfortable and was already making inroads on the tin of boiled sweets they kept in the glove compartment.

Roger grinned at her. "Caroline you're impossible," he stated affectionately.

"You wouldn't want me any other way." She settled back in her seat with a smile.

The journey from Hampshire to Cornwall progressed uneventfully, but when they finally crossed the border into the county, just east of Launceston, Caroline frowned and turned to Roger.

"What d'you think happened to Simon?" she asked, apropos of nothing. "Really, I mean, not the official story. Do you really think he got washed out to sea that night?" She shivered as her mind flashed back to the dreadful day, the previous summer, when Simon Dean, the unhinged former drummer of Gideon's band, had attempted to kill Abi and Natasha in South Wales.

Roger glanced at her in surprise, his eyes narrowed. "Whatever made you think of him, and what do you mean, *really*?" he asked.

Caroline shifted in her seat impatiently. "You know very well what I mean," she said sharply. "It was reported that he drowned and got washed out to sea, but I think we both know that may not be the case. Whenever we see Gideon and Abi I think of him, and I just wondered what you really think?"

Roger was silent for a moment. "I think he's alive," he said finally. "I'm not sure how he did it, but I believe he managed to cross the causeway after high tide without being spotted, and he's been lying low ever since." He paused and glanced sideways at his wife. "Gideon thinks the same."

Caroline pursed her lips. "Hmmm… So where can he be now?" she mused. "It could hardly be possible for him to leave the country. He'd be spotted." Roger didn't respond, and Caroline turned to him. "Roger? How could he leave the country? I'm sure the police were alerted to watch out for him."

"There are lots of ways," Roger said at last. "I suspect they're not keeping quite as close a watch now because the main consensus of opinion is that he drowned—but he could always be using a false passport, and a disguise."

Caroline peered suspiciously at him. "You know something, don't you? Roger, what d'you know? If that man is still at large, Abi and Tasha could be in danger…"

Roger put out a hand and gently patted Caroline's arm. "He won't do anything else," he said firmly. "He couldn't possibly risk that. But you're right, I do know something. Someone fitting Simon's description was seen to enter Seattle some months back." He paused again as Caroline caught her breath. "He wasn't travelling under his own name, and of course my informant may have been mistaken, but I think it's safe to say he's probably still alive."

"Does Gideon know?" Caroline asked, her face anxious.

"Yes." Roger nodded. "I thought he should be told. Apparently both he and Abi have never believed Simon drowned, so he wasn't very surprised. Angry still, and very keen I try to keep tabs on him, but not surprised."

"Honestly, Roger you might have told me,"

Caroline complained, leaning back in her seat. "Don't you think I want to know these things too? When my family is in danger—"

"They're not in danger now," Roger interrupted her firmly. "I told Gideon because it was his wife that Simon tried to kill, and anyway, you know I'm not really supposed to talk about information I get from my government contacts. You didn't really need to know."

Caroline fixed him with a baleful stare. "Anything that involves a member of my family getting shot at is something I need to know," she said firmly. "In future, Roger, you will tell me everything you find out about Simon, even if you risk getting into trouble over it," and she folded her arms and stared out of the window.

Roger smiled to himself and let her fume in silence.

****

Abi sighed, kicked off her very high heels, and slumped down onto the sofa. She closed her eyes and wriggled into a more comfortable position.

"That was the best party ever," she said in satisfaction. "Even having the bumps was fun." A giggle made her open her eyes to find Natasha curled up in a chair, grinning at her. "Are you still up?" she asked, smiling back. "Aren't you shattered? It's nearly four o'clock."

Natasha wriggled forward in her seat. "I'm not going to bed till you and Dad do," she stated firmly. "This is the first grown-up party I've ever been to, and I plan to make the most of it. Besides, even Grandma and Grandpa are still up." She nodded towards the conservatory, where Roger and Caroline were deep in animated conversation with Charles and Justin, the other two members of NightHawk.

Abi peered at her suspiciously. "You haven't been drinking, have you?" she asked, attempting to muster up a "responsible mother" tone.

"'Course not!" Natasha said indignantly. "Well, just some of that fruity punchy stuff. Earlier. Justin gave me some. Is that okay?"

Abi rolled her eyes. "Apart from the fact that it's full of vodka? I shall have words with him."

"Words with who about what?" asked Judy, bouncing down onto the sofa next to her friend.

Abi smiled sleepily at her. "Justin," she replied, glancing over at him. "Apparently he gave Tasha some punch. Are all drummers not to be trusted?"

Judy giggled and kicked her shoes off across the room. "If that's the worst thing he does, then he's fine in my eyes," she remarked.

Natasha sat forward in her chair and frowned at them. "Justin is very nice," she said. "And he is *nothing* like Simon." Her voice broke as she mentioned the name of the band's erstwhile drummer. Natasha had been badly affected by the experiences of the previous summer, and she suddenly got to her feet, squeezed herself onto the sofa between Abi and Judy, and cuddled up to them. "He's quite different," she reiterated. "You can trust him."

Abi glanced down at her fondly and dropped a light kiss on her curly head.

"I know, sweetie," she said. "I know he is. He seems very nice. But you still shouldn't be drinking alcohol."

Judy chuckled and squeezed Natasha's hand. "Don't listen to her, pet," she teased. "One drink won't hurt you. It's a special occasion. Not many thirteen-year-olds get to see their mother turn thirty."

Abi tutted as she reached over and slapped Judy's hand. "Stop undermining me," she protested mildly. She looked down at Natasha, adding with mock severity, "Don't make a habit of it, okay?"

Natasha looked up at her under long lashes and nodded demurely. "'Course not. I'm not stupid," she replied with a smile. She wriggled a little closer to her mother and bit her lip. "Mum...can I tell you something?"

Abi looked concerned at her change in tone. "Of course. What's wrong?"

"Nothing's wrong." Natasha shook her head. "It's just that...well, I've found something out." She paused and Abi looked down at her inquiringly. "It's 'bout Billy. Billy the farm hand," she added for further clarification.

Abi frowned. "Billy the farm hand?" she asked puzzled. "Who d'you mean?"

Natasha rolled her eyes, then glanced sideways at Judy, remembering they were not alone. "Doesn't matter," she muttered. "I'll tell you tomorrow," and she jumped to her feet and skipped into the conservatory to join her grandparents.

Abi stared after her, a slight frown creasing her forehead. She'd realised who Natasha was talking about and wondered what she'd found out.

Judy put her hand on Abi's arm. "Was that something secret?" she inquired curiously. "Tash clammed up when she remembered I was here."

Abi sighed and glanced round at her. "Yeah, I guess," she said. "Well, she thinks it is, anyway.

Something to do with that stuff we found out about my mum last summer."

Judy nodded. "The stuff you shouldn't have told me," she said with a smile. "Doesn't Tash know that I know?"

"Oh, I may have mentioned it in passing," Abi said with a grimace. "She probably wasn't listening. She ought to know I tell you everything, though," and she giggled like a teenager. Judy joined in, and when Gideon joined them a few minutes later, the two friends were almost rolling on the sofa in hysterics. He stared at them in surprise.

"That punch must have been strong," he remarked, catching his wife by the hand and pulling her to her feet. She swayed and fell forward to lean against him. He looked down at her and grinned. "Happy birthday, babe," he murmured as he bent his head and kissed her roughly on the lips. She snaked her arms up around his neck and pressed her body closer to his.

"I love you, Gid," she whispered, "and thank you for the best party ever."

Behind her, Judy struggled up from the sofa as the distant sound of a crying baby reached their ears. "There she goes," she grunted. "Not too bad tonight. At least I'm still up," and she gathered up her shoes from beneath the coffee table and headed off in the direction of the spare bedroom.

Gideon grinned at Abi. "What were you and Judy laughing at?" he asked quizzically, pulling her down onto the sofa and putting his arm around her shoulders. Abi slithered down, laid her head on his knee, and curled her legs up onto the cushions. "Dunno, really," she said, closing her eyes and trying to remember. "Oh, yeah. It started 'cause Tasha said she'd found something out about Billy, Billy the farm hand." She looked up at Gideon. "You know, from the diaries?" He nodded. "Then she realised Judy was here, so she went off, and I was just telling Judy that I thought Tasha knew that *she* knew—and for some reason we got the giggles." She wriggled her head on his knees and looked up at him solemnly. "It's good to laugh."

Gideon grinned at her and leant forward, his long dark hair swinging over his shoulders. "It certainly is," he agreed, tweaking her nose with his thumb. "Don't ever stop. So you don't know what Tash found out, then?"

Abi shook her head. "No," she said with a slight frown. "I thought we'd decided not to pursue him. The less people who know the whole story the better, but I know Tasha has always had the romantic idea that he's been pining for my Aunt Joan for the last sixty years…" She shrugged. "I don't want to think about it now. It's four thirty on the morning of my thirtieth birthday, and all I want to do right now is go to bed. With you," she added with a smirk.

In answer, Gideon gently rolled her off his knee onto the floor and stood up.

"Come on, then. I'll tell the rest of the guests to fend for themselves, and I'll see you in the bedroom."

He strode into the conservatory, where the remaining half dozen guests were congregated, chatting quietly, leaving Abi to scramble to her feet, retrieve her shoes, and scurry upstairs to wait for him.

Chapter 2

Wednesday 29th April, 2009

Abi turned to her daughter in frustration. "Tash, I thought we'd been through this a hundred times. The less people that know about Joan and Pauline the better, and it can't do any good at all trying to contact Billy after all this time. He's clearly made a life for himself in New Zealand and has probably forgotten Joan even existed. It won't help him and it won't help us if you tell him the story."

Abi thought back sadly to the story she and Natasha had uncovered the previous year. They had come across some diaries written by her mother and aunt when they were teenagers in 1950, and the tale they told was both shocking and heartbreaking. She had discovered her mother was not really the person she had seemed to be. Billy had been the young farmhand her aunt had fallen in love with all those years ago.

Natasha scowled and crossed her arms over her chest. "But he may have been pining for her all these years," she objected crossly. "He may not have been happy at all and may have thought she just abandoned him." She narrowed her eyes at her mother. "Like you thought Dad had abandoned you. Remember how that felt?"

Abi sighed and sat down on the edge of the bed.

"It's not the same, Tasha, and you know it," she said patiently. "First of all, Pauline wrote to Billy in Joan's name and explained why she couldn't see him again, and Dad and I were only parted for ten years. This has been nearly sixty."

"But she said in the letter that maybe when they were old she would explain everything to him," Natasha shouted, balling her hands into fists at her side. "Maybe he's been waiting to hear from her ever since. He's old now, but he probably checks the post every day for news of her…" She sat down on the bed next to her mother. "Please, Mum, please. Just let me tell him what really happened all those years ago. Tell him that she really did love him. Please, Mum?"

Abi put her arm around Natasha's shoulders and rested her chin on the child's head. "If we tell Billy," she said gently, "then there's a chance the whole story could come out. That wouldn't be good. How would that make my mother look?" Natasha looked up at her and raised her eyebrows. Abi gave a slight smile. "I know, you didn't think much of her anyway, and neither did I, but I think we both understand her better now, don't we, and I certainly wouldn't want the circumstances surrounding those deaths to be dragged up again." She paused and tightened her arm around her daughter. "And of course, there is the perennial problem of Dad's fame. If another story about this family gets out, imagine the field day the press would have with it."

Natasha pulled away from her mother's arm and sighed heavily. "I guess so," she muttered eventually, her slim fingers picking at the frayed edges of her denim shorts. "I just hate to think that he's been pining for her all these years."

Abi sighed, leaned over, and dropped a light kiss on her daughter's head. "I know how you feel," she agreed, "but I really think we should leave well alone. I'm sure Billy's had a very happy life. You said his sister says he has a family?" Natasha nodded. "Well, there you are then. It would only upset them if you started telling him about a lost love."

Natasha dropped her head forward so her hair swung over her face. "Okay," she murmured. "I s'pose you're right." She looked up at her mother. "He probably was happy, wasn't he? If he had kids and stuff." She managed a slight smile and got to her feet. "All right, you win. Can I help with the packing now?"

Abi laughed and nodded. "'Course you can," she said, getting to her feet and pulling a suitcase down from the top of the wardrobe. "We need to take a bit of everything; I really don't know what the weather'll be like."

Natasha pulled open a drawer and began to load underwear into the suitcase. "Lydia says it's nearly winter over there," she said, wrinkling her nose. "Couldn't we have gone when they have summer?"

"Not really. Dad's tour starts in May in Auckland, so it wouldn't be much good if we didn't go over there till October, now would it?" Abi laughed, adding a pile of shirts to the case. "But I'm fairly sure what passes for winter in New Zealand is much warmer than we have here."

"It better be," muttered Natasha darkly. "We're gonna be there for ages. How long is this tour, anyway, and are we going for all of it?"

Abi sat down on the bed again. "It starts in

Auckland on the fifteenth of May, then Wellington on the seventeenth, and Christchurch on the nineteenth. After that they're off to Australia for three weeks, then over to the U.S. and Canada for the beginning of July." She paused and glanced at Natasha. "We're going to New Zealand because it was a good excuse to go and see Penny and her family, and from there we'll go with the band to Australia." Natasha wriggled a little. "It'll be a brilliant experience for you, Tash. You'll get to see hundreds of new places."

Natasha looked up at her. "I guess so, and I get to miss school for a couple of months," she added with a grin.

"Actually..." Abi hesitated. "Dad and I thought you could go to school with Lydia while we're in New Zealand, so you don't miss too much."

Natasha stared at her in horror. "Mum!" she shrieked, "you can't be serious! Go to school in another country? Not a chance." She shook her head violently, causing her unruly curls to swing over her face. "And Lydia's younger than me anyway."

"Only a matter of months," Abi pointed out. "She'll be thirteen in October. I'm sure your lessons will be on a similar level. And think about it—what else are you going to do? Lydia'll have to go to school, so she won't be around to hang out with; so will the younger children. Dad and I'll be catching up with Penny and James, and I'm sure you won't find that much fun. You may as well go to school and at least get to hang out with people your own age."

Natasha looked unconvinced. "But I won't know them," she complained with a frown. "Only Lydia, and even though she's my cousin I've only met her twice."

She narrowed her eyes at Abi. "All right, I'll give it a go, but if I hate it I'm not going back. Deal?"

Abi laughed and reached over to pull a lock of curly hair. "Deal," she agreed. "Now come on, let's get on with this packing. We're leaving on Friday, and there's so much still to do."

****

Simon Dean pressed the phone close to his ear and sucked in his breath in annoyance. "It's really quite simple," he said impatiently. "How can you not get it? I've been through the details five times now. All you have to do is make the one phone call, and everything should carry on from there." He paused and listened intently, his ruddy face beginning to bead with sweat. His patience, never very good, was wearing extremely thin, and he was desperate for a drink. He cut off the flow from the other end of the line with a curt, "Right. You got it now? I'm off. Make sure you get it right," and he disconnected the call and flung his phone onto the bed.

Running a chubby hand through his untidy curls, Simon stalked over to the window and glanced down at the road below. The always busy Seattle street was thronged with Saturday shoppers, but he felt disinclined to go and join them. Instead, he moved over to the mini-bar located by the bed and rummaged inside. Eventually deciding on a beer, he snapped it open and took a long swig, then wiped the back of his hand across his mouth and took a deep breath. The final arrangements had now been made, and he just had to be patient and wait it out. If everything went to plan, he would need to think about leaving Seattle in the next week.

He threw himself down on the bed and pulled his old canvas sports bag up beside him. He felt in the outer pocket and pulled out a passport. He flicked it open and studied the image that stared back at him. It was not flattering, and before he used it he needed to have a haircut and reapply some dye, but it would serve his purpose. He glanced at the name on the page and gave a slight smirk. He had managed to live incognito as Paul Martin for the last nine months, and so far it had worked like a dream. Getting the passport in the first place had been the most difficult thing, but once he had managed that, his only problem had been financial. He had been unable to access most of his bank accounts, since the debacle in Wales the previous summer, and had been forced to exist solely on the money he had secreted in an offshore account, which he was hoping was untraceable. That money was rapidly running out, and Simon had realised he needed to do something drastic to sort his life out. He was fed up with being Paul Martin, and fed up with having to hide from everyone who had known him previously. He was actually taking rather a chance staying in Seattle, but the application of a little hair dye and the growth of a moustache had helped his disguise.

He tossed the passport back into his bag and took another swig from his can. If his current plan worked, he would be able to resume his former life with no worry of the police, and to reconnect with all his friends and family. His thoughts strayed briefly to his mother, and he felt the tiniest twinge of guilt. As far as he was aware, she thought him dead since the previous August, and he had done nothing to disabuse this notion. He shifted impatiently on the bed, drained his can, and kicked off his shoes. He'd been living in the shadows for too long and wanted it to end. If his latest scheme worked, then his quite justified—in his mind—actions of the previous summer would be pardoned and his normal life could resume. He lay back on the pillows and closed his eyes. If only he didn't have to rely on someone else for it to succeed, then he would be able to relax, but this was one plan he couldn't carry out alone.

****

Gideon glanced up as Abi entered the room. "How's the packing going?"

She sank down onto the sofa opposite him and raised an eyebrow. "Okay," she replied with a smile. "And when are you coming to help?"

Gideon looked aggrieved. "I've got far too much to think about with the tour," he said innocently. "I can't pack, as well! I'm still sorting out the final details with the guys. It's going to be hard, with a new drummer."

Abi tutted and curled her feet up underneath her. "Are you excited?" she asked. "This'll be the first abroad tour since '05. Does it seem weird?"

"Ye-es." Gideon chewed his lip. "In a way it does. The weirdest part being that you'll be with me." He glanced over at her, pain showing in his blue eyes. "You should've been there all those years ago, and now you will be. I think it might bring back some old memories."

"Yeah." Abi frowned, nodding slowly. "I've been thinking that too. I was so excited about going with you back in '95, and then when it never happened I couldn't even bear to think about what you were doing…" Her eyes filled with tears. "Oh, Gid, it was so dreadful. I just imagined you with all those awful groupies. I thought you were sleeping with them all. I even had to stop looking at the papers in the end. I just couldn't bear to think about what you might be doing when it should have been with me." She stopped speaking and shifted position on the sofa, self-consciously picking at her thumbnail.

Gideon watched her closely. After a moment he moved across the room and sat down beside her, sliding his arm around her shoulders and pulling her close. "You know it wasn't like that, don't you, Abs?" He rested his cheek against her shiny dark auburn hair. "I didn't look at another girl for about eighteen months after I finally stopped writing to you." He hooked a finger under her chin and tilted her face up to his. "I was completely, totally, and absolutely in love with you," he stated firmly, staring her in the eyes.

Abi wriggled closer and put her head on his shoulder with a sigh. "Were you?" she asked sadly. "I really want to believe that, 'cause that's certainly how I felt about you." She paused and glanced up at him. "I guess you were. I read the letters. But I'm sure you can understand how I felt not knowing any of that. I just imagined you sleeping around and having a whale of a time."

Gideon snorted and his arm tightened around her shoulders. "You've just described Simon," he said with a frown. "And yeah, he did try to get me to join him, but I wouldn't. I honestly couldn't think of anyone except you. Even after I finally realised I wasn't going to get any letters."

Abi snuggled closer still and entwined her fingers with Gideon's. "There's something else that worries me," she said eventually, in a very small voice. He looked down at her enquiringly. "I worry that if I *had* been there...and with a tiny baby to look after...what would have happened?"

Gideon frowned and pulled back slightly to look at her. "What d'you mean, Abs?" he asked. "Isn't that what we wanted?"

Abi shook her head. "No, we planned I should join you...but neither of us knew about the baby then. Suppose I *had* managed to come when I was pregnant. How would we have managed with a tiny baby on tour?" She paused and stared at him. "And suppose I couldn't cope with the attention you got from the groupies? What would have happened?"

Gideon sat up straight and looked at her in concern. "What are you saying, Abi? Are you suggesting we might not have made it? Are you suggesting it might have split us up?"

Abi sat forward and wrapped her arms around herself. "I don't know what I'm saying." She shook her head. "It just worries me, that's all." She turned and stared at him. "But it would have been really, really hard with a baby. I was sixteen, you were nineteen. You were totally caught up in the band and the fame and the touring...and everything. I think I would have got in the way." Her eyes filled with tears again, and she dipped her head forward to let her hair conceal her face. "Just me alone would have got in the way. Imagine what it would have been like with a baby, as well. I'm not coping well with the groupies you've got now, and I certainly wouldn't have done all those years ago."

Gideon stared at her in consternation and got to his feet. "Abi, of course we would have been all right," he said emphatically, standing in front of her, his gaze on her bowed head. He reached out and pulled her roughly to her feet. "We would always be all right, wherever and whenever we were. I can't believe you could doubt that, after all we've been through."

Abi raised her head. "I know," she murmured, "but I'm beginning to realise just how jealous I get when I see those dreadful girls running after you…when I was sixteen I should probably have done them some damage. You know what I was like."

Gideon threw back his head and roared with laughter. "Abs you really haven't changed." He grinned. "I keep expecting you to do them damage now! But honestly, you would have had nothing to worry about then, and you don't now. Simon and Charles tried to get me to go out with them to pick up girls, but I wouldn't do it." He paused and gently stroked her cheek with his index finger. "In fact, I'll tell you about a time when one of the fans came to my room…" He paused as Abi caught her breath. "And then maybe you'll believe me."

Chapter 3

Friday 17th May, 1996—Seattle, USA

Gideon slammed the hotel bedroom door behind him and leaned against it with his eyes closed. He had spent the hour following the concert explaining to Simon and Charles that he didn't want to go clubbing with them, that he had no interest in "picking up girls," and that all he wanted to do was go to bed. And write to Abi. But he hadn't told them that. Since the others had picked up on the fact that Gideon hadn't actually received any replies to his letters to Abi, he had kept his continuing one-sided correspondence to himself.

He walked slowly over to the bed and flung himself down, burying his face in the pillows. Even with his eyes screwed tightly shut, all he could see was her face. Everywhere he looked he saw her face. Sometimes smiling; sometimes sulky; sometimes angry; but always loving. Always loving to him. Always in love with him. Just like they'd promised each other. Just like it was meant to be. He rolled onto his back, pulling the pillow with him and clutching it tightly to his chest. Why had she not written? What had gone wrong? It was—he calculated rapidly—just over eleven months since he saw her last, and he still felt the same about her. But she'd abandoned him. He screwed his eyes shut again and tried to recall her face the last time he'd seen her. To his dismay he couldn't quite capture it. He could see her standing on the pavement waving frantically as he drove away, but the expression on her face eluded him. It was almost there—just at the edge of his memory. Like something one sees out of the corner of one's eye but can't quite keep. With a muttered oath, he swung his legs over the side of the bed and ran a distracted hand through his long hair. It was still damp with sweat from the gig, and his T-shirt and ripped jeans were beginning to stick to him unpleasantly. Sighing, he stood up, snatched a towel from the chair by the bed, and headed for the shower.

Fifteen minutes later, he emerged from the en-suite, a towel wrapped around his waist and his hair dripping over his shoulders. He grabbed another towel from the pile by the bed and began to rub his hair vigorously. He pulled on a clean T-shirt and a pair of old track suit bottoms, then reached into the mini-bar and selected a can of lager. Snapping it open, he carried it over to the window and peered down into the dark Seattle street. The sound of revellers floated up to him, and he smiled mirthlessly to himself as he thought about Simon and Charles and the throngs of girls they were banking on attracting.

He shook back his still-damp hair impatiently and took a long swig of his lager. At least they'd eventually given up trying to persuade him to accompany them. That thought had just entered his mind when there came a loud tap at the door. Gideon clenched his teeth and briefly closed his eyes, then strode over and pulled the door open.

"For fuck's sake, Simon, leave me…" He tailed off at the sight of the very young teenage girl who stood in the doorway. He rolled his eyes. "Oh, sorry. Thought you were Simon."

The girl stared up at him, brown eyes huge in her pale face, her very long strawberry blonde hair wild and dishevelled. She licked her lips nervously, then smiled at Gideon.

"Hi. I'm Sadie," she said, her West Coast accent sounding harsh to his ears. "I was wondering…could I get your autograph?"

Gideon took a deep breath and nodded. "Okay," he agreed, "hang on." He moved over to the bedside table to fetch one of the signed photographs the band used in such situations. As he turned to hand it to her, he found she'd sidled into the bedroom and was standing directly behind him. "Here you are," he said curtly, holding out the photo.

Sadie made no move to take it but gently pushed the door shut behind her. "Aren't you going to ask me in?" she asked, gazing up at him, her heavily kohl-rimmed eyes huge.

Gideon looked down at her. "No," he said shortly, and took a step past her towards the door, pulled it open, and stood waiting for her to leave.

She stood her ground and smiled shyly at him. "Please," she said. "I just wanna talk to you. I managed to get past security and made it up here. The least you can do is talk to me for a few minutes."

Despite himself, Gideon grinned slightly and slowly let the door close again. He gestured towards the bed. "Okay. Take a seat. D'you want a drink?"

She sat down on the edge of the bed and nodded. "Yeah. Beer, please."

Gideon raised his eyebrows. "How old are you?"

Sadie tossed her hair back. "Sixteen," she said, her eyes challenging him. "How old are you?"

"Nineteen," he replied, watching her carefully.

"Well, there you go," she shrugged. "Neither of us is old enough to drink legally. You're not in Britain now."

Gideon gave a short laugh and tossed a can of lager to her. She snapped it open, closed her eyes, and took a long swig. He watched her cautiously. The last thing he needed was a drunken teenager in his room, and he wanted to stay alert in case she tried anything. He walked over to the armchair in the corner of the room and slumped down in it.

Sadie pouted at him. "Come and sit by me," she invited, patting the bed beside her.

Gideon shook his head. "No. Thank you," he said politely. "You're just here to talk, remember."

She giggled, and flashed him a seductive look from her huge eyes. "Yeah, right. To talk."

Gideon sighed and crossed his legs. "Well that's all we're gonna do," he said, narrowing his eyes at her.

She shrugged and curled her legs up underneath her on the bed. "You say that now, but you don't know me yet."

With an impatient grunt, Gideon got to his feet and strode over to the bed. He stood hovering over Sadie, his piercing blue eyes flashing dangerously. "No," he agreed. "I don't know you. And I don't intend to know you. Not now, not ever. Now I think you'd better leave." He held out his hand to pull her to her feet. She reached up, grasped his large hand in hers and swayed to her feet. She looked up at him under her extended lashes.

"Aw, come on," she chided. "You know you want to, really. We could have such fun together." She pressed her hand against his crotch and moved her body closer to his.

Gideon stepped back abruptly and pushed her hand away. "I said no," he repeated through gritted teeth. "I'm not interested. I have a girlfriend."

Sadie tossed her head. "Oh, yeah? And where is she then?" she asked with a sneer. "She can't be much of girlfriend if she isn't with you."

Gideon felt his face begin to flame, and a red hot anger began to burn in his chest. He reached out and caught her by the wrist. "She's in England," he hissed, pushing his face close to hers. "And she's the best person in the world."

Sadie flinched slightly as he spat out the words, but she stood her ground. "When's she comin' to join you then?" she asked cockily. "She can't care that much if she's letting you tour without her."

"She's still at school," Gideon muttered, aware as he said the words how hollow they sounded. He could provide no better reason for Abi's absence, and he began to feel hot and cold as he realised just how much he'd been kidding himself these last months. With a smothered oath he grabbed Sadie by the wrist and propelled her towards the door. He pulled it open and pushed her out into the corridor, tossing the signed photograph after her.

"Go home," he ordered her. "Go home, grow up, and stop cheapening yourself." Then he slammed the door and locked it securely. He leaned back against the hard wood and took a deep breath.

It was time to face reality. Abi didn't want him.

She'd made that perfectly clear by her continued silence, but he'd been choosing to ignore it. The curious little interlude that had just taken place had given him a wake-up call. She wasn't coming to join him. Ever. He exhaled slowly and walked over to the bed. Unconsciously he straightened the covers and sat down on the edge, his hands hanging loosely in his lap. She wasn't coming. He'd lost her, and he needed to face it. Moving slowly in an almost dreamlike state, Gideon reached out and pulled a pad of paper from next to the bed. He began to write.

Dearest Abi, I've realised tonight you're not coming to join me. I realise finally what your silence over the last months has meant. I'm so sorry not to have understood sooner, therefore bombarding you with unwanted mail...but I found it too painful to face. When we parted, I believed we would be together forever, and I truly thought you believed that too. Now I realise I was wrong. That the tension I detected in you that last day was because you wanted to tell me it was over but didn't know how. I understand, Abi. I understand, and I forgive you. But I'll always love you and I'll never forget you. Maybe one day we'll meet again and you'll explain to me what went wrong, 'cause for the life of me I can't think what it was. So I'll finish now, my darling, and let you go and live your life. I'll never stop loving you but realise now I have to let you go. All my love for ever, Gideon.

He put down his pen, gently folded the paper in half and slid it into an envelope. He scribbled her name and address on the front and popped it into the pocket of his leather jacket. Then he turned off the lights, lay down on the bed, and attempted to sleep.

****

Saturday 18th May, 1996

Gideon stared at Simon in disbelief. "You did what?" he demanded, his face visibly registering his shock. "Simon tell me you're joking…please."

Simon grinned mockingly at his friend, and brushed his fair curls out of his eyes. "What's the problem?" he asked with a shrug. "You didn't want her. What d'you expect me to do? There she was, hanging around in the corridor, looking all rejected—all big eyes, sexy hair, and tits. I'm only human, Gid." He narrowed his eyes speculatively. "Can't see why you turned her down, actually. It's not like you've got a girlfriend or anything…" He dodged out of the way as Gideon's fist came flying towards him.

In a flash Charles leapt between his friends and diverted the flailing arm. "Hey, hey, hey!" he cried, catching Gideon's elbow and squeezing hard. "No brawling. You're meant to be friends." He raised a quizzical eyebrow at Gideon. "Can't quite see your problem, Gid," he admitted. "You didn't want the girl, and you know how Simon works. He always cleans up your leftovers."

Simon chuckled, and Gideon turned away with a muttered oath. He swung round again to face the others. "She was a vulnerable kid, guys," he said through gritted teeth. "She said she was sixteen, but I doubt she was even that old. I sent her away to save her from herself. I have *some* moral standards."

Simon leaned back against the doorframe and shoved his hands into his pockets. "Not what she told me," he said with a shrug. "She said you had a girlfriend. In England. Still at school." He paused for a moment. "She said when she asked why she wasn't here with you, you went berserk and threw her out." He paused again and watched as Gideon stalked over to the window and rested his forehead against the cold pane. "Are you still writing to Abi, Gid?" he asked at last.

Eventually Gideon turned to face them, his face dark and drawn. "I was," he admitted bleakly. "I couldn't bear to think she'd abandoned me." He sighed and ran a hand distractedly through his hair. "After that…incident…with the girl, I wrote a final letter to her. A letter letting her go. Saying I understood." He turned away again, the pain clear in his eyes, adding bitterly, "I posted it this morning. Are you happy now?"

Simon and Charles regarded him silently, unsure what response would be appropriate. Eventually Charles took a step forward. "Sorry, Gid," he said sincerely, pushing his shaggy black hair out of his eyes. "I know how hard that must have been for you. I'm really sorry things didn't work out between you. I liked her." He put out a hand and patted his friend awkwardly on the shoulder.

Simon pushed himself upright away from the door and nodded to Gideon. "Sorry, Gid," he echoed Charles. "So does this mean you'll come out on the town with us tonight then?"

Gideon swung round to face him, his eyes blazing. "No, I fucking won't!" he exploded. "Have you no sensibilities, Simon? Have you never loved anyone?" His eyes bored into Simon's. "You don't just get over it in an instant. It doesn't just stop. Now get the fuck out of my room if that's all you can say." He advanced on him menacingly, and Simon took a couple of steps backwards.

"Okay, okay, mate," he said hurriedly, holding up a hand in front of him. "Didn't mean to upset you. We'll go now. C'mon, Chas." He opened the door and stepped out into the corridor.

Charles hesitated a moment, then frowned at Gideon. "Will you be okay?" he asked quietly.

Gideon nodded, and touched his friend on the arm. "Yeah," he said, "just need to be alone. And, Chas?" Charles looked quizzically at him. "Don't pressure me. This could take a long time. Keep Simon off my back. I'm going to go away for a couple of days as soon as this run of gigs is over. Just to the Vineyard. Need a complete change."

****

Friday 25th May, 1996—Newbury, Berkshire

"You're the only person I know who's not pleased it's half-term." Judy grinned at Abi as the two of them wandered along the road towards Judy's house. "We have a whole week to do what we want—well, revising apart—and you'd rather be at school."

Abi, disconsolately trailing her school bag along behind her, flicked her unruly hair over her shoulder impatiently. "Well, I don't want to be at home with *them*, do I?" she muttered miserably. "Which means I shall spend all week at your house and probably piss your parents off big time."

Judy glanced covertly at her friend, and her heart clenched at the sight of the pain in her eyes and the complete change her personality had undergone over the past year. Her once round, happy face now had hollow cheeks and dark shadows under the eyes, and her whole demeanour was one of mild despair. Judy caught up with her and took her arm.

31

"Of course you won't piss off my parents," she said with forced cheerfulness. "We can hang out in my room and listen to music…and stuff." She was suddenly aware that Abi wouldn't want to listen to music. She wouldn't want to do anything, but especially not listen to music. Judy took a deep breath. "How about we go away for the week?"

Abi stopped walking and peered suspiciously at her. "What d'you mean?" she asked with a frown. "Go where, with whom?"

"Mum and Dad's caravan," suggested Judy brightly. "What d'you think? Just us."

Abi stared at her in amazement. "On our own?" she echoed. "Who on earth is gonna let us do that? And how d'you propose we get there?"

"Dunno," Judy admitted with a grin. "Maybe Dad would take us?"

Abi managed a slight smile. "I doubt he'd do that," she remarked. "That's rather a lot to ask of someone. Anyway, he has to go to work."

Judy looked a little crestfallen and wrinkled her nose. "I guess," she agreed reluctantly. "But maybe we could do something fun. I know there's a party one of the boys in the Upper Sixth at King Edward's is having. Nearly all our class are going."

Abi sighed. "I don't do fun anymore," she stated rather dramatically. "And certainly not parties." She heaved her bag further up onto her shoulder. "I'll just spend the week in my room." She walked slowly along.

Judy gritted her teeth and stamped her foot in frustration. "Abi, you're impossible!" she shouted. "You have to start living again. You have to get over him."

Slowly Abi turned to face her, her face contorted with pain. "Judy, I can't," she said quietly, her voice beginning to shake. "You know what I've been through. I can't ever get over that. I lost my baby, Jude. I lost my baby, and I lost the only man I'll ever love. I thought you understood."

The two girls stood facing each other on the pavement, the spectres of Gideon and the baby hanging between them.

Judy swallowed. "I know," she whispered eventually. "I know. But I love you, Abs, and I can't bear to see you suffer so much. I just want to help you." She took a tentative step towards Abi and held out her arms. After a momentary hesitation, Abi stepped forward and clung to her friend, the ever-ready tears beginning to flow down her sallow cheeks. "One day, Abs," whispered Judy gently, "one day you'll feel better. Until then I'm always here for you."

Abi hiccupped quietly and shook her head sadly. "I hope you're right, Judy, but right now I can't imagine it." Her blue eyes stared despairingly over Judy's shoulder.

****

Friday 25th May, 1996—Martha's Vineyard, USA

Gideon stood at the long window and stared out over the harbour. The weather was disappointingly wet and windy, and he watched as the boiling sea tossed and almost overturned the numerous small boats anchored in the bay. The spray flew towards the house, splattering foam onto the glass in front of him. He sighed and leaned his forehead against the cool windowpane. He had arrived at Martha's Vineyard the previous evening and had spent most of the day sleeping. His hosts had welcomed him without question and had left him to his own devices, happy to wait until he was ready to talk.

He sighed and turned back into the large, high-ceilinged room. It was sparsely but chicly furnished, with a polished wood floor and a collection of deep cushiony sofas, upholstered in cream cotton, clustered around a large wood-burning stove set into an alcove. Gideon wandered over to the nearest sofa and flung himself down onto its welcoming cushions. He leaned back and closed his eyes, still unable to banish the picture of Abi's face from his mind.

A hand gently touched his arm, and he opened his eyes to find his hostess hovering in front of him, holding out a steaming cup of coffee.

She smiled encouragingly. "Take this, Gid. You look like you need one."

He took the proffered mug and clasped his hands around its warmth gratefully. He mustered a smile. "Thanks, Sonia. Yeah I could do with waking up." He took a sip, then leaned back against the cushions again. "Are you gonna join me?"

Sonia curled up in the opposite corner of the sofa and surveyed her guest quizzically. "You were in a bad way when you arrived last night," she stated bluntly, shaking her long dark hair over her shoulders and narrowing her eyes at him. "I take it this is something to do with Abi?" She said the name softly, and Gideon could feel her intense gaze. He had met Sonia and her husband Kurt back in September of the previous year when he'd been performing in Boston, and the three of them had become firm friends. The older couple had taken pity on the tortured young man who was desperately unhappy away from the girl he loved but so caught up in his whirlwind new life that he was finding it hard to cope. They had made it clear to him that their home was always available to him as a bolt hole, should he ever need one, and Sonia had listened on many an occasion as Gideon poured out his feelings about Abi.

Finally Gideon raised empty eyes. "It's over," he stated bleakly. "I finally realised. She's never going to write." He took a long slurp of his coffee and turned to stare over at the rain-lashed window. "I wrote to her. A final letter. To say goodbye." He fell silent, his blue eyes staring blankly at the window and his fingers tapping nervously on the side of his mug.

Sonia watched him closely. She desperately wanted to reach out to the beautiful young man slumped in despair on her sofa—reach out, put her arms around him, and mutter soothing words of encouragement—but she felt it would not be appreciated. Instead she slid along the sofa until she was sitting next to him, and gently laid her beautifully manicured hand on his arm.

"I'm sorry, Gid," she said softly, staring straight into his piercing eyes. "I'm so sorry. I know how much you loved her."

Gideon's eyes flashed dangerously. "Love her," he barked out angrily. "Love her. I still love her. This has changed nothing." He ran a distracted hand through his hair and took a deep breath. "All that's happened is I've finally accepted she doesn't want me." He scowled at Sonia, his dark brows drawn together. "It doesn't mean I want to start looking for someone else. Don't you start trying to fix me up. I get enough of that from Simon and Chas. I come here to get away from it."

Sonia smiled at him. "Of course I won't, Gid," she

assured him, her long fingers gently caressing his arm. "Neither Kurt nor I would do that. I understand you come here to escape, and that's absolutely fine with us. We just want to be here for you, to help you when you need it. Nothing more."

Gideon looked down at her and nodded briefly. "Okay, then. Now can we go out and get clams? I'm starving."

Chapter 4

Sunday 3rd May, 2009

Simon glanced at his watch impatiently. His flight was running nearly half an hour late, and his patience was wearing thin. The SeaTac departure lounge was very noisy, crowded, and smelly, and he was desperate for a cigarette. He was just making his way over to the bar for yet another beer when the announcement came that his plane was ready to board. With a muttered, "Finally," he hitched his flight bag over his shoulder and marched, head down, towards the gate in the wake of the other passengers. Getting through with his false passport always gave him a bad stomach, and he could feel the beginnings of telltale gurgling deep within him. He swore under his breath and prayed his current plan would work, so he would be able to give up the charade he'd been living for the last few months. He slid his passport over the counter, waited while it was scrutinized, then followed the long stream of passengers towards the waiting aircraft.

Half an hour later, and thirty-five thousand feet higher, Simon was enjoying his first drink of the twenty-hour flight. He leaned back in his window seat and closed his eyes. He hadn't been able to afford to fly first class and was already finding the conditions extremely cramped, and, seated next to a middle-aged lady who looked keen to talk, he was going to have to spend much of the journey pretending to be asleep if he was to get through it without upsetting anyone. The thought of making small talk with a complete stranger had him shuddering with distaste, and he slumped further down in his seat and turned his face to the window. Hopefully she would engage the man to her right in conversation instead, and leave him in peace. Just before boarding the aircraft, he'd managed one last call to finalise the finer details of his plan and was feeling relatively confident it would succeed. That he had completely lost touch with reality had failed to register in his warped mind, and he smiled to himself as he sleepily stared out at the thick white clouds below him. Everything was going to turn out fine this time.

Chapter 5

Monday 4th May, 2009

Abi sighed and stretched her arms above her head with a little wriggle. She smiled over at Gideon's sister Penny, who was relaxing with her on the veranda of her beach-side house at Papamoa on New Zealand's North Island.

"Penny this house is so gorgeous! It surprises me each time I see it. That view is to die for," she murmured as she gazed out across the shimmering waters of the Bay of Plenty towards distant Motiti Island.

Penny chuckled and lay back in her deckchair. "It is lovely, isn't it?" she agreed, tilting her sunhat to cover her eyes. "And you're very lucky to have this weather. It's not usually this warm in early May. This is nearly winter for us."

"I told Tasha not to worry about the weather. I was pretty sure winter here would be like summer in England." Abi grinned, stretching her long brown legs in front of her and wiggling them in the sun.

Penny turned and peeped at her under the brim of her hat.

"It does get cold," she warned, "but the forecast for the next week is pretty good. Should get some beach time. We'll probably find it a bit chilly, but to you it'll feel fine."

Penny and her husband James MacRae had emigrated to New Zealand shortly after their marriage in 1994, and all their three children had been born there. It was a source of extreme irritation to Penny's mother, Caroline, to be so far from three of her grandchildren, but she and Roger tried to get over to visit them at least once a year. Abi had seriously wondered whether they would suggest tagging along with them on this occasion.

Penny sat up and adjusted her sunglasses. "So, how's everything going, then?" She gave Abi an intent look. "Are you looking forward to the tour?"

Abi was silent for a moment, then shrugged. "Heh…well, sort of." she said slowly. "But I do have a few issues about it."

"Thought you might," Penny said, with a half-grin. "Bet the groupies bother you, don't they? They would me. I'd hate it if James got followed everywhere by adoring girls."

Abi nodded vigorously. "Yeah, I've discovered I get really, really jealous." She paused and glanced over at Penny. "In fact, I was worried…"

Penny looked at her curiously. "Go on."

"I was worried…and I said this to Gideon…I was worried that had I gone on tour with him back in '95, when I was pregnant…that I would have got too jealous, and it would have split us up." She finished in a rush, and bent her head forward, letting her hair swing over her face.

Penny was silent for a moment, then leaned forward and touched Abi gently on the hand. "That wouldn't have happened, Abi," she assured her quietly.

"Do you have any idea what my baby brother thinks of you? I may have been over here, back in the mid-nineties when you two got together, but I was left in no doubt about his feelings. He was devastated when he thought you'd abandoned him." She paused, leaned back in her seat again, and took a deep breath. "I'm not saying you wouldn't have had problems—any teenage relationship with the addition of a baby is bound to have problems—but from what I know of you both, I'm absolutely sure you would have weathered any storm that came your way." She lowered her sunglasses and stared intently at Abi, her piercing blue eyes so similar to her brother's. "Honestly, Abi, you mustn't let it worry you."

Abi raised her head and pushed her hair back off her face. "Really? Oh, Penny, I do hope you're right. I feel so awful even to have been thinking it. It's just that I'm finding the groupies so hard to cope with now—imagine what I would have felt like when I was sixteen." She gave a wry grin. "You didn't know me then, but I was very…excitable. Had a very short fuse. According to Judy and Gideon, I was very high maintenance."

Penny threw back her head and laughed out loud. "So I gather," she said, her eyes sparkling. "But so are most teenagers, I believe. Not looking forward to Lydia reaching that stage, actually." Her mouth curved into a grimace. "Has Tasha shown any teenage signs yet?"

"Tasha was born teenage," Abi stated firmly. "But luckily, so far, she's a nice teenager. She's extremely strong willed, of course, and rules us all." She sighed and wriggled back into a more comfortable position. "We let her, because of the years we didn't have her…"

She gazed across the long expanse of lawn to where Natasha and Lydia could be seen making their way slowly towards the house. "Penny, you have no idea what the last three and a half years have been like," she continued, her eyes following the progress of the two girls. "I keep thinking it's all a dream. That if I don't hang on tight it will all fly away and leave me alone again, and I'll find myself in that terrible place where I believe Gid has abandoned me, and I've been told Tasha is dead." She looked away and bit on her lip. "That's why this whole worry about the jealousy thing is getting to me so much. I couldn't bear it if anything happened to spoil our happiness now."

Penny got to her feet and stretched. "I totally understand." She put her hand on Abi's shoulder. "But believe me—nothing is ever going to come between you and Gideon—or you and the children. Trust me." She gave a short laugh. "I'm nearly thirty-nine, and I've been around long enough to recognise the perfect relationship when I see it. Now, it's nearly six o'clock. I think it's time for wine. How about you?"

Abi looked up and smiled her assent, and Penny disappeared into the house to fetch the glasses.

****

Natasha and Lydia were fully aware their mothers were watching them from the veranda, and for that reason they slowed their pace still more and veered off towards the summerhouse. Natasha caught Lydia by the elbow and steered her towards the dilapidated wooden building.

"Can we go in there?" she asked, gesturing towards it with her head.

Lydia shrugged. "If you like. It's a bit cobwebby.

Nothing much in there. Why can't we talk out here?"

Natasha sighed and gave her cousin a gentle shove forward. "Because it's private, and our mothers are sitting just up there watching us, and goodness knows where everyone else is. No one'll be in the summerhouse, will they?"

"Guess not," muttered Lydia doubtfully, following Natasha up the two wide wooden steps to the double doors. She leaned around her cousin and pushed the right-hand door hard. It swung open with a crash, and the walls shook.

Natasha frowned. "Careful," she admonished, "you'll break something."

Lydia shrugged again. "Dad was talking about knocking it down and getting a gazebo," she said, staring round the mostly empty room with little interest. "We never use it."

Natasha stood in the middle of the room and looked around her. The summerhouse was old, showing signs of bad decay. It had clearly been neglected over recent years, and the only items left inside were covered in a thick film of dust and a network of fluffy cobwebs. The front wall was almost completely made up of small-paned windows, which were all either cracked or too grimy to see through. She shivered slightly as an ancient memory attempted to catch at her subconscious, but then she moved purposefully to the far corner and after a little rummaging produced two very old deckchairs that she proceeded to unfold.

"Well, I like it," she said firmly, pushing the half-formed memory to the back of her mind. "It could be quite cosy if you put more stuff in it. You could have a rug maybe, and some proper chairs. You know the sort you have in conservatories?" She sat down carefully in one of the deckchairs, wiggling her bottom a bit to make sure it wasn't going to collapse, then looked expectantly at Lydia. "Sit down, and then I can tell you all about Billy."

After subjecting the old chair to a careful spider check, Lydia perched on the edge and stared at her cousin. "Well?" she asked, flicking her long dark hair over her shoulder. "Who's Billy, and why is it so secret?"

Natasha watched her solemnly for a moment, then leant forward and regarded her sternly. "You must promise you won't tell another living soul what I'm about to tell you," she said. "In fact, you must swear it. Okay?"

Lydia nodded, her eyes widening, and she leaned forward expectantly. Natasha looked over her shoulder as if expecting to see listeners lurking in the dark cobwebby corners of the little room, then lowered her voice and rapidly related the story of Pauline, Joan, Billy, and poor little baby Sarah, a story she and her mother had discovered only the previous summer.

She told her how they had learned her grandmother had had a twin sister they knew nothing about, and one of them had a baby at sixteen. In order to avoid the child being taken away from her, the twins arranged for Pauline to go to London with the baby. Unfortunately, before Joan could persuade her parents to let them come home, Pauline accidentally smothered the baby whilst trying to keep her quiet. When Joan arrived the next day to fetch her, they had an argument, and Joan tripped and hit her head. When Pauline realised her sister was dead, she panicked, thinking she would be blamed for both deaths, and took on her twin's identity, managing to live as Joan for the rest of her life.

The experience had scarred her so much that when her own daughter, Abi, had also given birth at sixteen, she had taken the baby away and led Abi to believe she'd died. In addition to that she had also concealed the letters Gideon had written to Abi, making her think she had been abandoned. It wasn't until nearly ten years later that Abi, Gideon, and Natasha were all reunited.

As Natasha spoke, Lydia hung on her every word, her big brown eyes growing wider and more excited as the story progressed, and when it finished, she sucked in her breath and sat back in her chair. "Wow, Tash! What an amazing story! Your mum's family are so cool. So your grandmother killed two people. That's so awesome!"

Natasha tutted and slapped Lydia's hand. "No, she didn't!" she said crossly. "Well...okay, I guess she did...but they were both accidents. She didn't mean to kill them. She loved them both. But you see why you mustn't tell anyone? I'm not s'posed to tell you, really, but I'm going to need your help with something." She glanced around again to make sure no one was peering through the grimy windows as she leant even closer to her cousin. "You see, I've found out where Billy lives. Here in New Zealand, an' I want to go an' visit him to tell him what really happened to Joan."

Lydia caught her breath and stared at Natasha in horror. "You can't do that!" she exclaimed. "S'pose he tells someone? Anyway, won't it make him sad?"

Natasha sighed. "I'll tell him not to tell anyone," she said patiently. "And no, I think it would make him happy to know she loved him and that she didn't leave him 'cause she wanted to but because she died. He's probably been waiting for nearly sixty years to hear from her. I need to tell him."

Lydia considered her words, then slowly nodded. "Okay, I guess so. He must be really old by now anyway. Where does he live?"

Natasha delved into the pocket of her shorts and pulled out a crumpled piece of paper. She smoothed it out and scanned quickly to the end of the page. "Kaipaki," she pronounced carefully. "His sister says it's near Cambridge."

Lydia nodded enthusiastically. "Oh, I know where that is," she said in excitement. "You can get a bus to Cambridge. Not sure how you get from there to Kaipaki—may need to get a taxi or something. Have you got some money?"

Natasha nodded and grinned. "Yeah, Grandma gave me loads of spending money before we left. It should be plenty for bus and taxi fares." She paused and chewed thoughtfully on her bottom lip. "Only problem is how to do it without Mum and Dad finding out."

Lydia considered for a moment. "You could go one day when we're at school. You know, you leave at school time and get back for when we come home. D'you think that would be enough time?"

Natasha wrinkled her nose. "Hmmm…that doesn't give me very long. Maybe we could look up the buses and see what times they are and then try to work it out from there? What we need is for Mum and Dad to go out somewhere for the day so they get back late. D'you think your mum and dad will take them anywhere?" she suggested hopefully.

Lydia shook her head. "Doubt it," she said

dismally. "Dad has work every day, and Mum can't go far 'cause of the little ones." Lydia's younger brother and sister attended the local primary school and finished earlier in the day than the older girls. "She has to pick up Nathan and Josie at two forty, so that doesn't give her much time to go very far."

Natasha got to her feet and began to fold up her deckchair. "We'll sort something out," she said with confidence. "'Cause I'm not going back to England without seeing Billy. I won't get an opportunity like this again. Will you help me?" She raised her eyebrows at Lydia, who was struggling to collapse her chair.

"'Course I will," she said immediately, her eyes shining. "I love planning stuff. Let's go to my room now and look up the bus times." She heaved the chair into the corner and grinned at Natasha. "It's quite lucky we went back to school today, actually. If you'd been here last week, we were still on holiday, and then we wouldn't have found it so easy for you to sneak off."

Natasha gave a wry grin. "Oh, well, I s'pose there are some advantages to school after all," she said, pushing the door open and emerging into the afternoon sunshine. "Come on, let's go and do some investigating."

****

Abi lay back on the pillows and watched as Gideon prepared for bed. They were sleeping in Penny and James' largest spare room, which looked out over the bay towards Motiti Island. Natasha was sharing a room with Lydia, and little Oliver had been put in with his cousin Josie. She had been less than delighted with the idea, being nearly six years old, but had finally agreed, on the understanding that he mustn't get into bed with her. Abi was fully expecting Oliver to appear in their bed before morning. She wriggled into a more comfortable position and watched as Gideon peeled off his jeans, pulled his T-shirt over his head, and dropped them both in the middle of the floor. Then he turned and threw himself onto the bed beside her. He looked up at her with a grin, his dark hair flopping across his face,

"Good day?" he asked, reaching out and running his index finger down her cheek.

Abi smiled back. "Yeah. Pretty good," she said with a nod. "Just spent most of the time chatting to Penny. She's okay, your sister."

Gideon watched her with interest. "What'd she tell you, then?" he asked suspiciously. "Horrible things about me as a child, I s'pose?"

Abi chuckled and leaned down to kiss him on the nose. "Not at all," she said. "I think she actually likes you. No, she kind of put me right on a few things." She glanced at him from under her lashes. "A few things I was worrying about."

Gideon rolled onto his stomach and looked up at her. "The tour and the groupies?"

Abi shrugged. "Well, yeah. Sort of. And what I said to you about what might have happened if I'd been with you in '95." She paused and let her hair swing in front of her face. "She told me not to be so silly, and that you were totally besotted with me and nothing could ever come between us."

Gideon was silent for a moment before he gently pushed Abi's hair behind her ear and tilted her chin up to face him. "So you believe her, if not me, then? She's right, of course. You do know that, don't you?"

Abi looked at him coyly. "Yes," she whispered. "I know. I guess I already did. I just worry," and she wound her arms around his neck and pulled him down on top of her. "Can you forgive me?"

Gideon raised an eyebrow, then brought his lips down hard on hers and slid his arms round under her shoulders. "Maybe," he murmured, his lips still pressed onto her mouth. "We'll have to see if you're a good girl or not."

He rolled off her and pulled her over on top of him. She pushed herself up on her hands and gazed down at him, her long hair swinging over her shoulders and brushing his face. "Let's find out, shall we?" she said as her hands began to slide down his lean tanned body, her tongue tracing a path down his chest.

Chapter 6

Monday 4th May, 2009

"I wish we'd gone with them." Caroline sighed and pushed her glasses up onto the top of her head. "Don't you, Roger? We really should have. We should be supporting Gideon at his first concert."

Roger regarded his wife, an amused smile playing about his mouth. "I think it's called a gig, Caroline," he said. "And why on earth would you want to do that? You hate his music."

Caroline frowned. "Hate is too strong a word," she objected. "I prefer other things, but I don't hate Gideon's music. I just think it would be nice to show our support."

Roger grinned. "No, you don't," he said wickedly. "You just want a trip to New Zealand to see Penny and the children. Caroline, we're going in September. Can't you wait till then?"

Caroline smiled. "Well, there is that, of course," she agreed. "I always want to go and see them, but it's something else, too. I noticed before they left that Abi was a little upset about the tour, and I just thought a bit of support from us might make her feel better."

"Why was she upset?" asked Roger in surprise. "Isn't she pleased NightHawk are back together? I thought she wanted Gideon to get back into the business."

Caroline nodded vigorously. "Oh, yes, she does. Of course. She was the one who kept pushing him to do something. It's not that." She paused and frowned. "I think she's finding those dreadful groupies a problem. She gets very jealous when they follow Gideon around. And I did overhear her say she'd been worrying she wouldn't have coped very well if she *had* been on tour with him when she was sixteen."

Roger shrugged. "Probably wouldn't have," he agreed. "But they're not kids now, Caroline. She'll be all right. Now, turn the television on, there's a good girl. It's time for the news," and he sat back in his chair and looked expectantly at her. With a click of her tongue, Caroline got up and switched the television on, then resumed her seat and popped her glasses back on her nose.

"It'll just be bad news as usual," she remarked pessimistically, peering at the screen. "There never seem to be any nice things happening any more."

They sat in silence for a few minutes, watching the various news reports from around the world. Then, as the end of the programme loomed, the presenter smirked and leaned slightly forward in her seat. "One final item tonight," she began, as a large picture of Abi and Gideon appeared behind her. "Gideon Hawk and his family have arrived in New Zealand prior to the start of the tour of the newly re-formed NightHawk." Caroline gave a little squeak of excitement and shifted slightly in her chair. "The arrival coincides with a story that has just broken." The picture behind the presenter changed to that of a red-haired woman standing in the garden of a townhouse, holding the hand of a small child who was wearing a baseball cap pulled well down onto his head. The presenter continued, "News is just in that Nancy Adams, a former girlfriend of Gideon Hawk, has announced he is the father of her son Josh, eight, and that he has ignored the child since birth. Miss Adams, thirty-two, lives in New Zealand with her son and has told the press she's struggling to support him. She's hoping Hawk will contact her whilst he's in the country."

Roger reached over, picked up the remote control and muted the sound. Caroline remained staring at the screen, a look of absolute horror on her face. She swallowed audibly. "Oh, Roger," she whispered. "Not again! Why can't they leave them alone? Now they'll be besieged by the paparazzi again. How could she tell such lies?"

Roger leaned back and crossed his legs. He surveyed his wife over the top of his glasses. "How do we know it's a lie?" he asked reasonably. "We don't know everything Gideon got up to when he was away. He certainly had a few girlfriends."

Caroline's head shot round, her face shocked. "Roger! How can you think such a thing?" she demanded, thumping her fist into the cushion beside her. "If Gideon had fathered a child, he would have taken responsibility for it. Even if it was a dreadful mistake."

"Okay," conceded Roger. "He would have done that. If he knew about it. Maybe she didn't tell him…that bit could be a lie." He frowned thoughtfully. "I think we must consider the possibility that we have another grandchild, though."

Caroline got to her feet and began to pace the

room, her arms wrapped tightly around her body. "But not one we want," she snapped. "Not a child born because of some sordid little affair our son didn't even bother to tell us about. No, Roger, I don't believe it. She's lying. She has to be."

She walked over to the drinks cabinet and poured herself a sherry without offering one to her husband. Roger watched her silently, his mind working overtime. He too considered it unlikely Gideon had fathered a child he knew nothing about—again, he thought ruefully, thinking of Natasha. His son was so famous that if he had got some girlfriend pregnant, the chance she would remain silent for eight years was extremely unlikely. On the other hand, he had to acknowledge it could be true. He knew Gideon had had a few wild years when he thought Abi had deserted him, and he might well have a few secrets his parents knew nothing about.

He sighed and got to his feet. "Caroline, don't worry. It's probably not true. After all, why would she wait eight years to say something? It seems to me more likely that someone is cashing in on the fact that he's just started a tour and is very high profile just now. Let's wait and see what he says, shall we?"

Caroline spun round, her arms still clutched around her. "All the more reason we should be there with them," she said firmly. "We must go tomorrow. Abi will need us."

"Abi? What about our own son?" asked Roger with a small laugh. "Doesn't he need us too?"

"Gideon can look after himself." Caroline nodded briskly. "But Abi is vulnerable already. Roger, we must book a flight. Will we be able to get one tomorrow?"

Roger sighed and ran a hand over his thinning hair. "Okay, you win, we'll try to get a flight. It would be nice to see Penny, and I suppose you're right about Abi. You're the nearest thing to a mother she's got now. But I think we should ring them first. What time is it over there?" he asked, glancing at his watch.

Caroline frowned in concentration. "Well it's eight o'clock now, and they are eleven hours ahead of us. That means it'll be seven in the morning. We can phone; the children will be getting ready for school."

****

Tuesday 5th May, 2009

Penny snatched up the phone from its cradle as she hurried past with the contents of the children's packed lunches.

"Hello?" she said breathlessly, tucking the receiver under her chin and beginning to butter the bread. "Oh, hi, Mum. This is a surprise. Can I call you back in a bit, rather busy…Oh, right. Yeah, hang on. I'll get him. He's still in bed—you do realise how early it is here, don't you?…Okay, hang on." She stopped in front of Abi and Gideon's bedroom door and knocked lightly. There was no reply, so she cautiously opened the door a crack and peeped in.

Abi was lying facing her, and as Penny stepped quietly into the room, she opened her eyes and looked blearily at her. "Wassup?" she muttered indistinctly. "Is Ollie all right?"

Penny nodded and stepped further into the room. "Yeah, nothing to worry about. Mum's on the phone. Wants to speak to Gid," she whispered, her hand pressed over the receiver.

Abi sat up and nudged Gideon with her foot. "Gid,

wake up. Your mother's on the phone." There was no reply, so she shook his shoulder and put her mouth close to his ear. "Gid, your mum's on the phone. Now. Wake up."

This time there was a muffled grunt from the other side of the bed, and Gideon's arm reached up, his hand grasping at the air. Penny leaned forward and put the receiver in his hand, then grinned at Abi and backed out of the room again.

"Mum?" Gideon grunted down the phone. "D'you realise what time it is here? This better be important." He struggled into a sitting position while he listened to Caroline speak, then froze in horror, his face hardening. "She said what?" he bellowed. "No, of course it's not true...Well, I just know it's not...Hang on..." He nudged Abi. "Abs, turn on the TV, quickly. On a news channel."

She glanced at him in surprise, then leapt out of bed and did as he asked. She flicked through several channels, finally landing on 3 News. Staring at the screen, she froze as she noticed a picture of Gideon behind the presenter. She glanced back at him, and he gestured for her to turn up the sound, whilst at the same time continuing the conversation with his mother.

"You don't have to do that...Well, if you really want to, but we'll be fine. We're used to this sort of shit following us around...Okay, I guess that'd be nice for Abi. I'll tell Penny to expect you...No, I don't know what we'll do about it. Maybe have to see her, I don't know." He paused and stared intently at the television screen. "Can I call you later? Yeah, I know, eleven hours. Talk later."

He disconnected the call and tossed the phone onto

the bed. Abi was staring transfixed at the screen, her arms wrapped around her waist and her eyes wide with disbelief.

She glanced back at Gideon. "Gid?" she managed to croak. "Is it true?"

In a single bound, Gideon left the bed and was standing beside her, his arm thrown protectively around her shoulders. "Of course not!" he said in horror. "How could you even think it? There is no way that's my child."

"But you did date her?" Abi asked, her eyes roaming reluctantly back to the pictures on the screen. "This Nancy Adams…she was your girlfriend?"

Gideon sat on the end of the bed and pulled Abi down beside him. "Yeah," he said with a sigh. "I did date her. For about six months. But it wasn't serious, and there's no way she could have got pregnant."

"There was no way I *should* have got pregnant." Abi spoke very quietly, her head bent forward so her hair concealed her face. "But I did."

Gideon caught her by the shoulders and turned her to face him, pushing her hair off her face with one hand. "That was different," he stated firmly, staring her in the eyes. "You know how that happened: The condom was old; I was young. There's no way on earth Nancy"—Abi flinched at her name—"could have got pregnant. I was very careful."

Abi wriggled out of his grasp and got to her feet. She walked over to the window and stared out over the bay, her mind doing somersaults as she attempted to process this new information. Amazingly, it had never occurred to her before that Gideon could possibly have a child conceived during their years apart, but she forced herself to realise it could easily be true. She spun round to face him, her eyes huge in her pale face.

"Did you love her?" she asked, her voice brittle.

Gideon shook his head violently, his eyes anguished. "Of course not," he said emphatically. "I only ever loved you. Even after I knew—believed—I'd lost you. The other girls were just a distraction. A way of attempting to forget you, to try to make myself not care. To show you I didn't care…" He dropped his head into his hands forlornly.

Abi stood and watched him from across the room, wondering how much more there was she didn't know about this man she had loved since she was fifteen. She knew he'd had other girlfriends during their time apart. She had had other boyfriends. But to consider that a child could have come out of one of those unions made her feel physically sick. She picked her dressing gown up off the chair and shrugged it on.

"I'm going to make sure Tasha goes to school," she said flatly, "and to check Ollie is all right. We'll talk later." She walked out of the room, leaving Gideon slumped on the edge of the bed, his head bowed.

Penny glanced up as Abi entered the kitchen, immediately taking in her appearance. She raised her eyebrows, but Abi shook her head ever so slightly and walked over to where Natasha and Lydia were tucking into their breakfast.

Natasha looked up and narrowed her eyes. "What's up?" she asked, spraying toast crumbs all over the table. "You look dreadful, and Aunty Penny said Grandma rang. Are she and Grandpa all right?" A slight edge of panic sounded in her voice, and she stared wide-eyed at her mother.

"Grandma and Grandpa are fine," Abi assured her, with a forced smile, sitting down at the table and pouring herself a cup of coffee. "She just needed to talk to Dad about something."

Natasha looked unconvinced. "But you look dreadful. Are you ill?" she persisted, frowning.

"Just got a bit of a headache," lied Abi smoothly, taking a long slurp of coffee. "This'll make it better."

"Coffee's not the best thing for a headache," Lydia stated severely. "In fact, it'll probably make it worse. Have a glass of water and some painkillers."

Abi summoned a smile. "This'll be fine, thank you, Lydia. Water never tastes right in the morning."

Penny joined them at the table and poured herself a coffee. She sat back in her chair and smiled at Natasha. "So you approved of school enough to go back today, then?" she asked, attempting a subject change.

"It was all right." Natasha shrugged. "I'll go today, anyway. Some of the kids were a bit of a pain when they found out who Dad was, but it was nothing I couldn't cope with. I get that everywhere," she added with a tone of resignation.

Abi stared at her in consternation as she realised that some of the children would probably have seen the news bulletin she and Gideon had watched in the bedroom. She couldn't let Natasha go off to school unprepared. She got to her feet, and her chair scraped noisily on the tiled floor.

"Tash," she said, biting her lip. "I need to talk to you before you go to school. Come to the sunroom when you've finished your breakfast." She picked up her coffee mug and left the room.

Natasha began to get to her feet, but Penny waved

her back into the seat. "Finish your toast, Tasha," she said firmly, getting to her feet. "Then you can go and see your mother."

She followed Abi to the sunroom and found her standing staring out over the sea, her eyes blank and her body tense.

"Abi?" she ventured, stopping just behind her. "What's happened?"

Abi half turned towards her, her shoulders slumped. She indicated to Penny to sit down, and then briefly outlined the story on the news.

"So I can't let Tasha go to school and find out from some cocky little kid who'll think it great sport to taunt her with it. If she's prepared, she can deal with it."

Penny looked concerned. "Maybe she should stay home today?" she suggested. "I can keep an eye on her while you and Gideon sort things out."

Abi shook her head. "No, she should go to school. Otherwise, people will think it's true. We need to behave as normally as possible," she said tightly.

"It's not true, is it?" Penny asked eventually.

"He says not." Abi shrugged. "But how can he know for sure? It was an accident when I got pregnant with Tasha. It can happen too easily." She took a long, shuddering breath and stared out the window again. "I don't think I could bear it if it was true," she said very quietly. "It just wouldn't be right. It would spoil everything."

Penny got to her feet and went to stand next to her, putting her arm around Abi's shoulders and giving her a squeeze. "It would be hard to take," she agreed. "But it wouldn't change anything between you and Gideon. If it is true, then it happened when you two were not together. It doesn't affect your relationship at all. You must try and keep it in perspective. It may not be true anyway."

"It's not true," Gideon's voice, charged with emotion, echoed from the doorway. "I told you, Abi, there is no way it's true. Why can't you trust my word?"

"What's not true?" Natasha's voice was loud and brittle as she marched into the room and stood staring at her parents. "What's going on?"

Abi spun round and attempted to smile at her. "Come and sit down, Tash," she said, holding out her hand.

Natasha shook her head and remained where she was. "No. What's going on?" she repeated, even more loudly, barely concealing the fear in her voice.

Gideon sighed. "Tasha, there was a news item just now that says one of my former girlfriends thinks I'm the father of her child. I'm not, but we don't want you to go to school and have someone else tell you," he said walking over and standing next to Abi. "Your mother's rather upset about it—as am I—but there's nothing to worry about. These things happen if you're famous."

Natasha stared at him impassively, then shook her head and sat down on the nearest chair with an exaggerated sigh. "This means we'll get besieged by the paparazzi again, doesn't it?" she said in annoyance. "Well, I could have done without that. Honestly, Dad, why couldn't you have been an accountant or something?" Then with another shake of her head, directed at both her parents, she got to her feet again and headed back to the kitchen. "You two sort it out. I'm going to school."

Abi, Gideon, and Penny stared at her retreating back in shocked surprise.

Abi gave a slightly nervous giggle. "An accountant," she said faintly. "She wishes you were an accountant. That child never ceases to amaze me. I guess she can deal with things better than I can."

Gideon reached out and put his arm around her shoulders. "It'll be fine, Abs, you mustn't worry. It's not my child."

Abi pulled away from him and walked over to the window. "How do you know for sure?" she asked without turning round. "You had no idea I was pregnant with Tasha, and you never even considered the possibility. You're not infallible, Gideon."

"Abi, that's just not fair." Gideon strode over and stood beside her. "You know why that happened. The condom was out of date, and I didn't know any better. It was my first time, remember."

Penny's eyes widened, and she coughed apologetically. "I'll leave you two to sort this out," she said. "I need to make sure the kids get off to school okay. I'll be around if you need me." She hurried out of the room and headed back to the kitchen.

Abi stared out over the sea and sighed. "I hope you're right," she said finally, "because I don't think I could cope if it's true." She glanced briefly at him, her face sombre. "Now I'm going to get Ollie up and dressed."

Gideon put out a hand to stop her, but she shook it off and walked over to the door. She turned and surveyed him solemnly. "Sort this, Gideon," she said, "and sort it fast."

He watched her go, his face inscrutable. His

shoulders slumped, and he dropped heavily into a deeply cushioned chair. This was the first time anything had come between them, and he was beginning to feel out of his depth. He needed to sort it out fast, but he had no idea how to do that.

Chapter 7

Tuesday 5th May, 2009

Natasha kicked the gate shut behind her with an annoyed grunt, and Lydia glanced at her in concern. "You all right, Tash?" she asked. "D'you think it's true?"

Natasha threw a quick glance over her shoulder. "No," she replied shortly. "Dad said it's not, an' I believe him. It's the bloody paparazzi who bother me." She slung her bag over her shoulder and marched off down the road, leaving her cousin standing on the pavement staring after her.

Lydia ran to catch up with her and took her arm. "Don't worry, we can deal with them," she said with confidence. "They don't scare me."

"They don't *scare* me," Natasha said darkly. "I'm more concerned I may hurt them. We just can't escape them. I sometimes really wish Dad wasn't so famous." She looked at Lydia. "I mean, how would you like it if your dad got followed everywhere by screaming teenagers, and photographed by the gutter press?"

"I guess that would be weird." Lydia grinned. "He works in a bank. I don't think that's very sexy," and the two girls giggled at the thought that their fathers might be sexy.

"I s'pose it's quite fun that he's famous...usually."

Natasha sighed. "But he can't do anything normal without it being reported on. Not that having someone claim you're the father of their child is really normal. I hope it's not true."

Lydia wrinkled her nose. "I thought you said it wasn't?" she objected.

"Well, I do believe Dad," Natasha said slowly, "but I guess he could be mistaken. I know he had loads of girlfriends during the years he and Mum were separated. Obviously he did—he was a famous rock star in his twenties. Apparently he's good-looking, too. But I'm sure he would have been careful not to have a baby." She went silent, and a closed look came over her face.

"What?" Lydia looked at her curiously. "You look weird. What have you thought of?"

Natasha shook her head. "Nothing," she said, quickening her pace and hurrying across the road towards the school entrance. Lydia caught up with her and grabbed her elbow.

"Tash?" she said severely. "What is it? Tell me. We need to stick together, and I need to know everything if I'm going to be able to do that."

Natasha stopped walking and looked round at her. "Okay," she conceded. "It's just that, well, Dad can't have been very careful when Mum got pregnant with me. They didn't really mean that to happen. She was only sixteen. If he was careless then, maybe he was again with that woman." Her nose wrinkled with distaste as she said the words.

Lydia bit her lip thoughtfully. "Well…" She looked doubtfully at her cousin. "He was only eighteen when he and your Mum—you know. He must have been lots older with that woman. You can make a mistake at eighteen that you wouldn't do at twenty-something, can't you?"

"Yeah, maybe." Natasha shrugged, tossing her hair back over her shoulders. "I s'pose you're right. Hope so, anyway. Now let's get to school and face the questions there!" She took a deep breath, caught Lydia's arm, and together they marched through the gates and into the playground.

****

Simon's plane touched down at Auckland nearly two hours later than expected, due to a string of unforeseen events that had caused delays all along the way.

As he exited into the warm autumn sunshine, he felt a slight disturbance in his stomach again. He frowned and dismissed the nervous qualms that threatened to overwhelm him, then hailed the nearest taxi and jumped in. He barked out his destination, sat back, and closed his eyes. He had managed to sleep for much of the flight but would still appreciate a long soak in the bath, followed by a nap in a proper bed. After that he felt he would be up to planning his next move.

He had purchased a newspaper from a stand at the airport, and his face took on a look of mild satisfaction as he read the headlines. He quickly scanned down the front page, then flipped over to page four to finish the story. He sat back with a sigh and a smile. Looked like Gideon was about to get besieged by reporters again. Served him right.

****

Gideon finally found Abi and Oliver playing on the beach, surrounded by a barricade of sand castles and deep holes. The little boy was wet, sandy, and very happy, and Abi was industriously digging a large hole for him to sit in. He looked up as his father approached, a huge grin on his ice-cream-encrusted face.

"Daddy!" he cried. "Look, Mummy's made big hole!"

Gideon smiled at the little boy and squatted down on the sand next to his wife. She continued to dig her hole, her bare tanned back towards him. After a couple of minutes of silence, she sat back and surveyed her handiwork.

"Will that do, sweetie?" she asked Oliver, brushing sand off her hands. "If I go any deeper, we'll be back in England." Oliver giggled and jumped into the hole with an ear-splitting cry of delight. Abi stretched her legs out in front of her in the sand. She arched her back and wriggled her shoulders. "That was harder work than it looked," she remarked, glancing sideways at Gideon. He reached out and gently began to massage her shoulders, brushing her long hair out of the way as he did so.

As his long fingers worked their magic, Abi sighed and began to relax. "That's nice," she murmured, bending her head forward, her hair swinging down and brushing against her legs. "What are we going to do, Gid?"

Gideon sighed and relaxed slightly as he realised she didn't seem quite so mad at him any more. "Don't know, babe," he admitted, his hands continuing their soothing movements. "I'm at a loss. It's no good just doing a press release to say it's not true. They'll never go for that."

Abi swung round to face him, knocking his hands

from her shoulders. "It really isn't true, is it?" she asked, anguish sounding in her voice. "You really were always careful?"

Gideon put his hands back on her shoulders and stared her straight in the eyes. "Yes, Abs, I was. That first time with you...that was completely different. By the time I was going out with Nancy, I was twenty-three, and I knew what I was doing. There's no way that's my child."

Abi stared back at him, then slowly nodded. "Okay, I guess I believe you. So long as you weren't trusting her to be on the pill...?" The whole idea was distasteful to her.

Gideon shook his head forcefully. "God, no!" he said at once. "I never trusted anyone about that. Much safer to use a condom anyway." He paused for a moment. "I also think Nancy would have told me if she was pregnant. She was pretty keen on me. Far keener than I was on her. She would have jumped at a chance to trap me."

Abi got to her feet abruptly and walked a few steps away, staring out towards the island in the distance.

"I hate to think of you with other people," she said quietly. "It's so wrong. Usually I can put it out of my mind, but something like this just brings it flooding back." She turned back to face him. "So if it's not true, what's she playing at? What does she want from you?"

"Money, I guess." Gideon shrugged. "She will have seen the band are back together and decided now was the time to make a move. Specially since she apparently lives in New Zealand now. Very convenient."

"Where was she from?" Abi asked reluctantly, not

really wanting to know.

"Seattle. Seems odd she's over here, actually. Unless she got together with someone from here." He paused and frowned slightly. "That's probably it. She probably met someone and moved here with him and now he's left her. She's short of money and thinks I may be a meal ticket for her."

Abi wrinkled her nose with distaste. "Gideon, this is sordid," she said sharply. "Whatever will your parents be thinking?"

Gideon sucked in his breath. "Oh, yeah, nearly forgot. Mum says they're coming over. I must tell Penny."

"What? Coming here? Now?" Abi stared at him in amazement. "Why?"

"Apparently Mum thinks you'll need her," Gideon replied with a crooked grin. "Not worrying about me, just you."

"Quite right, too." Abi gave a reluctant smile. "But they really don't need to bother. I can look after myself. I did it for long enough."

Gideon strode over to her and put his arm around her shoulders. "And you never need to again. I'll always look after you. I'm so sorry this has happened." He looked down at her seriously. "Might be nice for Tasha if they're here, though."

"Oh, yes, and it'll be nice for me, too." Abi nodded. "But it's a lot of trouble and expense for them to go to."

Gideon grinned down at her. "I think they just wanted an excuse to visit Penny. I know they were very envious of us coming over just now."

A sound behind them made them turn to see Penny

making her way across the beach towards them. "There you are!" she exclaimed, stopping beside them and placing a large wicker basket on the sand. "I've been looking everywhere for you. I've brought lunch. Thought you might be peckish, and I also thought we needed to talk." She laid a striped blanket on the sand and sank gracefully down onto it. She looked up at her brother and his wife over the top of her sunglasses, and patted the ground beside her. "Sit down. We need to sort things out."

Silently Abi and Gideon sat down on the blanket beside her, and little Oliver toddled over to join them, his chubby face hungrily expectant.

Penny laughed and handed him a chunky cheese sandwich, then turned to the other two. "Right. Have you decided what you're going to do?" She came straight to the point, her piercing blue eyes fixed on Gideon in a very big-sisterly way. "You can't just ignore it. Gideon, is there any chance it's true?"

He shook his head. "No, no chance at all. She's just trying it on." He frowned. "We could just go on air and deny it, but I don't think that's enough."

Penny nodded in agreement. "Oh, definitely not," she said at once. "I think you need to go and see her."

Abi stared at her in surprise. "Go and see her?" she echoed. "How can we? Would that be a good idea? Gid, what d'you think?"

"Dunno," he said slowly. "The paparazzi'll be everywhere. We'd never get there unnoticed. Always supposing we can find out where she is."

Penny shrugged. "The papers'll know that. There were photos of her at her house. You only need to ring them."

"Definitely not." Gideon shook his head emphatically. "Then the whole world'll know we're going. No, if we do go and see her, it has to be done secretly. Get her to go to a different location and arrange to meet her there. It won't be easy, but it may be possible."

Abi shook her head. "But how on earth do we get in touch with her without using the press? I presume you don't still have her phone number?" she added, scowling at Gideon.

He shook his head, then shrugged. "No, I don't, but I know a couple of people who may have," he said, watching her nervously.

She narrowed her eyes at him suspiciously. "Who?"

"Maybe the tour manager we used in the late nineties, a couple of friends of mine in Seattle…and possibly Chas," Gideon replied.

"Well, there you go, then," said Penny cheerfully before Abi could pass comment. "If you can get her number, you're half way there. That's good, isn't it, Abi?"

Abi bit her lip. The thought that Charles or anyone else she knew might have the phone number of one of Gideon's ex-girlfriends made her feel physically sick, and she turned to face him. "Chas has her number?" she asked softly, her eyes boring into him like lasers. "Why would Chas still have her number?"

"She toured with us," Gideon said. "She worked for the band. She did wardrobe, stuff like that. We all had her phone number."

Abi inclined her head. "Fine, at the time, of course you did. But now? Nearly ten years later? Why would

Chas still have her number? Did he go out with her too?" she asked, her voice brittle and slightly too loud.

"No." Gideon sighed. "He didn't go out with her. Some of the roadies did, though." He watched Abi carefully. "And Simon."

Abi sucked in her breath and stared at him, her eyes like flint. "Simon?" she repeated. "She went out with Simon…and the roadies? After you, I assume? Well, she sounds like a right little slapper, doesn't she? How's she getting so much of our attention? How does she have the right to fuck up our lives like this? A worthless piece of crap like that. Get rid of her, Gideon. Get her out of our lives!" She turned on her heel and ran down the beach towards the sea.

Gideon moved to go after her, but Penny laid a restraining hand on his arm. "Let her go, Gid," she warned. "She needs to get it out of her system. This has been a hell of a shock for her."

Gideon raised his eyebrows and ran a distracted hand through his dark hair. "Not just for her," he muttered savagely. "I'm not exactly enjoying myself either, you know!"

Penny pulled him back down onto the blanket beside her and handed him a can of cola. "I know," she said with a sigh. "But this is *because* of you. Even if it's not true, it's still because of your actions. Abi feels disconnected from that because it was during a time when she wasn't with you, when she had no idea what your life was like." She paused and laid a hand on his arm. "She told me yesterday how happy she'd been these last three years, and how much she fears that if she lets go it will all fly away and leave her alone again. I think this has given her a taste of what that might feel like. And it scares her." She paused again and gave a wry smile. "And Abi doesn't like to admit she's scared, does she? She likes to appear tough and self sufficient. You need to be very understanding, Gid, even if this is hard for you too. You need to face this together, and whatever happens, she needs to feel you're totally devoted to her, and that nothing can ever come between you."

Gideon looked at her solemnly. "Nothing ever could come between us," he said immediately, his eyes straying to where his wife was wandering along the edge of the water. "How could she even think that? God, Penny, what shall I do? Should I call Nancy, or will that freak Abi even more?"

"Of course you should call her," Penny said. "No question. And Abi must go with you to see her. Then she'll see for herself there's nothing between you and that the child is not yours. You need to do this as soon as you can. Go and see if you can get her number. I'll stay here with Ollie and wait for Abi."

"Okay," Gideon agreed reluctantly, getting to his feet. "I'll try Chas first, then some people in Seattle." A few steps from where she sat, he paused and looked round at her. "Oh, yeah. Mum and Dad are coming over. I forgot to say." Then he escaped up the beach away from her startled exclamation.

****

Down by the water's edge, Abi watched as Gideon made his way back up to the house, leaving his sister on the beach with Oliver. She kicked at the sea savagely with her bare foot and ground her teeth together in frustration. Why did it have to be that every time she thought her life was sorted—and in this case perfect—

something happened to disrupt it? She realised she was probably overreacting to this latest piece of sensationalism from the press, but it had brought to the fore all her un-dealt-with issues about Gideon and former girlfriends. She realised it all stemmed back to the day in August '95 when she had seen him on the news with another girl and had thought he was being unfaithful to her. He wasn't, but the feeling had never left her, and it had been very easily triggered again by this latest piece of news.

She turned and stared out across the shimmering blue ocean towards the distant hump of land that was Motiti Island. The gentle waves lapped over her feet, and a light breeze ruffled through her already beach-tangled hair. She closed her eyes and raised her face up to the sun, revelling for a moment in its welcome warmth; then she took a deep breath and turned to make her way back up the beach. It was no good hiding away from things. This was something that needed to be sorted, and she wasn't about to let Gideon face it alone.

****

"Roger, you really do amaze me sometimes." Caroline leaned back in her seat and adjusted her headrest. "How on earth you managed to get these tickets I'll never know. I suppose I shouldn't ask, either," she added, raising her eyebrows.

Roger smirked at her and attempted to stretch his long legs out in front of him. "You said you wanted to fly to Auckland today, so I sorted it," he said smoothly. "You give the orders, I carry them out. That's how it works, isn't it?"

"Quite right, too." Caroline smiled, patting him affectionately on the hand. "If a system works, why change it?" She leant back in her seat with a satisfied sigh. "It will be nice to see Penny and James again. And I'm so glad Gideon phoned before we left. I think they're doing the right thing, don't you?"

Roger shrugged. "I suppose so. Doubt it'll be much fun for either of them, though. Abi's going to hate meeting one of Gideon's ex-girlfriends. Just hope he's right," he added with a grimace.

"Oh, Roger, I'm sure he is. He seems so certain. Surely he would have made sure that sort of thing couldn't happen. Wouldn't he?" she said doubtfully. "He was very young when he and Abi... Surely he would have been more responsible all those years later?"

Roger smiled at her. "I'm sure he was, Caroline," he said firmly. "I'm sure it'll all turn out all right. Now, we have a very long flight ahead of us. I hope you brought plenty to read, because I don't intend to listen to you talking all the time." With a chuckle, he leant back, closed his eyes, and listened in amusement to her indignant tutting.

****

Abi couldn't sleep. She rolled onto her back and stared up at the high white ceiling with its flickering shadows cast by the light of the moon. She sat up and gazed out of the long window at the nearly full moon that hung huge and luminous over the bay, illuminating the beach and the distant island. She sighed and rested her head on her knees. She was dreading the next day.

Gideon had managed to get a mobile number for Nancy from one of his contacts in Seattle—Charles hadn't had it after all, rather to Abi's relief—and after a few attempts he had finally spoken to her. She had reluctantly agreed to meet with them the following afternoon at a ranch outside Christchurch, where she assured him she wouldn't get tracked by the press. Gideon had then managed to book them both on a flight from Tauranga, leaving just before midday, which would arrive in Christchurch about two thirty. They had arranged to meet Nancy at four and had booked into a small rural hotel for the night to allow for the possibility of seeing her again the next day if need be. Abi got out of bed and walked to the window. The view was spectacular, but she couldn't help wishing she were back home in her house overlooking Sennen Cove. She would be safe there. Safe and secure, with nothing threatening her happiness.

She turned and stared at her sleeping husband. He lay on his back, with one arm hanging off the edge of the bed and the other covering his eyes. His mouth was slightly open, and he was snoring gently. Abi smiled affectionately at him. Once this was sorted, she wasn't going to let him or the children out of her sight. Nothing was ever going to come between them again.

Chapter 8

Wednesday 6th May, 2009

"Mum, we'll be fine, stop fussing." Natasha shook her curly head at Abi and picked up her school bag. "You'll be back tomorrow anyway, won't you?"

"Should be." Abi shrugged. "If all goes according to plan, but it'll probably be pretty late in the evening. Grandma and Grandpa are arriving tomorrow morning, though. You'll have them to amuse you," she said with a smile, giving her daughter a hug. "Now, off you go or you'll be late. And Tash? Thanks for doing the school thing—I know you didn't want to."

Natasha wrinkled her nose and gave a wry grin. "Actually, you were right," she admitted reluctantly. "It's more fun spending time with people my own age. Lydia and I get on really well, too. It's not too bad." She grinned more widely. "And I'm ahead of most of the class, so that's good, too."

"Good." Abi laughed. "Now off you go, and we'll see you tomorrow night, or Friday at the latest. Be good for Penny, and keep an eye on Ollie, won't you?"

Natasha nodded and, waving a hand, followed Lydia out of the door and down the drive.

They walked in silence until they reached the main road. Then Lydia glanced around before whispering, "Maybe we should have done it today? They'll be away all night. Tomorrow they'll be back in the evening, and Grandma and Grandpa will be here by then, too."

Natasha shook her head impatiently. "We couldn't have," she objected. "You said the bus leaves Tauranga at seven thirty, so we would've had to leave home at quarter to seven for me to get it. Mum and Dad would have thought that suspicious when they're leaving today. No, it'll be much easier tomorrow morning. Your Mum'll be fussing about the grandparents coming, and no one will notice if we leave home half an hour early." She glanced at Lydia and raised her eyebrows. "It'll work, you'll see."

Lydia looked unconvinced and caught Natasha by the arm. "But the bus back doesn't get in till six thirty," she objected. "How are we going to explain your absence that long? Even if your mum and dad aren't back, the grandparents will be here and'll be wanting to see you. What excuse can we use?"

Natasha frowned. "There is that earlier bus. The one at one twenty, that gets back at five to five. But we decided I wouldn't have enough time to get that one. If I get to Cambridge just before nine, I've then got to get a taxi to Kaipaki, so it'll probably be half nine by the time I get there. I need a couple of hours, at least, to talk to Billy. More, probably. Then I have to get a taxi, back to Hamilton this time, and that's further." She paused and wrinkled her nose. "I'd have to rush to get the early one. And you'd still have to say I'd gone somewhere after school anyway. No, let's stick to the plan, and I'll get the later one. You can say I've gone home with someone."

Lydia looked confused. "Who?" she asked, wide-eyed. "You don't know anyone."

Natasha gave a snort of annoyance. "I've met your friends. One of them might have invited me for tea or something," she said vaguely with a wave of her hand.

Lydia looked doubtfully at her. "Without me? I don't think Mum'll go for that. Better if I say you stayed for some after-school club or something. What d'you like?"

Natasha rolled her eyes. "Oh, I don't know! This was s'posed to be easy. Now it's getting complicated. You think of something."

Lydia sighed. "If we don't do it properly, you'll get found out and get into loads of trouble, and so will I for helping you," she said patiently. "If we can think of a really good reason you haven't come home with me, then we may get away with it." She thought for a moment. "I guess I could go to a friend's house and call Mum and say we've both gone, and then I could come home at the same time the bus gets in? How does that sound?"

Natasha grinned. "Sounds brill!" she said admiringly. "Will your mum go for it?"

"Maybe." Lydia shrugged. "Best I can come up with, though. Tomorrow morning leaving early will be a doddle. Mum'll be so stressed about the grandparents arriving she won't even notice us. Now come on, we'd better get a move on, or we'll be late," and they dodged across the road and hurried towards the school gates.

****

Abi glanced back at Penny as she and Gideon mounted the steps to their flight to Christchurch. She raised her hand and gave a little wave, then followed her husband onto the aircraft and to their seats.

They had been seated near the back of the plane,

and as Abi slid into the window seat, she realised just how much she was dreading the trip. She had eventually got to sleep at around three o'clock, and having risen again at seven, she was beginning to feel tired, restless, and irritable. She settled into her seat and attempted to get comfortable, then glanced around to see if the drinks trolley was in sight; a coffee was probably just what she needed to wake her up. Gideon slid in next to her and folded his long legs into the tiny space.

"This is going to be comfortable," he remarked with a grimace. "Good job it's not too long a flight."

Abi wrinkled her nose. "I wish it was longer," she said. "I'm dreading getting there."

Gideon reached out and put his arm around her shoulders, pulling her closer towards him. "It'll be fine," he attempted to reassure. "By tonight you'll be wondering what all the fuss was about."

Abi raised an eyebrow and looked at him dubiously. "I hope you're right."

Twenty minutes later, they were in the air and had both partaken of large cups of very strong coffee.

Abi sat back with a sigh. "That's a bit better," she said, closing her eyes and wriggling in her seat in an attempt to get more comfortable. "Might manage to stay awake for the rest of the flight now. I really didn't sleep well last night." She glanced at Gideon with a slight grin. "You, on the other hand, were snoring contentedly away. Hope that's the sign of a clear conscience!"

"Of course it is," he retorted with a smile. "I was sleeping the sleep of the innocent. Honestly, Abs, there's nothing to worry about."

Abi was silent for a moment before she sighed and spoke without looking at him. "I know that, but it's the whole deal of having to meet someone you had a relationship with. Having to meet her in person. That's never happened before. It keeps reminding me of that time I saw you on the news in August '95—you know, with that skinny girl in Seattle? I was pregnant, and scared, and desperately worried because I hadn't heard from you... Then I saw that—God! I was a mess afterwards. This has brought it all back, all the feelings of betrayal, of loss, of panic and aloneness." She turned to look at him, and her blue eyes reflected her pain. "It's not a feeling I ever wanted to have again."

Gideon watched her as she spoke, his heart torn apart by her obvious distress. He wished he could tell her he had never been with any girl except her. That he had kept himself for her, all the years they were apart; but of course he hadn't, any more than she had. They both thought they'd lost each other and had acted accordingly. He realised that, under the circumstances, they'd probably both had fewer lovers than one might have imagined, but they had each had several, and it was important they accept the fact and move on. He reached over and took her hand in his. As usual, it was cold, and he closed his large hand around it and squeezed gently.

"Abi, I'm sorry," he said, his fingers caressing her palm. "But I think we need to accept the fact we both had lovers during the years we were apart. It was inevitable, but it in no way detracts from our relationship. Nothing can harm that. You do understand that, don't you? We need to move on and put our pasts behind us."

Abi wiggled her fingers in his hand and raised her eyes to his. "It's hard," she said simply. "I love you so much I just can't bear to think of you with anyone else. It tears me apart. I know it was inevitable. I know I did it, too. But that doesn't make it any better." She turned and stared out of the window beside her. "And somehow actually having to meet one of them..." She pulled her hand away from his. "What are you going to say to her? What will she think of me being there? Gideon, this is intolerable. I don't think I can come with you."

A look of intense pain crossed Gideon's sharp features, and he recaptured her hand and held it tightly in his. "Abi, you must," he said. "I can't do this alone. I need you with me."

"Maybe you should have thought of that nine years ago," she muttered unfairly, attempting to free her hand again. Gideon held on tightly and, catching her chin with his other hand, turned her to face him.

"You're upset," he said, his eyes flashing. "So I'll let that one go. But Abi, I need you with me. I want her to see us together. To see how strong we are. I don't want her to be able to find a chink in our armour. We need to do this together." He stared her in the eye, daring her to argue.

Abi stared back. "I know," she said simply. "I'm being unreasonable. Sorry. Of course I'll come." The ghost of a smile played around her lips. "Just don't expect me to be nice to her. One false move on her part, and I'll have her."

Gideon grinned at her. "That's more like it," he approved. "That's more like my high maintenance teenage Abi! I think I could do with her today." He squeezed her hand again, and she looked up at him. "You do know just how long it was before I had a girlfriend, don't you? I told you about the time I threw that girl out of my room in May '96? Well it was another eighteen months or so before I actually…did anything."

"Winter '97?" Abi bit her lip. "That's about the same time I first got together with someone." She shook her head as if to rid herself of the memory. "It was not an encounter I'm very proud of, either."

Gideon let go of her hand and settled back in his seat. "Maybe we should tell each other about those occasions," he suggested tentatively. "Maybe that would help to lay the ghosts? Much as I don't want to know details of your sex life, it may help us understand how we each felt during that time." He paused and glanced over at her. "What d'you think?"

Abi looked solemnly at him, her eyes dark. "Maybe it would help," she said at last. "I've imagined so many different scenarios…maybe the truth won't be as bad. Just so long as I know it won't change anything between us. Won't make you like me less…" She suddenly looked very young and very vulnerable.

Gideon stared at her in dismay. How could she even consider that? He shook his head. "Abi, when will you finally get it into your head that nothing on earth could ever make me like you less? I adore you. I always have and I always will. Anything you did while we were separated bears no relation to our life together. If anything, it'll probably make me love you even more." He reached out and pulled her hand into his lap. "Abi, I love you more than you could ever imagine, and nothing can ever change that."

Abi stared at him. "Okay, then," she said with a nod. "I feel the same about you, but I do worry what you'll think when you know what I was like at the end of the nineties. I wasn't very nice for a while."

Gideon laughed out loud. "Neither was I," he admitted immediately. "I didn't treat my girlfriends very well at all. I judged them all against you, and none of them fared very well!" He paused and gently stroked her hand. "If we both bear that in mind, I really think it might help if we actually knew the truth. I certainly think it would make me feel even closer to you."

Abi took a deep breath and nodded. "Well, then, you go first. When was your first time?"

Chapter 9

Sunday 30th November, 1997—Newbury, Berkshire

Gideon stared up at the house, his heart in his mouth. The day was cold and dreary, the sky sullen and threatening, and the wind was whipping the fallen leaves around his feet. He shivered and turned up the collar of his leather jacket. With his hands thrust deep into his pockets, he slowly crossed the quiet tree-lined suburban street and walked towards Abi's childhood home. Taking a deep breath, he squeezed past Arthur Thomson's old Saab and made his way up the narrow path to the front door. He stood for a moment on the doorstep, his breathing suddenly shallow; then he raised his hand and pressed his index finger firmly on the bell. Nothing happened for a while, and he was about to press it again when he became aware of a dark shadow coming closer behind the frosted glass. He stepped back onto the path and waited, unconsciously brushing his hair back over his shoulders. The door opened with a slight creak, and Abi's father stared out at him. The man had aged a little in the two and a half years since Gideon had last seen him, and he peered out at the young man hovering nervously on his path.

Gideon stepped forward again. "Hello, Mr. Thomson," he said politely, his mouth dry and the words feeling alien. "I was wondering if Abi was at home?"

Arthur stared impassively at him, then stepped back and started to close the door. Gideon jumped up onto the step and put out his hand.

"Please, Mr. Thomson... Don't shut me out. I just want to talk to her."

Arthur paused and pulled the door slightly more open. "She doesn't live here anymore," he said bleakly, his stare hostile. "And if she did, she wouldn't want to see you."

Gideon recoiled slightly at his tone, and swallowed. "Why?" he asked, his voice sounding hollow in his own ears. "Why wouldn't she want to see me? Where is she now?"

Arthur sighed. "She's gone away to college. She never wants to see you again. Don't come back. We don't want you here. You ruined her life." He very slowly and deliberately closed the door.

Gideon stepped back onto the path and stared in dismay. That she was no longer there was not that much of a surprise. He knew she'd planned to go to art college. But that she thought he'd ruined her life and never wanted to see him again? His head was reeling. How could she feel like that? What had happened? He stared up at the dark windows of the house and felt a furious anger welling up in him. He could sense the hand of her mother in this. She must have influenced Abi after he'd gone away. Turned her against him in some way. He moved forward to ring the bell again, to try and demand some answers, then slowly let his hand drop to his side.

She hadn't written. He'd sensed something wrong that last day before he left. Now this from her father.

Maybe it was time he accepted it. He really had lost her. He'd been trying to force himself to believe that, ever since he stopped writing to her, but deep inside he'd still harboured a tiny flicker of hope that all was not lost. He'd been waiting for this first trip back to England for a chance to do something about it. Now that flicker had finally been extinguished.

Shoulders drooping, he turned and walked slowly back down the path, squeezed past the Saab, and stepped out onto the pavement. He started walking back to where he'd left his mother's car. Just as he reached it, he glanced to his left and realised he was on the corner of the road Judy had lived in. He stared along it thoughtfully. If anyone would know what had gone wrong between them, it would be Judy. Abi told her everything. Maybe he should have one last try. He took a deep breath and started walking quickly along the road towards the Cromwell's house. Of course they may have moved, he thought as he walked, they may be out...but it was worth a try.

As he approached the house, he became aware of a dark green estate car edging out of the drive. He stopped walking and studied it closely to see if it was the Cromwell's. The car appeared to be loaded with luggage and three passengers. 'L' plates were prominently displayed, and as Gideon watched, Judy carefully drove the car out onto the quiet street, and turning left, drove slowly away from him.

He turned and walked back to his car. There was no point in waiting; they were clearly going away. He had to fly back to the USA the next day, so he would have no time to come back. Something heavy and cold settled in his stomach, and a wave of pure loss swept over him. It was over. It was finally time to move on.

****

Friday 5th December, 1997—Seattle, USA

The screaming and applause carried on long after the boys had left the stage, and as they were hurried backstage and into the dressing rooms, they could hear the demanding fans attempting to break through the security barriers. Gideon turned as he entered his dressing room and found himself staring into the faces of dozens of crying and screaming girls who were desperately trying to get past the guards. He flicked his sweat-drenched hair back off his face and glowered at them, before striding into the room and slamming the door behind him. He tossed his guitar onto the sofa and snatched up the tall bottle of mineral water standing half-drunk on the table. He downed it in one huge gulp, then tossed the empty bottle into the trash, peeled off his smoky, sweaty clothes, and headed for the shower.

As he stood under the scalding water, letting it run all over his head and body, his eyes tightly closed, he wondered again if he was doing the right thing. They had been back in the US for nearly a week and had just completed a three-day run in Seattle. A huge party had been arranged for after the last gig, and Gideon had reluctantly allowed himself to be persuaded into attending with his friends. He had got himself a reputation over the last couple of years of being extremely antisocial, a reputation that had greatly enhanced his attractiveness in the eyes of the adoring teenage fans. He was moody, enigmatic, and unattainable. That made him by far the most popular member of the band.

As the water ran down his body and pooled at his

feet, he relived again the conversation he'd had with Abi's father nearly a week earlier. It was the primary reason he had agreed to go to the party. His heart was still broken, but he'd realised life had to go on. He poured shampoo onto the top of his head and began to rub vigorously. He needed to wash all memory of the performance from his body. He always felt like that. He loved to perform. He loved playing the music, he loved the atmosphere, the adrenalin rush. He loved it all. But once he was offstage it all changed. He stopped being Gideon Hawk, frontman of NightHawk, sex symbol to thousands of teenagers, top guitarist and song writer. He became just plain Gideon, the boy from Newbury who'd made it big. Who'd made it big at the expense of the love of his life. Who could never go back. This evening he was going to try and combine the two personas, and he was nervous.

He stepped out of the shower, shook his head violently to get rid of the worst of the water, then rapidly towelled himself dry. He wandered back into the dressing room and pulled on a clean pair of ripped jeans, a black T-shirt, and a very old tatty check shirt. He pulled on a pair of socks, then shoved his feet into his holey baseball boots. He peered into the mirror and made an attempt to sort out his hair. Still wet, it flopped onto his shoulders limply. With an annoyed sigh, he picked up the hair dryer and quickly got it to a state where it no longer made his clothes wet, then, picking up his distressed leather jacket and stuffing his wallet and cigarettes into his pocket, he swung out of the room and went in search of Simon and Charles.

The party was being held in one of Seattle's largest and most prestigious hotels, and the band had been staying there since they'd arrived on Monday. A limousine had been laid on to take them back to the hotel; they would need to be smuggled out the back of the theatre to avoid the fans. Gideon arrived at Simon's dressing room and walked in without knocking. Simon was sprawled on the sofa wearing only his boxer shorts and a sweaty T-shirt, with a can of beer in one hand and a joint in the other. Gideon walked over, took the beer off him and nodded to the shower.

"Get showered and dressed," he ordered shortly. "We need to get going. Plenty of time for beer later."

Simon rolled his eyes. Then, running a hand through his damp fair curls, he got to his feet with a grunt and slouched over to the shower, dumping the joint in the ashtray on the way past.

He grinned at Gideon. "You looking forward to this party, then?" he asked as he peeled off his remaining clothes and opened the door of the shower. "Gonna make a lot of little girls happy."

Gideon scowled and ran a hand through his hair, then picked up the discarded joint and took a long toke. He carried it over to the sofa Simon had vacated and sank down into the cushions. He took another toke on the joint, then tossed it back into the ashtray. He was feeling very unsettled and found he was drumming his fingers on the arm of the chair.

"Hurry up, Si," he called. "I wanna get to the hotel before all the other guests. Hate making an entrance."

After a few minutes, Simon reappeared from the shower, rubbing his hair vigorously with a towel. "Chill out, man." He grinned. "You really are in a state, aren't you? What's up? It's only a party." He began to drag on a pair of faded jeans and a very old rugby shirt, then thrust his bare feet into a pair of ancient trainers. He picked up his jacket from the back of a chair and raised his eyebrows at his friend. "So why the stress?"

Gideon stood up and glowered at him. "I don't do the party thing," he muttered. "You know that. I usually leave after the first five minutes. This time I'm gonna stay."

Simon opened the door of the dressing room and walked out into the corridor, ushering Gideon before him. "Finally planning on getting laid, are you?" he teased, locking the door behind him. "'Bout time, if you ask me."

Gideon growled and aimed a blow at Simon's head. Simon ducked and laughed, just as Charles emerged from the next room, his jacket slung over his shoulder and his dark hair artistically dishevelled.

"Hi, guys." Grinning, he fell into step beside them. "What's up?"

"Gid's gonna pull tonight," said Simon with a wicked smile. "'Bout time, eh?"

Charles raised an eyebrow. "Never thought I'd see the day! Well, you'll have plenty to choose from tonight. Just make sure you ask their age." He caught Gideon by the arm and pulled him towards the back door, where several security men were waiting to escort them to the limousine.

****

An hour and a half later, the party was in full swing, and Gideon found himself cornered by a posse of impossibly young and skinny girls. They all had ridiculously long messy hair and looked like they'd got dressed in the dark. He scanned the throng for any that might be just that little bit different from the others. He sighed. He knew exactly what he was looking for, and he wasn't going to find it here. He glanced at them all again, and this time a girl of about his own age, with waist-length auburn hair, caught his eye. She was dressed in jeans and a bright green T-shirt, and as he looked she caught his eye and smiled widely. He closed his eyes briefly, then opened them and looked at her again. She was still smiling at him, and something in that smile had just a tiny hint of what he was looking for. He pushed through the throng of girls and reached her side. He looked down at her. She was quite tall but still had to tilt her head to look up at him. He noted with mild relief that she had green eyes. He didn't think he could have coped if they'd been blue. She was still smiling, and he took her by the hand and led her out of the main room and into a smaller, more intimate bar. He ordered a beer for himself and raised an eyebrow at his companion.

"Screwdriver," she said to the barman, her accent proclaiming her to be local to Seattle. She slid up onto a bar stool and smiled at Gideon again. He leaned against the bar and took a long swig of his beer.

"Hi," he eventually said, rather inadequately.

The girl laughed. "Hi," she replied, tossing her hair back over her shoulders. "I'm Amanda." She picked up her drink and took a sip, watching Gideon over the rim of the glass.

He gave a half smile. "I'm Gideon. But I guess you already knew that."

She grinned back at him, her green eyes flashing. "Yeah," she agreed. "I guess I did. You don't usually stay long at these parties. Why this one?"

He watched her closely, answering her with

another question. "Do you come to them all?"

"Whenever you're in Seattle, yeah, I do. I don't follow you all over the country like some of those losers, though." She laughed and indicated the throng of girls in the other room. "That's just lame." She stared at him for a moment, her eyes narrowing slightly. "So why tonight? Why haven't you escaped to your room? Done the whole moody enigmatic star thing?"

Gideon finished his drink and put the empty glass down on the bar. "Just felt like it," he said guardedly. "Had enough now, though. You wanna come up to my room for a drink? Get away from the 'losers'?"

"'Course I do." She shrugged. "Thought you'd never ask. I'll bring this with me." She picked up her drink and slid off the bar stool, looking at him expectantly. "Come on, then, let's go."

He stood up and led the way to the elevator, uncomfortably aware of her eyes on his back. She followed him in, and they stood side by side but not touching as they rode up to the sixth floor, where all the band were accommodated. A uniformed security guard stood outside Gideon's bedroom door, and he whisked it open as they approached.

"Mr. Hawk." He nodded as they passed through the door. "Enjoy your evening."

Gideon tossed his jacket onto the bed and walked over to the mini-bar. "What d'you want?" he asked, not turning round.

Amanda moved over and stood beside him. "Still got my screwdriver," she said, waving her glass at him, and wandered over to peer out the window.

Gideon watched her as he snapped open a beer and took a long swig. She was definitely attractive. She had something the other girls didn't. He didn't want to think too hard about what that might be. He was just glad her eyes were green. He walked over to join her, and together they stared down into the busy Seattle street below. The pavement outside the hotel was thronged with fans who'd been refused admittance to the party— ever hopeful and waiting for just a glimpse of their heroes.

Amanda grinned and turned to Gideon. "Sad, aren't they?" she drawled, finishing her drink and placing the glass on the windowsill. She glanced up at him expectantly, then walked over to the bed and sat down. Moving his jacket out of the way, she patted the quilt beside her. "Come on, I wanna hear all about you. The enigmatic Mr. Hawk." She laughed. "I guess all the girls say that." Gideon didn't reply and remained standing at the window. "Aw, come on, Gideon, don't be shy. I didn't come up here for the view."

He turned round and moved slowly across the room towards the bed. "What did you come up for?" he asked at last.

"You, of course." she said raising her eyebrows. "And I guess you wouldn't have brought me up here if you didn't want me." She patted the bed beside her again. "So tell me about you. You're so private, all I ever hear are rumours. You can tell me which ones are true."

Cautiously Gideon sat down beside her and placed his can on the bedside table. "What rumours?" he asked. "What do they say about me?"

"Oh, all sorts," she said with a grin. "That you're gay, that you're married, that you're a virgin...that you have a girlfriend in England...that she broke your heart…" She paused as she saw his face. "Anything? Any of them close?"

Gideon looked her directly in the eyes. "No," he said. "None of them close." Then he put his hand behind her head and pulled her face up close to his. They stared at each other for a moment before his lips came down on hers with a savagery that surprised them both. She responded by winding her arms around his neck and pushing him back onto the bed. With a swift and practised movement, Amanda undid Gideon's jeans and pulled them off, flinging them across the room. Then she ripped off her own clothes and pinned him down on the bed with her leg. She grinned down at him, her long auburn hair swinging over her shoulders and brushing lightly across his face.

"Okay," she murmured, "show me what you got."

****

The midmorning sun finally broke through the clouds, and as the gentle warmth reached Gideon's face, he opened his eyes and rolled onto his back. He lay for a moment in that just-wakened state, wondering where he was, and then suddenly it all came rushing back to him.

With an intake of breath, he turned his head to his right to find a sleeping auburn-haired girl lying next to him. He closed his eyes tightly, and the events of the previous evening came rushing back to him. The meeting at the party. The retreat to his room, followed by the very brief but passionate sex. He rolled onto his side, so that his back was towards her, and attempted to get his thoughts in order.

He had taken a stranger to his room and had sex with her. His first sex since Abi. His only sex apart from Abi. He screwed his eyes up tightly and felt his whole body go hot and cold. It must have been patently obvious to the girl—Amanda was her name, he recalled—just how desperately inexperienced he was. The whole encounter had been over in less than two minutes. He had assumed she would then leave, but she had poured them both a drink and insisted they get into bed and watch television together.

The next thing Gideon knew was waking up. He sat up and glanced over at her. She was lying on her side, her long hair spread out around her, her mouth slightly open. A half-drunk vodka and orange juice sat on the table beside her, along with a partly-smoked joint. Gideon leant forward and put his head in his hands. God, what on earth must she have thought of him? She had sought him out, looking for a night of passion with a famous rock star. What she had got was very quick teenage sex, followed by an episode of *Seinfeld* and a good night's sleep!

He got out of bed and padded into the bathroom, taking care not to wake her. He stripped off his boxers, unsure why he was still wearing them, and hopped into the shower. He turned it on very hot and with a lot of force and stood directly under the jet in an attempt to wash away the events and memories of the previous night.

He had been unfaithful to Abi. At least that was how it felt to him. For the last two and a half years he had remained totally loyal to her, always at the back of his mind hoping they would be reunited. His encounter with her father had finally shown him that was not going to happen, but he still felt dirty and ashamed. He snatched up the soap and scrubbed vigorously at his body, leaving his skin red and angry. Eventually he turned off the water and towelled himself dry. He walked quietly back into the bedroom and pulled on his jeans and T-shirt. A slight sound from the bed made him glance around to find a pair of sharp green eyes watching him. Amanda propped herself up on one elbow and grinned at him.

"Morning," she said with a yawn. "Good sleep?"

"Yes. Thank you. And you?" he asked politely, awkwardly pulling on a pair of socks.

"Yeah, haven't been to bed that early in years!" She laughed, and sat up, pulling the quilt up over her breasts and linking her arms around her knees. "Did it help?"

Gideon looked at her in confusion. "What?" he asked with a frown. "Did what help?"

"The sex. Did it help you forget her?"

In a single movement he had shot across to the bed, caught her by the wrist and pulled her out to stand naked in front of him. She stood with her feet planted firmly apart, and stared up at him with confidence.

"How dare you," he hissed. "I will never forget her…and what the hell do you know about it anyway?"

Amanda shook Gideon's hand off her wrist and walked over to the window. "You talk in your sleep. Probably best you know that, if you're gonna make a habit of this." She turned round and raised her eyebrows at him. "She's the only one you'd been with, isn't she?"

Gideon stared at her in horror. "Talk in my sleep…?" He sat down heavily on the edge of the bed. "Oh, fuck. What did I say?"

Amanda watched him for a moment in silence, then

took pity on him. "Not much. Just muttered her name and said 'sorry.' " She glanced at him under her lashes. "Then I think you thought I was her, because you muttered you loved me and would never leave me."

Gideon put his head in his hands and groaned. "Oh, god, I'm so sorry." He spoke without raising his head. "I said her name?"

"Just once...Abi," she said, sitting down beside him and putting her arm gently round his shoulders. "Don't worry. It'll get easier. And I won't tell anyone."

"Thank you," he muttered, still not raising his head. "Not sure I want it to, though."

Amanda glanced down at his bowed head. "Yes, you do," she said firmly. "If your relationship with her is really over...is it?" He hesitated, then nodded briefly. "Then you need to get over it. Keep doing what we did last night, and it *will* get easier. Trust me, I've been there." She paused for a moment, chuckling slightly. "And you need all the practice you can get, believe me!"

Gideon raised his head and looked at her. She was grinning, and her green eyes were sparkling.

He gave a reluctant smile. "I guess I do," he admitted. "It's been a while."

Amanda leaned over and planted a light kiss on his cheek. "Well, next time you're in Seattle, if you want a bit more practice, give me a call. I'll be around. No strings." She indicated a piece of paper by the bed, with a long number scribbled on it. "If you want to." Then she flashed him a dazzling smile, got to her feet, and wandered into the bathroom.

Gideon stared after her, his mind in a whirl. A very beautiful, confident girl had just told him he was crap in bed, and offered him some more practice. He couldn't help a small chuckle of his own. Maybe he'd take her up on the offer one day. He could never forget Abi, and didn't want to, but maybe Amanda had helped, just a little bit, to make it easier.

Chapter 10

Friday 5ᵗʰ December, 1997—Bath College of Art, Bath, Somerset

"I really don't want to, Jess." Abi laid down her pen and looked over her shoulder at her roommate. "You know me. I'd much prefer an early night with a cup of cocoa and a good book."

Abi had been in residence at Art College in Bath for nearly three months, and she'd settled in very well. She was thoroughly enjoying her course, had made a lot of good friends, and was enjoying the freedom of being away from her parents and the confines of their claustrophobic existence. Her roommate Jess had become a very good friend—not a substitute for Judy, of course, who was now reading European Studies at Exeter—but a good friend nonetheless. However, Abi had been leading a very quiet life since she'd been at college, and had been deliberately avoiding most social occasions, preferring to stay in her room or maybe just go out for a coffee with a couple of girlfriends. She had told no one, not even Jess, about her relationship with Gideon, or about her pregnancy, and consequently her fellow students regarded her as something of an enigma. She was talented, beautiful, and friendly, but she steadfastly refused to go to any parties.

Now Jess was attempting to make her change her

mind. "But Abs, it's the Student Union Christmas do. Oh, please come! Even for just a little bit. You don't have to talk to any boys. You can stay with me and the girls," she wheedled, her big brown eyes pleading.

Abi gave a short laugh and spun her chair round to face her friend. "It's all right. I'm not scared of the boys, you know. Just not interested in starting anything," she said with a shrug.

Jess nodded in agreement. "Oh, neither am I," she said, catching Abi's hands in hers and pulling her to her feet. "But you can still socialise with them. Doesn't mean you have to sleep with them!"

Abi smiled and surveyed her friend's pretty, round face, framed by a wild mass of curly black hair loosely held back with a red hairband. She was fairly sure Jess and her other friends believed she was a virgin, and she'd done nothing to disabuse them of the assumption. She had no intention of telling any of them her recent history, so it served her purpose well. But even so, she could probably risk a foray to the student union for a Christmas party.

She grinned at Jess. "Okay, just for a little bit then," she said, rolling her eyes. "But no trying to fix me up with anyone."

Jess squeaked and flung her arms around her friend. "Oh, Abs, thank you! You won't regret it. It'll be brilliant, you'll see." She let go of Abi and stepped back, taking in her friend's attire of jeans and striped jumper. "You might want to get changed, you know, wear something a bit more partyish?"

Abi laughed out loud. "Yeah, okay! I do know what to wear to a party. I'm not that out of touch. Just got to make a quick phone call, and then I'll be back to get ready. Don't leave without me." She gave Jess's hand a quick squeeze, slipped out of the large room they shared on the second floor of the accommodation block, and hurried down the corridor to the payphone that hung on the wall at the far end. She snatched up the receiver and shoved her hand into the pocket of her jeans to search for some coins. She came up with four tenpence pieces, quickly dialled a number, and waited impatiently until the person at the other end answered before pressing her four coins into the slot. "Judy?" she spoke loudly over the slightly crackly line. "Hi, it's me...you okay?" She paused, and a grin spread over her face. "Really? Well, have fun...Guess what I'm going to do tonight...no! Judy, what do you think I am?...No, I'm going to a party..." She listened again. "Yeah, I think so. D'you think I should? Am I doing the right thing?... I know, I know...but it's not that easy." She leaned back against the wall, the telephone cord winding around her neck. "I guess you're right. I've got to do it sometime...Okay. I s'pose if I'm gonna do it, I should do it properly. I'd better go and dig out my gear. No one here has met Grunge Abi. Hope they can cope!" She ended the call with a promise to meet up soon, then trotted back to her room to get ready.

Jess had disappeared into the shower, so Abi went over to her chest of drawers and started going through clothes. Eventually she found what she was looking for and pulled on black woolly tights, a short, very faded denim skirt, a baggy black T-shirt, and an oversized blue-checked shirt. She scrabbled under her bed, pulled out a pair of very worn Doc Marten's and thrust her feet into them, then walked over to the mirror and carefully applied a fairly large quantity of black eyeliner and mascara, let her long wavy auburn hair out of its restraining scrunchy, and messed it up with her hands. She stood back to survey herself in the long mirror screwed to the back of the door, and very nearly lost her nerve. She was transported straight back to the night three years earlier when she'd first met Gideon at the school Christmas dance. She was just about to tear off the clothes and climb into the safety of her bed when Jess emerged from the shower, her hair wrapped in a towel and wearing only her pants. She stopped short and emitted a tiny squeak when she saw Abi.

"Abi!" she finally managed. "You look amazing! You should always dress like that."

Abi spun round to face her. "I'm not sure," she said, her voice shaking slightly. "This has brought back some memories…" She walked across the room and sank down on the edge of her bed.

Jess ran over and knelt down in front of her. "Abs, you look amazing," she repeated. "Whatever the memories, you still look brilliant." She paused and looked closely at her friend. "D'you want to talk about anything?"

Abi shook her head. "No. Thank you. I can't. The memories are too raw." She turned her face away and bit down hard on her lip.

Jess caught her hands in hers and squeezed tightly. "Abi, it helps to share. Please, try me. I know I'm not Judy, but I still love you."

Abi glanced round at her, her blue eyes wide with pain. She shook her head. "I love you too, Jess. You're a brilliant friend, but I don't know if I can. It still hurts too much." She stopped and bent her head forward, letting her hair swing in front of her face. "I'll tell you some of it. I had a boyfriend when I was at school. We met three years ago at the school Christmas dance"— she paused as Jess caught her breath—"and we were really, really in love." She lifted her head and stared at Jess. "But he left. And that's it."

Jess frowned. "Really?" she asked gently. "That's it? There must be more. Who was he? Where is he now? Why did you split?"

Abi shook her head. "No more," she said firmly as tears threatened. "Oh, except I'm not the pure little virgin you all think I am."

Jess grinned at her. "I did wonder," she said. "Just one or two things you said. But Abi, how long has it been? When did you split from him?"

"Two and a half years."

"And in all that time you haven't looked at another man?"

Abi shook her head. "No. I kept hoping…for ages. For years. But I guess I don't hope any more," she said quietly, surreptitiously wiping a tear from the corner of her eye.

Jess caught her hands again and pulled her to her feet. "Right," she said with a smile, "time to get you back out there. You're much too pretty to keep hidden in your room. You look totally amazing in those clothes. Shall we go and party?"

Abi bit her lip again, then nodded. "Okay. Let's do it. And Jess…thanks for listening. Sorry I can't tell you everything."

The party was in full swing when Abi and Jess arrived, and they made their way through the throngs of over-exuberant students towards the bar.

Jess leaned forward. "Vodka and Coke," she

shouted above the noise of the music. "What d'you want, Abs?"

Abi slid onto a bar stool next to her friend and smiled at the student manning the bar. "White wine spritzer," she said loudly, then glanced curiously around the room. The student union was housed in a large building containing a number of rooms, one of which was fully equipped as a bar. It was currently almost completely full of partying students, many dressed in a Christmassy theme.

Abi nudged Jess. "Is it meant to be fancy dress?" she asked with a grin, watching a tall gangly boy she recognised from her photography class dancing wildly whilst sporting a set of antlers and a large red nose.

Jess shook her head. "Nah, anything goes, as they say." She downed her vodka in one gulp and indicated to the barman that she wanted a refill. She watched Abi curiously. "You don't really drink much, do you?" she asked, narrowing her eyes. "Have you ever got drunk?"

Abi smiled, a faraway look in her eyes. "Not much," she admitted. "Judy and I drank a whole bottle of wine at New Year's when I was fifteen. We were definitely a bit tiddly! Had a dreadful head in the morning. Other than that...not really. I never really went to parties or stuff during sixth form...I was still too upset...you know." She stopped talking and looked away from Jess, letting her hair conceal her face.

Jess squeezed her arm. "You're better off staying sober," she assured her. "Can't accidentally do something you shouldn't." She gave a little laugh. "I wish I'd followed my own advice a couple of times. How about that school dance you mentioned? Did you drink there?"

Abi looked at her in surprise. "No. It was in the school hall. They're not going to allow alcohol for a group of fourteen- to eighteen-year-olds, are they? What sort of school did you go to?"

Jess grinned wickedly. "Oh, the school didn't provide it, but we always managed to smuggle some in. The boys were very good at that."

"Mine was an all-girls school," said Abi dismally. "They just shipped the boys in from the boys' school for dances and stuff."

"Did your boyfriend go to the boys' school?" Jess couldn't help but be curious.

Abi glanced at her. "No. He used to, but he'd left by then. He's three years older than me."

"How come he was at the dance, then?" Jess persisted, her second vodka disappearing almost as rapidly as the first.

There was a long silence, until finally Abi sighed. "He was in the band they hired for the night."

Jess sat up straight. "Cool," she said, her eyes shining. "He's a musician? What does he play?"

Abi shook her head. "I said no more info," she said firmly. "I don't want to talk about it," and she took a long swig of her drink.

Jess watched her. "Sorry, Abs," she said contritely, pouting her full red lips. "Didn't mean to upset you. Now knock that back and have another. Then I think it's time to dance."

"You're a bad influence on me, Jessica," Abi said with a little laugh, dutifully draining her glass and replacing it on the bar. "But I guess this is more fun than staying in the room again."

"Might help you forget him," added Jess

ingenuously, handing Abi another tall glass of wine and soda.

Abi's head shot up, and she narrowed her eyes. "I will *never* forget him," she snapped, flicking her hair back over her shoulders. "I don't *want* to forget him. I still love him." She paused and stared bleakly around the room. "But I guess I can't let it stop me living. Life has to go on—Judy's been telling me that for the last two years. Come on, then, let's dance." She slid off her bar stool, caught Jess by the hand, and pulled her into the middle of the dance floor.

The two girls very soon caught the attention of a number of other students, none of whom had seen Abi emerge from her room before. By the third dance, they'd attracted quite a crowd, and Abi overheard a few muttered comments.

"Is that Abi Thomson?"

"Yeah. She looks so different."

"She actually looks quite cool."

On hearing the last comment, Abi swung round to face the speaker and scowled at him. "You sound surprised," she snapped, her eyes flashing. "What do you actually know about me? Nothing. I am cool." Then she jerked her head at Jess and stalked back towards the bar. Jess tottered after her on her stilettos, catching up with her as she slid back onto the bar stool and ordered another drink.

"Abs, they didn't mean any harm," she gasped, shaking Abi's arm. "They thought you looked cool. That's nice."

Abi stared at her and downed her drink in one go. "Memories," she muttered. "Too many memories. I shouldn't have come."

Jess clambered unsteadily onto a bar stool and grabbed Abi's hand. "Yes, you should," she said firmly. "Fuck the memories, you look cool *now*, and you need to have a life. Get on the floor and dance…it's doing you good."

"Not sure you're right," Abi said, taking another long swig of her wine and wondering why the room seemed to be rotating. "But I can't be bothered to leave now."

As she spoke her eyes fell on the back view of a young male student who was leaning nonchalantly against the wall, beer can in hand. He was dressed in faded, ripped jeans and a checked shirt with the sleeves rolled up to just below the elbow. His hair was very dark and just long enough to have got hooked inside his collar. Abi's heart did a little flip. He looked just as Gideon had looked when she first met him. She slid off the stool and made her way unsteadily across the crowded floor towards him. Stopping just behind him, she reached out and tapped him on the shoulder. He turned, and she saw at once that any resemblance to Gideon was only from behind. His dark hair flopped across his forehead, and his eyes were a deep brown.

He looked quizzically at her. "Hi."

Abi swayed slightly and steadied herself by holding onto his arm. "Hi," she said, enunciating carefully. "I'm Abi Thomson, and I look cool."

The boy grinned and held out his hand. "Hi, Abi Thomson. I'm Mike Prentiss, and yes, you do look cool." They shook hands solemnly, and Mike raised his eyebrows. "D'you wanna dance?"

"Maybe." Abi nodded. "But I do feel a bit wobbly."

Mike gently took her hand and led her out into the middle of the dance floor. "You'll be fine," he assured her. "Just hold on to me." He put his arms around her waist, and she leant her head on his shoulder. "I don't think you're very used to drinking, are you?" he asked, amusement in his voice.

"Only coffee," came Abi's muffled reply.

He chuckled and rested his chin on her head as they moved rhythmically around the room. "Maybe we should go and get you a cup?" he suggested.

Abi nodded sleepily. "That'd be nice," she agreed, raising her head from his shoulder and peering blearily at him. "Think I might be a bit drunk."

He laughed and, putting his arm around her shoulders, steered her towards the door and out into the cold night air. She shivered as the wind whipped around the side of the building and caught her unawares. Mike held her close to his side and hurried her across the wide expanse of tarmac towards the accommodation block. He turned left as soon as they entered the building and guided her up the stairs to the third floor. Holding her securely by the hand, Mike led her along the corridor to his room, and she leant against the wall with her eyes closed while he unlocked the door.

"Here we are, then," he announced, pushing her gently through the door and turning on the light. "Take a seat, if you can find one, and I'll put the kettle on."

Abi pushed aside a pile of clothes and sat down heavily on the bed. The room was a lot smaller than the one she and Jess shared, and she realised at once it was a single room. It had a desk covered in books and papers, a chest of drawers with none of them closed, a single wardrobe, and the bed she was currently sitting on. She wriggled backwards so she could lean against the wall and close her eyes. She was beginning to feel slightly sick, and everything was spinning wildly. She opened her eyes again and found Mike standing in front of her, holding out a steaming mug of coffee.

"Didn't know how you took it," he said, "so I guessed and put milk but no sugar?"

Abi attempted to smile, and nodded. "S'right," she said, holding her hand out to take the mug. "Thanks."

Mike sat down beside her, cradling his own mug, and smiled. "Feeling okay?" he asked, surveying her closely.

"Not really," Abi replied honestly. "Feel a bit sick. Really not used to drinking."

"I haven't seen you around," he said after a minute. "Where have you been hiding?"

"In my room." Abi looked at him under her lashes. "I'm not very sociable."

Mike wriggled back on the bed until he was leaning against the wall next to her. He sipped his coffee and glanced sideways at her. "Have you got a boyfriend?" he asked at last.

Abi stiffened, and frowned at him. "Why?" she asked suspiciously.

Mike laughed. "'Cause if you haven't I might ask you out," he said candidly.

Abi surveyed him blearily. "I wouldn't be much fun," she said, slurring slightly. "I have a broken heart."

"Ah." Mike nodded, and took another slurp of coffee.

Abi frowned at him. "What d'you mean…ah?" she asked, slightly belligerently.

Mike shrugged. "That explains why you've been

hiding in your room." He smiled at her. "You're far too pretty—and cool, of course—to stay shut away. You'll never get over your broken heart that way."

Abi spoke without opening her eyes. "Don't wanna get over it," she muttered. "But I wouldn't mind forgetting it sometimes." She opened her eyes and looked directly at him. "D'you wanna help me forget it?"

Mike frowned at her. "Maybe," he said cautiously. "Now drink your coffee, and try and sober up a bit. I'd prefer to have this conversation when you know what you're saying."

Abi dutifully finished her coffee and handed the empty mug to Mike, wiping her mouth on the back of her hand.

"Thank you," she said. "Please could I have a glass of water now?"

With a chuckle, Mike slid off the bed, disappeared into the bathroom, and returned with a tall tumbler of water.

Abi thirstily drank it down, then sat back with a sigh. "That's a bit better." She looked up at him under her lashes. "Sorry if I was a nuisance. I don't often drink."

"I could tell." Mike took the glass out of her hand, placed it on the bedside table, and wriggled back on the bed until he was sitting beside her. When he slipped his arm around her shoulders, she instinctively stiffened and inched away from him. "Do you mind?" he asked, keeping his arm in place.

Abi took a deep breath and shook her head. "No, it's fine." she said, relaxing a little.

Mike shifted closer to her, and rather stiffly she

rested her head on his shoulder. "That's better," he said with a small smile. "Now tell me about you. Apart from the fact that you look cool, of course."

Abi groaned. "Did I say that?" she asked in anguish, sitting up, her face flushing a fiery red. She bent her head forward so she could hide behind her hair as she muttered, "I'm so sorry. What must you think of me?"

Mike chuckled. "I think you're very pretty, very funny, very sad, and very drunk," he replied, watching the way her long hair swung around her shoulders. "Not so drunk now, though. D'you want some more coffee?"

Abi shook her head and peeped at him through her hair. "No. Thanks. I'm okay now." She licked her lips. "Umm…did I also tell you I have a broken heart?"

"Yep. And you asked if I wanted to help you forget it."

"Oh, dear, I really shouldn't drink at all. I just can't hack it," she said with an embarrassed giggle. "I think you asked me out."

Mike shrugged. "Well, I said I might," he said, watching her in amusement. "Then I thought I should maybe wait until you were sober. I'll try again. Would you like to go out with me?"

Abi chewed on her bottom lip and stared at him. "Maybe," she conceded. "But I'm still in love with someone else…"

Mike held up a hand to stop her. "I know, I know, and you don't want to get over it. You already said. But I think we could still have some fun together. And when we're together you can forget your broken heart." His eyes sparkled mischievously, and he brushed her hair off her face. "What d'you think? Shall we give it a go? Nothing serious. Just a bit of fun."

Abi wriggled round and sat facing him on the bed, her eyes serious. "Okay," she said, "but nothing serious. And there is one other thing…" She paused, feeling awkward. "Can we have sex? Now."

Mike stared at her in surprise. "Now?" he repeated. "That's a little soon, isn't it? What's the rush?"

Abi blushed and clambered off the bed. "It doesn't matter," she muttered. "I shouldn't have asked. Forget I said it." She walked over to the window and stared out into the dark night sky.

Mike slid off the bed and went and stood beside her. He gently took her hand in his and squeezed it tightly. "Why now, Abi?" he persisted. "You're not a virgin, are you?"

She shook her head and spoke without looking at him. "No, but the only person I've slept with is my boyfriend. My…ex-boyfriend." Her voice caught as she uttered the words. "And I think I have to break the spell." She shook her head impatiently. "That sounds stupid, but I know what I mean. I don't think I can move on and be with anyone else until I've actually…done it…with them." Her head suddenly shot up, and she stared at him, her eyes worried. "I'm not a slut. I don't do this all the time. In fact, I haven't done it at all for two and a half years."

Mike looked down at her, his face serious. "Abi, I know you're not a slut. You don't need to tell me that." He took a deep breath. "But I'm not sure you really know what you're asking. You don't even know me. Wouldn't it be better to get to know each other first?"

Abi shook her head. "I don't expect you to understand," she said sadly, "but I don't think I can

112

move on and 'go out' with anyone until I've slept with them. Sounds stupid, but if I don't I shall just be thinking about what it was like with…with…my boyfriend, and I won't be able to move on. I still love him, and at the moment I think I always will—but I do want to start living again, and I think that if I do that I might be able to." She tilted her head and looked up at him with a half smile. "And I do like you. You've been very nice to me. I think I would like to go out with you. But nothing…"

"But nothing serious. I know." He smiled down at her. "Well, it's not what I'd normally do, but if that's really truly what you want, and it's not the drink talking…"

"It's not the drink talking," Abi assured him, flicking her hair back over her shoulders and standing up straight. "But it does feel weird. I haven't even kissed anyone since…he left."

In answer, Mike bent his head and gently touched her lips with his. After a moment she responded, and reaching up, put her hands on his shoulders, tentatively pulling him down towards her.

Chapter 11

Wednesday 6th May, 2009

"I should have known this was a bad idea." Abi swung her bag off the carousel and scowled at Gideon. "We each agreed to tell our stories, and now you're mad at me. Do you see me being mad at you? No. Because I'm more mature." She swung the bag over her shoulder and flounced off towards the exit, not waiting to see if he was following her. He caught up with her just as she was about to step out onto the pavement, grabbed her arm, and pulled her back into the building.

"Abi, I'm not mad at you," he said with a sigh. "Now come on, we need to get out of here. We're attracting attention."

Abi glanced around at the small throng of sightseers and paparazzi who had gathered near them, and rolled her eyes. "What's new," she muttered. "Come on, then. We'll discuss this further at the hotel." She dived through the huge glass doors and headed for the nearest taxi.

Gideon followed more slowly, his mind totally consumed with the unwelcome vision of Abi and Mike and their first encounter. It had affected him even more than he'd thought it would, and he was beginning to wish he hadn't suggested telling the stories. He was well aware he was being grossly unfair, and that Abi was probably having the same feelings after hearing about him and Amanda. The difference was that she seemed to be able to cope with her feelings better. Maybe she was right. Maybe she *was* more mature. He glanced at her out of the corner of his eye as they rode in silence in the back of the taxi, noting at once the slightly increased rate of her breathing, and her heightened colour. He smiled to himself. She wasn't handling it any better than he was. He reached out and took her hand in his. She shifted slightly in her seat, and continued to stare out the window, but she didn't pull her hand away.

"I think we should go to the hotel, get booked in, and have a rest before we go anywhere else," Gideon suggested, sliding along the seat until he was sitting right next to her. "The hire car should be there waiting for us, too."

They had booked into a small hotel in the names of Mr and Mrs Thomson in the hope the paparazzi wouldn't find them, and had arranged for a hire care to be delivered there for them, to avoid any delays at the airport.

Abi shrugged. "If you like," she said, slightly sulkily, sounding very like the Abi he remembered from years ago. She glanced at him, narrowing her eyes. "We need to talk about this."

"Okay." Gideon nodded. "Guess we should both have a good shout about how we feel, and then hopefully we'll feel better."

Abi stared at him suspiciously. "I feel fine," she said firmly. "As I said, I am mature. I understand your need to have sex with a stranger and then spend the whole night in bed with her. Watching television. Very cosy." She snatched her hand out of his and folded her arms across her chest. "And no doubt you visited her each time you were in Seattle, didn't you?"

"Actually, no." Gideon shook his head. "I never saw her again. Next time I was in Seattle I was seeing someone else." He grinned at her. "I don't think you're as mature as you think."

Abi grunted and folded her arms even more firmly. "Hmm. Maybe not," she admitted. "I must confess I just want to go and rip her head off."

Gideon chuckled and put his arm around her shoulders. "Now you can see how I feel about that...Mike bloke," he said, his eyes flashing. "I want to take him to the edge of a cliff and watch as he bounces down the rocks. And you probably *did* see him again."

Abi nodded. "Yeah, we sort of dated for a couple of months." She paused for quite a long time, and Gideon was just about to speak when she continued quietly, "I wasn't really what he wanted in a girlfriend. He was hoping I'd get over you and we could be a proper couple. It never happened. I was just using him, really, and in the end I told him it wasn't fair on him, and we decided to be just friends." She looked up at Gideon, her eyes sad. "I told you I wasn't very nice for a while."

"That doesn't sound too bad," he said with a shrug. "You were honest with him. You could have kept stringing him along."

"I just used him for sex, Gid, like a teenage boy in a brothel. I don't think that was very nice of me. And he was a nice boy. He deserved better."

Gideon moved closer and put his arm around her shoulders. "It was what you needed at the time," he said philosophically. "I guess I did too. That was certainly what Amanda was about, and if I'm honest, so were all the others."

A look of pain crossed Abi's face, and she turned to look out the window. "All the others?" she asked. "How many were there?"

"Probably not as many as you're imagining," Gideon said with a lopsided grin. "The papers had me sleeping with everyone. I think it was about eight."

Abi turned to face him. "That's only one a year," she said in surprise. "I thought there would be more. I never read about you in the papers. I couldn't bear to."

Gideon shrugged again. "We were on the move a lot. I went quite long periods with no one." He paused, and glanced cautiously at her. "Nancy…the woman we're going to see… I was with her the longest, I think. We went out for about six months. How about you? How many were there?"

Abi's face fell, and her eyes grew dark. "Too many," she said. "Probably about six or seven."

Gideon raised his eyebrows. "That's not as many as me," he said. "Don't worry."

"You don't understand." Abi shook her head. "They were all in the space of just over two years. Mike was the first…and all the others were between about March '98 and early 2000. After that I had a life change, and had no one else until I met you again." She looked up at him. "So it was rather a lot in a short period of time. That's why I'm not very happy about that period of my life."

Gideon tightened his arm around her shoulders and rested his head against hers. "It was just what you needed," he repeated. "We were both feeling very hurt and vulnerable, and not making a very good job of getting over each other." He paused, and smiled down at her. "Quite clearly we were meant to be together. I hated hearing your story, I don't mind admitting that, and I suspect you hated hearing mine, but I think it's probably shown us just how much we were both missing each other. It's very weird that our first times were on the same day." His face darkened, and his left hand balled into a fist at his side. "God, I could fucking kill Simon, and your mother, for their part in this! None of that needed to happen but for their actions in trying to keep us apart."

Abi snuggled closer to him and put her hand on his chest. "Me too," she said sadly. "And I never got the satisfaction of even talking to my mother about it." She raised her head. "And Simon. Wonder where he is? D'you think we'll hear from him again?"

"Undoubtedly." Gideon snorted. "He'll know the police are after him at the moment, so he will have gone to ground, but I'm sure he'll resurface eventually. And when he does…" He gently moved the thin strap of Abi's top to one side and kissed the small scar that adorned the top of her left arm. "I will never forgive him for doing that to you," he muttered, in his mind reliving the moment he saw Simon shoot at Abi, luckily inflicting only a minor injury.

"I'm fine." Abi smiled at him and dropped a light kiss on his nose. "I also drank too much in those two years. And smoked a lot of weed. You wouldn't have liked me so much then."

"Abi, I was living the rock star life. What the hell d'you think I was doing? Going to bed each night with a cup of cocoa?"

"Going to bed each night with a different girl," muttered Abi.

"Now you know that's not even true," pointed out Gideon patiently. "Eight in eight years? I think we should probably not tell each other about our other encounters...unless you want to, of course."

Abi shook her head. "No. I really don't. I don't want to think we're not being totally open with each other, but we really don't need the gory details, do we?" She wrinkled her nose. "We've managed so far without knowing."

Gideon nodded. "Fine with me. You may need to find out some more about my relationship with Nancy, though. Is that all right?"

"Have to be," said Abi shortly. "Not looking forward to that at all." She took a deep breath. "So when was it you were with her? Just so I know."

"For about six months, from...July '99 to January 2000. She was on tour with us. Doing costumes and stuff."

Abi frowned as the hint of a memory tugged at her mind. It fluttered away again, and she shook her head. "Okay. So the dates do work for this child of hers, then? What did it say? He was born in September 2000. She must have got pregnant in December '99." She glanced at Gideon. "Unless he was early, she conceived when she was going out with you. Was she faithful to you?"

"How the hell should I know?" Gideon snapped, running a hand through his hair. "I just know it's not my child. Now look, there's the hotel." He pointed to the building nestled at the foot of the mountains, just outside the little town of Springfield. "Let's hope no one's got wind of our arrival."

He opened the taxi door, jumped out, and handed a wad of notes to the driver. They retrieved their luggage and made their way up the path. It was noticeably colder than it had been in Tauranga, and Abi shivered as they approached the low building.

"Hope it's got heating," she muttered, hitching her bag more firmly onto her shoulder. "And I could really do with a bath or shower before we go out."

Gideon glanced at his phone. "It's half three now," he said. "That took longer than I'd anticipated. We arranged to get to Nancy's ranch at four. You can have a quick shower."

Abi stared balefully at him. "Let her wait," she said dangerously. "I am not foregoing being clean and comfy for that woman," and she pushed the double glass doors open and strode into the reception area.

****

Caroline looked around her with distaste. "Roger, six more hours is far too long to have to wait here," she said firmly, fixing her husband with a stern gaze. "We've been here for three already. What can we do for all that time?"

"You wanted to fly over today," Roger pointed out with a shrug. "This was the only flight I could get, and we were lucky to get it. Surely nine hours' layover is a small price to pay." He leaned back in his chair and opened his paper. "Didn't you bring a book?"

Caroline tutted loudly. "Of course I brought a book, Roger," she said with a sigh. "But that's not the point. Maybe I could do some shopping?" She glanced vaguely around the huge airport at the enormous array of shops available for her perusal. She and Roger were currently sitting in one of the many cafés at Tokyo Narita Airport, sipping large cups of cappuccino, and although Roger seemed content to remain there reading his paper, she was already bored. She got to her feet. "I'm going shopping, Roger," she said firmly. "You stay here so I don't lose you." She picked up her bag and headed off in the direction of the most enticing emporium.

Roger watched her go over the top of his glasses, a fond smile playing on his lips. Caroline never liked to sit still for long. She was very like her son in that way, and when she was already slightly het up and worried about something she was even worse. He watched as she disappeared into a brightly lit gift shop, and sighed at the thought of the numerous trinkets she would return with to distribute around the various female members of the family. He glanced at his watch—only one o'clock. Still another six hours to wait. He did a quick calculation and realised it must be four o'clock in New Zealand, the time that Gideon and Abi were due to meet with the woman. Roger had forgotten her name and had no interest in trying to remember it. He mentally crossed his fingers that Gideon was correct in his assumption the child wasn't his. He didn't feel quite so confident of the fact as Caroline, but Gideon had been so happy since he and Abi had re-connected, it would be a shame to see anything spoil it.

****

Natasha was sitting cross-legged on Lydia's bed, watching while the younger girl located a map of the Cambridge area on her computer and set it to print.

Lydia spoke without turning around. "This is a good clear map," she said. "You should have no problem following it You can show the taxi driver exactly where you want to go." She jumped up and caught the sheet of paper as it emerged from the printer, then handed it to Natasha. "You just have to find a taxi when your bus gets to Cambridge. Shouldn't be too difficult. That's the only thing we can't organise in advance. Your ticket on the morning bus is booked, and so is the return one from Hamilton." She grinned at her cousin. "I'm so excited for you. I just hope we can pull it off without getting found out."

Natasha was impressed. "You're very organised," she said with a grin. "I have a tendency to wing it a bit more. Act before I think sometimes. Bit like Mum. I get carried away with the excitement of a plan and sometimes ignore the important bits. Thank you for helping me."

Lydia bounced onto the bed beside her. "No problem," she said happily. "I love doing stuff like this. I'd be too nervous to have the actual adventure, but I love planning the details. We make a good team."

"Like Joan and Pauline," said Natasha, smiling. "And Mum and Judy."

"Who's Judy?" Lydia asked curiously.

"Mum's best friend. Judy's the one who always got Mum out of scrapes when they were children. Stopped her from doing the really stupid things...well, most of them, anyway." Natasha giggled.

"Oh, I'd like to be your Judy!" said Lydia, her eyes shining. "Pity we don't live in the same country, though." She thought for a moment. "Maybe we could Skype whenever you want to plan something, and I can tell you if it's a good idea or not?"

Natasha giggled again. "That sounds fun. We could

try, anyway. Not that I do this sort of thing very often."

Lydia looked doubtful. "How about that time you went to see your grandfather on your own?" she asked. "That was a bit like this, wasn't it?"

Natasha frowned. "Don't call him that," she snapped. "He doesn't deserve me as a granddaughter. Call him Arthur."

"Do you ever see him?"

"No, Not since the day he gave us the diaries and stuff. Mum doesn't want to see him either, not after what he did. Or didn't do." She paused and put her head on one side. "I don't think I actually hate him. I kinda feel sorry for him, but I don't like him, and I don't want him as a grandfather. I've already got a nice one of those. Don't need another." And the two girls smiled at each other conspiratorially.

Chapter 12

Wednesday 6th May, 2009

Abi climbed into the passenger seat of the hire car and strapped herself in. She had had her shower, and had dressed, after a great deal of thought, in skinny jeans, a low-cut green strappy top, and an open green-and-blue checked shirt. She wore flat black shoes on her bare feet and had fastened her hair up into a large tortoiseshell clip, leaving long tendrils hanging down on either side of her face.

Gideon glanced at her as he slid into the driver's seat. He thought she looked fantastic. He smiled at her as he started the engine. "Okay, babe?"

"I guess so," she replied a little doubtfully. "Just wanna get it over with now. Let's go."

The ranch Nancy was staying at was about ten minutes from Springfield, along the West Coast Road towards the Korowai-Torlesse Tussocklands Park, and as they drove through the town, past the giant pink doughnut erected in honour of *The Simpsons Movie*, and then sped along the road through the glorious countryside, Abi felt her stomach tightening into a knot. Suppose it was true, she thought, panic rising. What would they do? She knew Gideon truly believed the child wasn't his, but she had to admit he could be mistaken. Despite all their affirmations of love and the fact she absolutely adored Gideon, she still couldn't quite imagine how she would cope if it turned out he had fathered a child with another woman. Obviously it would in no way lessen her love for him. Nothing could do that, but it would definitely have some sort of effect on their marriage.

She sneaked a glance at his face as he drove. It showed definite signs of stress, and his lips were set in a thin line. Besides, he was clutching the steering wheel so tightly his knuckles were white. She reached over and put her hand lightly on his thigh. He flashed her a quick smile, then fixed his eyes back on the road ahead of them. After about five miles, he indicated to turn right down a narrow track that appeared to lead into the mountains. They drove slowly along the path, and eventually a long low house appeared on the left, bounded by a white post fence. Gideon slowed down and peered at the house.

"This is it," he said tersely, pulling the car onto a flat grassy patch to the side of the gate. He manoeuvred the vehicle carefully next to the fence, then turned off the engine and sat staring out at the mountainous backdrop. "Nice view."

"Yeah," Abi agreed, glancing at him. "This isn't actually her house, is it?"

Gideon shook his head. "No, she lives on the outskirts of Christchurch, but that would have been too public. We would have been followed there. This belongs to some friend of hers. They're away and said she could use it." He opened the car door and stood up, stretching. "Come on, let's do it."

He caught Abi's hand in his, and together they walked up the long dirt path to the white front door.

There didn't appear to be a bell, so Gideon raised his hand and knocked sharply on the glass pane.

Abi swallowed, and moistened her lips with her tongue. She squeezed Gideon's hand tightly and kept her eyes fixed on the small window in the door. Eventually they heard the sound of a bolt being pulled back, and the door opened.

Nancy stared at them. She wore a calf-length blue cotton dress and leather flip-flops. Her bright red curly hair was held loosely off her face with a blue scarf. She nodded at them and stood back to allow them access to the house.

"Gideon," she said formally as he passed by.

"Hello, Nancy," he replied curtly. "This is Abi, my wife."

Nancy held out her hand tentatively to Abi, who hesitated momentarily, then shook it.

"Pleased to meet you," muttered Nancy, narrowing her eyes at Abi, a curious look on her lightly freckled face.

Abi frowned; there was something familiar about the woman, but she couldn't quite put her finger on it. Maybe it was just the numerous pictures she'd seen in the paper. But she felt it was something more.

Nancy led them into a large light living room with huge windows looking out over the mountains. She indicated they should take a seat, then disappeared into the kitchen to fetch some tea.

"I think I've seen her somewhere before," whispered Abi as she sank down onto the deep red velvet sofa next to Gideon.

He looked at her in surprise. "In the paper?" he suggested, with an attempt at a grin.

"No…not that. Somewhere else." Abi shook her head, her brow creasing as she tried to remember.

"Don't see how you could have," Gideon remarked quietly. "I mean…when?"

Abi shrugged, and leaned back on the cushions as Nancy reappeared with a large tray holding tea and a plate of cupcakes. She poured them each a cup, handed round the cakes, and then took a seat in the chair opposite them and waited.

There was an awkward silence, until Gideon sighed and asked, "What's this all about, Nancy? You know that's not my child. It can't be."

"Firstly, he's not an 'it,' " she replied frostily. "And secondly, of course he's yours. He was born in September 2000. If you remember, we dated from July '99 until January 2000. I got pregnant in December '99. So he must be yours."

She was sitting forward in her chair, her hands clasped tightly together between her knees. Abi watched her closely. She looked very nervous, not at all at ease. Her knee was vibrating, and she had tiny beads of sweat on her neck.

"Maybe you were unfaithful to him?" she asked bluntly, staring directly at the other woman's face. "I gather you slept with all the roadies, as well. Maybe it was one of them." Gideon laid a warning hand on Abi's arm, but she shook it off impatiently. "Oh, yes, and Simon. You slept with him, too, didn't you? Or was that after Gideon? You really are a bit of a slut, aren't you?" She finished with a defiant look at Nancy.

"I didn't say she slept with *all* the roadies…" Gideon began, attempting to restore some semblance of order to the conversation, but Abi turned on him.

"Defending her now, are you? Don't you see what she's doing, Gid? She wants your money. She's a dirty little slut who couldn't keep her legs together and decided she wanted a famous dad for her kid. She's probably lied about when he was born and everything." She leapt to her feet and stormed over to the window, standing with her arms tightly folded and her back to the other two.

Gideon, who was beginning to seriously doubt the wisdom of having brought his wife with him, attempted to smooth the waters. "Abi's upset…understandably—"

Abi interrupted him. "Don't you dare apologize for me!" she snapped, swinging round to face them. "I meant everything I said."

Gideon sighed. "Abi's upset," he repeated, glaring at her. "But despite that, I think she's probably right. I know you had relationships with several of the roadies, and with Simon, and I'm now beginning to wonder if one of them was at the same time as you were seeing me." He paused and leaned forward in his chair. "I mean, why wait nine years to tell me? If you knew—or even thought—your child was mine, why didn't you tell me straight away? It's very suspicious that you choose to do it now when I'm very much in the public eye again." Noticing Abi start to move towards Nancy out of the corner of his eye, he reached up, caught her wrist, and pulled her down onto the sofa beside him where he could keep an eye on her. "What is it you want? I guess it's money, is it? And what are you doing in New Zealand, anyway?"

Nancy shifted in her chair, and looked down at her hands. "He is yours," she repeated softly. "I did have relationships—as you call it—with a couple of roadies, and with Simon, but not at the same time as you." She looked up and stared him straight in the eye. "Yeah, I do want money. I'm here in New Zealand because I came here with a guy I was with for a time. Then we split, and I've been finding it very hard to survive. I thought it was time you did your duty as a father."

Gideon sucked in his breath. "He can't be mine," he said quietly. "We always used protection, Nancy. You know that. I never trusted you were on the pill. I didn't trust anyone. I always used a condom, and you know it. And I still think you would have told me straight away if you'd got pregnant. I know how much you would have liked to trap me."

Nancy flinched but kept her head raised. "I didn't tell you because I didn't find out until we'd split up. By then you'd gone on tour somewhere else—I don't remember where, and I'd gone back to Seattle. I was too proud to tell you. I wanted to cope on my own." Her big green eyes filled with tears. "But now I can't cope, and I don't want Josh to suffer."

Abi rolled her eyes and made to get up. Gideon kept tight hold of her wrist, but he couldn't keep her quiet. "For god's sake, Gid, are you hearing this? What a sob story. She's making the whole bloody lot up. There probably isn't even a child. I mean, where is he?" She looked around as if expecting a small boy to emerge from behind a chair.

"Abi, quiet. You're not helping," Gideon hissed in her ear. "Of course there's a child. He was on the news. Where is he now?" He turned back to Nancy.

"At school, of course," she said defensively.

"It didn't occur to you that perhaps we might want to see him?" Gideon asked with a sigh. "Honestly,

Nancy, you can't expect me to accept your claim without even seeing the boy. If he's mine, I'm pretty sure I'll be able to tell by looking at him."

Abi pulled on his arm. "What d'you mean, 'if he's mine'?" she asked, her eyes wide. "Of course he's not yours. You said so."

"I know. I didn't mean he was mine. I just mean if she's trying to claim he is, then at least she should have him here." He turned back to Nancy. "We want to see him, Nancy, and not just a fuzzy photo, the real thing. When does he get home? Surely it's after school time now?"

"He goes to school in Christchurch. One of my friends picked him up, and I have to go and fetch him after I've seen you."

"So he won't be back here till later?" he asked, narrowing his eyes.

"Yeah, much later, and then he must go to bed. He has school again tomorrow." Nancy got to her feet, nervously twisting her hands together.

"No," said Gideon firmly. "He's not going to school tomorrow. We'll come back here tomorrow morning and meet him then."

"No, really, he must go to school. They get cross if the children stay off for no reason." Nancy's voice began to quaver.

Gideon got to his feet and stood looking down at her. "What are you trying to hide, Nancy?" he asked, watching her face closely. "Any school would understand the circumstances. You can't pull that one on us. Have him here tomorrow morning, or we go back to Tauranga and go to the press and tell them you were just trying it on."

"Okay, okay." Nancy held up her hands in submission. "He'll be here. I guess you do have to meet him."

"We'll be back at ten," Gideon said firmly. Turning to Abi, he held out his hand to pull her to her feet.

She was staring at Nancy, a very curious expression on her face. "I know where I've seen you before," she said, so quietly that Gideon had to strain to catch the words. "You were the girl in Bristol. Outside the Colston Hall. Oh, my god! I talked to you. I told you stuff." She paused, her face pale and her eyes wide. "Did you know who I was? You did, didn't you? You knew who I was and you never said anything...you total bitch!" and she launched herself out of the chair and flung herself at Nancy, arms outstretched.

With a cry of alarm, Gideon leapt forward and caught her around the waist just as her fingers were about to claw at Nancy's face.

"Abi, what the fuck?" he bellowed. "Control yourself! What the hell's going on? Sit down and stay there." He dumped her unceremoniously back onto the sofa, then turned to Nancy. "D'you know what she's on about?" he asked his eyes sparking dangerously.

Slowly Nancy nodded, and walked over to the window. "Yeah. I recognised you as soon as you walked in." She addressed Abi. "I was just hoping you didn't remember. Yeah, I was a total bitch. But you were a right mess. I don't think you would have wanted him to see you like that, would you?"

Abi stared at her. "That's not the point," she yelled. "You knew who I was and you didn't say anything."

Gideon stared from one to the other of them in total

confusion. "You two have met?" he asked, shaking his head in disbelief. "How? When? Someone tell me. Please."

Abi and Nancy exchanged glances, then Nancy shrugged. "It was in Bristol in January 2000. You remember you did a gig there on the European tour?" Gideon nodded. "Well, if you remember, I was with you, working on costumes. I went out the stage door for a breath of fresh air during the gig, and I…found Abi."

Gideon stared at Abi in horror. "You were in Bristol when I was there?" he whispered. "I didn't know."

Abi took up the story. "When Nancy says she 'found me,' she's right. I was sitting slumped on the pavement outside the theatre, very drunk and very stoned. Not a pretty sight, I'm sure."

Nancy gave a short laugh. "Even in that state you were pretty," she assured her. "That's one of the reasons I didn't tell him." She moved over to the chair again and sat back down with a heavy sigh. "I'm sorry, Abi. I behaved very badly that night. But you were hardly an angel yourself, were you?"

"I guess I'd better tell you the whole story." Abi curled her legs up under her on the sofa and looked at Gideon. "It's not very nice, I'm afraid."

Chapter 13

Wednesday 12th January, 2000—Bath, Somerset

"Abi, come on, we're going to a gig!" Jess burst into Abi's bedroom and jumped up and down in front of her.

Abi looked up from her book, grinning. "I'm not going anywhere tonight, Jess," she said firmly. "Got work to do, and anyway, it's not a good night for me."

Jess hopped up and down in frustration. "Oh, Abs, don't be so dull. Jason has got tickets to some gig in Bristol, and we're all going. You've got to come. It'll do you good. You've been looking miserable all day."

Abi raised an eyebrow. "That's because I *am* miserable," she said with a shrug. "As I said, today is not a good day for me. Just a bit of an anniversary."

Jess looked at her closely but knew not to ask any more. "Please come, Abi," she persisted. "I don't want to go without you."

Abi rolled her eyes. "Who's playing?" she asked with a sigh.

Jess looked slightly embarrassed. "Not sure. He didn't say. Someone big, though. He was very lucky to get the tickets," she said brightly. "Please, Abs, please!"

"Oh, all right then. Maybe it'll do me good to get out." Abi sighed and pushed her chair back. "Need a couple of drinks before we go, though. Not going in a car with that lot without a drink in me."

Jess giggled and gave her a quick hug. "I agree. I'll go and get us a drink, and you get dressed."

Now in their third and final year at Bath College of Art, Abi and Jess were sharing a house in the town with another girl and three boys, and life was pretty much one constant party. Abi wandered over to her wardrobe and flung open the doors. Her shoulders drooped as she surveyed the mess of mostly unwashed clothes piled in a heap on the bottom. Only three things were still hanging up, and she didn't fancy wearing any of them. A bit of rummaging produced a pair of wide flared jeans studded with rhinestones up the side, a figure-hugging black-and-green top, and a pair of high wedge sandals. She pulled them on, then examined herself in the long mirror. Not very practical for January, but she had never been very good on that score. She looked around, picked up a very old denim jacket and a brightly coloured knitted scarf, snatched up her bag, and left the bedroom to make her way to the kitchen.

Jess had just poured white wine into two very large glasses, and she held one out to Abi. "There, that should do the trick," she said with a giggle. "Should be enough to take the edge off Jason's driving."

Abi took the glass, downed the wine in a single gulp, then walked over to the fridge and poured another one.

Jess raised her eyebrows. "One of those nights, is it?" she asked.

Abi shrugged and surveyed her over the rim of the glass. "Yeah," she said briefly. "It is. If I'm going anywhere tonight, I do it my way," and she made short work of the second drink. "So where are the others?

Are we leaving?"

Jess walked to the kitchen door and peered out into the corridor. "I thought they were ready," she admitted with a frown. "It's just us, Jason and Pete. Kate and Damien are staying here. They have other plans."

Abi raised her eyebrows. "I thought they only did that at weekends," she said with a grin.

Jess rolled her eyes. "Oh, it seems to be all the time now. May as well advertise Kate's room. She's never in it."

Fifteen minutes later, the four students were in the car, speeding towards Bristol. Jason was driving, with Pete in the passenger seat and the two girls squashed in the back with quantities of very smelly sports kit.

Jess wrinkled her nose. "Jase, don't you ever wash your kit? It's almost gassing me an' Abi!"

Jason chuckled. "I save it till the holidays and take it home for Mum. Gives her something to do," he said, taking a very sharp corner far too fast.

Abi was thrown across the seat and cannoned into Jess. "God, Jase, your driving gets worse all the time!" she complained, struggling upright and disentangling herself from a pair of muddy rugby boots. She peered out the window to see where they were. "Is this gig in the Colston Hall?" she asked, delving into her bag and pulling out an already-rolled joint.

She lit it and passed it to Jess. Jess took a long toke on the joint, then passed it back to Abi. Pete turned round and raised his eyebrows.

"What are you two up to?" he asked suspiciously, his brown eyes narrowed behind his long blond fringe. He flicked his hair back and sniffed. "Can I have some?"

Abi handed him the joint. "Yeah, but not Jason," she stipulated, attempting to retain some semblance of responsibility.

"Yeah, his driving's bad enough already!" Pete said with a laugh. In response, Jason took the next corner too fast, and the girls once more ended up in a heap in the back.

"Christ, Jase, you'll get stopped by the police if you keep doing stuff like that," Jess admonished him, pushing Abi off her and wriggling back into position. "Aren't we nearly there anyway?"

Pete nodded and turned round to face them again, handing the joint back to Abi. "Yeah, there's the Colston Hall just over there. There's a car park that way, I think." He pointed vaguely to his left.

Abi squeezed the lit end of the joint between her thumb and forefinger to extinguish it, then dropped it back into her bag.

"Keep that for later then," she said with a slightly woozy grin. "Who're we seeing tonight anyway? Jess didn't know."

Jason manoeuvred the car into a parking space near the entrance of the multi-storey car park and turned off the engine. He spoke without turning round. "NightHawk. I was really lucky to get tickets..." He stopped as Abi emitted a piercing shriek.

"NightHawk! I can't go to see them." She turned to Jess in horror, and caught her by the shoulders. "Why didn't you tell me? I can't come in. You must take me home." She shook her friend, and stared wildly around the car as if a means of escape would suddenly present itself.

"Abi?" Jess spoke tentatively, her brown eyes wide

with concern. "Abi, what on earth's wrong?"

Abi stopped shaking her, and stared at her friends in slowly dawning horror. The other three stared back at her in shocked silence. Her hands dropped from Jess's shoulders and fell onto her lap. She bent her head forward and let her hair swing in front of her face.

"Nothing," she muttered. "Sorry, guys. Just freaked out there a bit. Didn't mean to scare you."

Jess reached out and took one of Abi's hands. "What's wrong, though? Why can't you come and see NightHawk? I thought you liked grunge."

Abi took a deep breath and tried to calm her frantically thumping heart. "I do," she said, attempting to keep her voice steady. "But I don't feel well. You go without me. I'll…I'll go and get a coffee or something."

Jess exchanged glances with the boys, and without a word they got out of the car and wandered a few yards away. She turned back to Abi. "Abs, it's more than that, isn't it? It was NightHawk that freaked you out. Not going into the theatre." She peered closely at her friend and put her hand on Abi's arm. "Tell me what's wrong. Is it something to do with the anniversary you mentioned?"

Abi raised an ashen face. "Sort of," she whispered. "Please don't ask, Jess. You just go and enjoy it. I'll be fine."

Jess hesitated for a moment, then leant forward and gave Abi a quick hug. "Have you got some cash?" she fussed. "You need to go and have coffee or something. Sober up a bit. The fresh air is going to get you."

Abi nodded. "Yeah. I got plenty of money. Now go, or you'll miss the beginning."

Together they clambered out of the car and joined the boys, who were leaning nonchalantly against the wall of the car park.

"All right now?" Pete raised his eyebrows as the girls approached.

"Abi doesn't feel well," said Jess firmly, squeezing her friend's hand. "She's gonna go and get a coffee while we go to the gig. We'll meet up afterwards."

Abi shifted her weight from one foot to the other and tried to keep her balance. Jess had been right about the fresh air. She was feeling very lightheaded and wobbly. She carefully focused on her friends. "I may go home," she said slowly. "I've got enough for a taxi. Don't wanna wait for three hours or more."

Jess frowned and moved a little closer to her. "Are you sure, Abs? Will you be all right on your own? I could stay," she said quietly.

Abi shook her head. "I'm fine. Honest. You go, all of you."

Pete pushed himself upright and shrugged. "Come on then. If she says she's fine, she's fine. She's a big girl," and he started off towards the exit, not waiting to see if the others were following.

"Abi, walk with us until we're outside the hall." Jess caught Abi's arm and propelled her after Pete. "I'm not leaving you here in that state. I want to make sure you're near a coffee shop or something."

Abi allowed herself to be led out of the huge multi-storey car park and dutifully followed her friends as they made their way towards the venue where NightHawk were playing. She was still in a state of shock and remained silent until they arrived at the door to the hall.

Jess turned to her, concern in her eyes. "Are you sure you'll be all right, Abs?" she asked, glancing around to make sure there were no visible threats lurking in the shadows. "You will go somewhere safe, won't you? Maybe getting a taxi home is the best option. Promise me you won't do anything silly?"

"Can't promise." Abi shrugged, her voice slightly slurred. "I'm always doing silly things." She looked at Jess. "Now go on. I'll be all right. Go and enjoy it." She gave her friend a little shove towards the door where the two boys were waiting impatiently.

With a final glance behind her, Jess trotted over to join them and disappeared amongst the thronging fans heaving around the entrance.

Abi watched her go, her face impassive, before she wandered unsteadily over to a bench in front of the hall. She sank down onto it and put her head in her hands. How could she have been so stupid as not to have checked to see who was playing? Although she tried to avoid reading about NightHawk's activities, even she had not failed to note that they were in the middle of a European tour that included several dates in Britain. The last of the audience had disappeared through the doors, and the street outside the hall had gone eerily silent.

Abi sat back on the bench, and rested her head against the wall. She felt so stupid. She had completely freaked out in the car, and now her friends would think she was mad. Jess had been very kind, but Abi knew she had been suspicious as to the reason for the outburst. Slowly she got to her feet and began to walk unsteadily along the wall of the huge building. When she got to the corner, she glanced both ways and sighed.

She had no idea where she was; her brain was addled from the wine and the dope, and she had completely forgotten which way it was to either the coffee shop or the nearest taxi rank.

She turned left and walked slowly along the side wall of the hall, pausing when she reached a plain grey door that was clearly a fire escape. She leaned against the wall, and stared at the door. Somewhere behind there was Gideon. Her Gideon. He was performing to her friends, and he had no idea she was there. She should have been in there. Not in the audience like Jess, Pete or Jason, but backstage. Helping Gideon prepare for his performance. Maybe helping with the costumes. Living her life...with him. Instead, she was outside in the cold...on her own...while his life went on without her.

Slowly she sank to the ground and sat on the cold pavement with her back against the wall. She fumbled in her bag and brought out the half-smoked joint. After a couple of attempts, she managed to light it, leant back against the wall, and took a long toke. She had hoped it would calm her down, but she already felt sick, and it only served to make that worse. She closed her eyes, and the world began to spin. A single tear trickled down her cold cheek as she recalled that same date four years before, when she had given birth to her baby. To Gideon's baby...Natasha. Natasha who hadn't even lived to see the next day. Another tear joined the first one, and within seconds Abi was sobbing silently, her head resting on her knees, the joint hanging loosely in her hand.

A sudden sound made her lift her head, to see the fire escape door open and a person step out onto the pavement. Abi blinked away her tears in an attempt to see more clearly, just in case it was Gideon... It was a girl, and Abi's head dropped back onto her knees. She listened as hesitant footsteps approached and stopped in front of her.

"Are you all right?" The accent was American, and the tone concerned. Abi slowly raised her head. The girl was squatting down in front of her, her pale freckled face serious. She had shoulder-length curly red hair and was wearing jeans and a NightHawk T-shirt. "Are you all right?" she repeated, slightly louder. "Can I help you?"

Abi shook her head dismally. "No one can help me," she muttered, sniffing.

The girl sat down beside her on the pavement, and leant back against the wall. "You don't look very well," she said bluntly, taking in the tear-streaked face and the half-smoked joint. "Are you sure I can't help in any way?"

Abi raised her head, and studied her more carefully. The world was still spinning, but she managed to get her in focus. "Did you come out of the hall?" she asked eventually.

"Yeah." The girl nodded. "I'm with the band. I do the costumes."

Abi groaned. That should have been her. "D'you know Gideon, then?" she asked.

"Of course. I know them all. I'm touring with them." The girl looked at Abi. "Are you a fan?"

Abi leaned towards her conspiratorially. "I used to know Gideon," she whispered. "Long time ago."

The girl smiled slightly. "Did you?" she whispered back. "How come?"

Abi looked at her suspiciously. "Can't tell you that," she said, her words slurring slightly. "No one else knows. Not even Jess."

The girl smothered a smile. "Who's Jess?" she asked.

"My friend." Abi glanced at her. "Judy knows, but she's not here."

"Okay. When did you know Gideon, then?"

"Years ago. 'Bout five years ago. Then four years ago today I—" Abi stopped, and the tears started down her cheeks again. "Gideon was my boyfriend. Then he left."

The girl frowned and stared more closely at Abi. Her eyes widened, and she leant forward. "What happened four years ago?" she asked. "Is that when Gideon left you?"

Abi looked at her and frowned. "No. 'Course not. He left ages before that."

"So...what happened four years ago?" the girl persisted.

"Nothing." Abi clammed up, suddenly becoming aware she was speaking to a complete stranger and telling her things she hadn't even told her friend. She looked covertly at the girl again. "Does Gideon have a girlfriend now?"

The girl hesitated for a moment, then nodded her curly head. "Yeah. Yeah, he does. He's very happy," she said at last.

"Oh." Abi digested this piece of information. "That's nice. I'm glad he's happy."

The girl took the half-smoked joint out of Abi's hand. "I think you should get rid of this," she said. "There are a lot of police around tonight. I wouldn't like you to get arrested."

Abi shrugged. "Who cares?" she muttered. "What would it matter? No one would even notice."

The girl sighed and got to her feet. "I think you should go and get a coffee to sober up." She held out a hand to pull Abi to her feet. "And then get yourself home to bed. There's a really good all-night coffee shop just around that corner. Go there and sort yourself out. D'you have any money?"

Abi swayed as she regained her feet, and steadied herself against the wall with her hand. "Loads of money," she said with a nod. "Gonna get a taxi home."

"Good idea," approved the girl. "But get a coffee first. Don't want you in a taxi in that state. Now go on. You'll feel better after that." She gave her a little push in the direction of the coffee shop.

Abi began to wobble along the road, then turned. "Don' tell anyone what I told you," she said with a frown. "'Bout Gideon. That's secret."

The girl nodded, and Abi turned and made her way slowly along the pavement.

****

Nancy watched until Abi had almost reached the corner, then turned and went back in through the fire door. She closed it behind her and leaned against it for a moment to get her thoughts in order. She could hear the sounds of the band on stage, and she hurried through the corridor and into Gideon's dressing room. She went straight over to where his old leather jacket hung on the back of a chair and thrust her hand into the inside pocket. She pulled out a battered black leather wallet and, with only a moment's hesitation, opened it and slid out a tatty photograph. She caught her breath. Despite the fact it had obviously been taken several years earlier, it quite clearly showed the girl she had just been speaking to outside.

So that was Abi. Gideon's lost love. He had never spoken about her to Nancy, but she had managed to glean a certain amount of information from Simon and Charles. She knew Gideon had had a girlfriend in England before he became famous, and that he'd been hoping she would join him when she finished school. Nancy wasn't sure what had happened between them, but she had always had the impression it had been Abi who'd dumped Gideon. Now, having spoken to Abi, she wasn't so sure. She was just sliding the photograph carefully back into the wallet when she became aware of a presence behind her.

"What the fuck are you doing with that?" Gideon's hair was soaked with sweat, and his face was like thunder. He was out of breath from performing, and his guitar was still slung around his neck. "Nancy? I asked you a fucking question!"

"Nothing, I was just… I was just looking for some cash. I wanna get a drink. Thought you might have some."

"You were looking at my photograph," he snarled. "Why were you looking at my photograph?"

"Didn't mean to." Nancy thought quickly. "I pulled it out thinking it was a fiver. Sorry. She's very pretty."

Gideon snatched the wallet out of her hands, and flung it onto the table. "If I *ever* catch you in my wallet again…" he barked at her, his eyes sparking dangerously, "you'll be back in Seattle before your feet touch the ground. Now get out of my dressing room! I don't want to see you again tonight!"

"But Gid, I'm sorry," Nancy stammered, realising she'd lost control of the situation. "Please forgive me. Is it the interval?"

"Well I'm not gonna walk off stage in the middle of a set, am I?" he said shortly, pushing past her into the corridor. "I'm going outside for some fresh air. Don't follow me," he added, seeing her start to fall into step with him.

"D'you want this?" Nancy called after him, holding out Abi's half-smoked joint. Gideon glanced round, then reached out and took it from her. He strode over to the fire door and disappeared.

****

As the cold January air hit him, the sweat began to cool on his body, and Gideon shivered. He stepped out onto the pavement, having first checked for fans or press, and leant against the wall with a sigh. He lit the joint and put it up to his mouth, glancing down the almost deserted street as he did. At the corner he could just make out the back view of a girl in a telephone box. She had long auburn hair, and Gideon found himself painfully reminded of Abi. Seeing Nancy with the photograph had upset him even more than he'd let on, and now the girl in the phone box had made it even worse. How dare Nancy go in his wallet? He took a long toke on the joint, wondering for a moment why Nancy had given it to him, then with another quick glance at the girl in the phone box, he turned and went back into the building, closing the door firmly behind him.

Chapter 14

Wednesday 6th May, 2009

"You smoked my joint!" Abi stared at Gideon in dismay. "You smoked my joint, and you never knew it was mine." She turned to Nancy. "You could have told him. When he saw you with the photo, you could have told him."

"Why?" Nancy shrugged. "I was his girlfriend then. I wasn't going to risk him running after some doped-up little loser I found on the street. I couldn't risk that." She stared defiantly at Abi. "I helped you, didn't I? I could have just left you there. I sent you to the coffee shop. You obviously got home okay."

Gideon was staring at her, an inscrutable look in his eyes. "You left her out on her own in the middle of Bristol when you knew she wasn't in a fit state to look after herself? You knew who she was, and you did that?" His voice was low and quiet.

Nancy glanced at him nervously. "You'd split with her years before," she said quickly. "You wouldn't have wanted her in that state. I didn't know you still wanted her. You were with me."

"Yet you knew I kept a picture of her in my wallet," he said, his eyes narrowing dangerously. "Why was that, d'you think? But you left her out in a city street, in the evening, when she could barely stand?"

"I told her where the coffee shop was," Nancy whined, writhing uncomfortably on her chair. "If you'd seen her, Gid—she was a real mess."

"All the more reason to take her somewhere safe," he snapped. "If some harm had come to her that night, it would have been your fault."

"Oh, right!" Nancy leaned forward in her seat. "My fault she decided to get too drunk and stoned to stand up straight? How is that my fault? I didn't even need to speak to her when I saw her. I stopped her getting arrested."

Abi got to her feet. "I *am* here, you know," she said, her voice deceptively calm. "I know what state I was in, and I know what happened to me next." She turned to Gideon. "Nancy actually couldn't have done more, unless she'd taken me into the theatre. To be honest, I wouldn't have gone with her. At that time I thought you'd left me, remember? I was far too proud to turn up drunk and crying in your dressing room. I hate that she didn't tell you she'd seen me…but I don't think she could have done much else for me." She spun round and faced Nancy. "You lied to me about him being happy. You knew he still liked me, and you should have told him you'd seen me. But you were in love with him, so of course you didn't." She turned and walked over to the window. "I don't know what I would have done in your place. I don't really want to think about that. Gid, I want to go back to the hotel now."

Gideon looked from her to Nancy, then back again. "This is too much to take in," he said, running a hand through his hair. "Abi, we need to talk. Nancy… whatever it is you want from me now means nothing. I will *never* forgive you for this. Abi and I could have been reunited all those years ago, but for you." He stood up and towered over her. "We'll be back tomorrow at ten. Make sure your kid is here."

He stepped over to where Abi was still staring out at the mountains, caught her hand tightly in his, and pulled her towards the door. She went with him silently, not looking at Nancy, and together they walked back to the car. Abi climbed in, did up her seatbelt, and leaned back, eyes closed. In her mind she was reliving the night in Bristol as vividly as if it had just occurred. She could feel the terrible pain that tore at her heart when Nancy had said Gideon had a girlfriend and was happy. She could even feel the effects of the alcohol and dope, and she felt the world begin to spin around her. She opened her eyes in a panic. Gideon was watching her.

"Are you all right, Abi?" he asked, starting the car but waiting for her reply before reversing out onto the track. "Is it okay if I drive?"

Abi nodded mutely, not trusting herself to speak. She had always remembered the girl outside the theatre. She remembered she'd been nice to her. Now, having discovered the truth—she shivered, and pulled her shirt more tightly around her. She still had a lot to tell Gideon about that night, but she wasn't ready yet. She needed to get back to the hotel and into a bath to wash off the feeling of dirt and betrayal. Gideon leaned forward and turned up the heating. Within seconds warm air was circulating around Abi's feet.

She turned her head and smiled at him. "Thanks. Feeling a bit out in the cold," she said with a shrug.

He reached over and put his hand on her leg. "I love you, Abs. I'm so sorry this has happened." He paused and glanced at her. "But I think there's more?"

Abi nodded. "Yeah, I want to tell you what happened next, but not till we're back in our room. I need to be clean and cosy."

They drove in silence until they reached the hotel, and then Abi ran a bath while Gideon organised for some food to be delivered to their room. He walked into the bathroom just as Abi was sinking beneath a sea of bubbles, her long hair tied up on the top of her head. She leant back against the end of the bath and smiled up at him.

"Stay and talk," she said. "I don't want you too far away."

Gideon's face darkened, and he squatted down next to the bath.

"I don't want to *be* too far away," he said tersely. "I can't believe what I heard—that you were outside the theatre when I was on stage...that Nancy didn't tell me... Oh, god, Abi! We could have met again that night! How different things would have been."

Abi watched him thoughtfully. "But would they have been better?" she ventured. "I was a real mess, just like Nancy said, and we were both still young. What would have happened if we'd got together then? I still thought Tasha was dead..." Her voice broke slightly. "We probably wouldn't have found out the truth about that until my mother died. Would we have made it? I was a very different person then...and so were you, I'm sure."

Gideon reached under the bubbles and captured one of Abi's hands. He pulled it out and held it against his face. "Don't," he said firmly. "This is like when you said we might not have made it if you'd been on tour with me at the beginning. Abi, we would always have made it. You must believe that."

Abi sighed, and closed her eyes. "Maybe," she said, "but you really wouldn't have liked me then."

"But if we'd been together," Gideon pointed out, "you would have been different. You would have been happy, and therefore not needing to resort to alcohol and drugs to escape your memories. I would have been different, too."

Abi opened her eyes and surveyed him solemnly. "I guess you're right," she conceded. "We would've been different. But if we'd met that night...I'm not sure. Right. I'm clean enough. I'll get dried, and then I'll tell you the rest while we eat." She stood up in the bath, bubbles still clinging to her naked body.

"Is there much more?" Gideon asked curiously, watching as she dried herself and slipped into her pyjama bottoms and a T-shirt.

"A bit," she said, looking at him from under her lashes. "The first thing I did was phone Judy."

Gideon grinned. "Of course you did..." He fell silent as the full significance of her words hit him. "The...the girl in the phone box..." he stammered. "It was you?"

"Yeah. That was me. No wonder she reminded you of me." Abi walked over to the window and pulled the curtains across, then jumped onto the bed and sat cross-legged in the middle. "Let's eat, and I'll tell you everything."

Chapter 15

Wednesday 12th January, 2000—Bristol

As Abi walked slowly along the side of Colston Hall towards the coffee shop, she felt a wave of desolation wash over her, and she realised she desperately needed to talk to Judy. Judy was the only one who would understand, the only one who knew everything that had happened to her. Approaching the corner of the building, she became aware of a telephone kiosk just to her left. She wobbled over to it and shoved the heavy door open. Once inside, she leant against the side and caught her breath. She closed her eyes. The world was still spinning. That girl had been right; she could do with a coffee. She would just phone Judy, then go and find the coffee shop. Fumbling in the pocket of her jeans, she brought out a handful of coins, then reached into the other pocket to pull out a crumpled scrap of paper. Judy had recently got a mobile phone, and Abi had still not managed to memorise the number. She propped the piece of paper up on top of the phone, got her money ready and, carefully attempting to focus on the numbers, dialled.

While waiting for Judy to answer, the full impact of the day caught up with her, and tears began to trickle unheeded down her cheeks. She slumped against the side of the phone box and let her head fall forward. She really needed Judy right now. She would know what to say. By the time the phone was answered, Abi was in floods of tears and found it very hard to speak.

"Judy?" she eventually managed to croak. "It's me."

Judy's voice echoed down the line. "Abs? God, you sound dreadful. What's happened?"

"I'm in Bristol. Don't know what to do. Need to talk to you."

"Abi, have you been drinking?" Judy's voice was suspicious. "Why are you in Bristol? Are you on your own?"

"Made a mistake," slurred Abi, sliding down the side of the phone box until she was sitting on the cold concrete floor, her knees raised. "Didn't mean to come. I didn't know they were playing. She didn't tell me..." Judy's gasp of realisation registered only vaguely.

"Oh, god, Abi! NightHawk! You haven't been to see them have you? Abi?"

"No," Abi managed to say. "No, but talked to some girl. She says Gideon has a girlfriend. Jude...she said he's happy."

"Oh, Abi!" Judy sounded very distressed. "I'm so sorry. And today of all days."

"You remembered!" Abi smiled slightly despite herself. "I love you, Judy."

"I love you too. How are you getting back to Bath?"

"Getting a taxi. But need to sober up first." She leant her head forward and rested it on her knees, still holding the receiver to her ear. "Needed to talk to you."

"I'm coming to get you." Judy's voice started to sound very far away. "Abi, did you hear me? I'll come and get you. You can come back with me. You shouldn't be on your own."

Abi listened to the words but found she couldn't form a reply.

Judy's voice came again, slightly more agitated. "Abi? Answer me. Are you all right?"

With an extreme effort, Abi raised her head and managed to croak, "Yeah. Thank you. That'd be nice."

"Okay, where are you?" Relief sounded in Judy's voice.

"Outside Colston Hall. Gonna go an' get coffee round corner. All-night coffee shop," Abi managed with an effort.

"Right, you do that. I'll find you. Don't go anywhere else. I'll be about an hour or so, though. I'm in Taunton. Promise you'll stay put, Abs?"

Abi found herself nodding, then forced herself to speak. "Yeah, I'll stay put, Judy. Thank you." She ended the call and sat with her hands dangling between her knees, her head resting against the side of the phone box.

After a moment she struggled to her feet, replaced the receiver in its cradle, pushed the door open, and emerged into the cold evening air. Shivering, she wrapped her arms around herself and pulled her thin denim jacket close to her body before heading unsteadily towards the well-lit coffee shop that she now saw was located just across the road. Walking very carefully, Abi crossed the road, let herself into the warm and welcoming café, and ordered a large cappuccino. She carried it to a small table in the window and made herself comfortable. She was beginning to feel very tired, both physically and emotionally, and was so glad Judy was coming to rescue her. A part of her felt very guilty and uncomfortable that she was allowing her best friend to drive all that way for her, but the desperately sad and broken part of her was very glad. She leant back in her chair and sipped her coffee. At least she had somewhere warm to wait.

An hour later Judy walked into the coffee shop to find Abi fast asleep, her head cushioned on her arms and three empty coffee cups littering the table. She sat down next to her and gently shook her arm. "Abs, wake up, I'm here."

Slowly Abi opened her eyes and raised her head. Her hair was tangled, her makeup was smudged, and her face was red and swollen from crying, but she managed to smile.

"Hi, Jude," she murmured. "Thank you so much for coming. I'm sure I'd have been all right, but…"

"Don't be daft," Judy interrupted, giving her friend a quick hug. "It's what I do. I rescue you. Always have, always will." She grinned affectionately at her. "You're coming back to mine for the weekend. D'you need to go back to Bath to get anything, or can we go straight back to Exeter? I have to pick up a couple of friends in Taunton on the way past."

For the first time, Abi noticed Judy was rather curiously attired in a very short, very tight red-and-gold dress, and extremely high gold sandals. She had flung a Barbour jacket over the top, and the whole ensemble looked rather ridiculous.

"Why are you dressed like that?" Abi asked with a frown. "Were you going out?"

"I was already out." Judy grinned. "I was in a night

club with some friends, in Taunton. I'm the designated driver, so I really do have to go back to pick them up."

Abi gasped, her blue eyes wide with horror. "Oh, god, Jude, I'm so sorry! You were having a night out, and I've ruined it. Whatever must you think of me? And your friends..." She tailed off, extremely uncomfortable.

Judy patted her hand. "It's fine, Abi. I really don't mind. I just told my friends my best friend needed my help, and left them to it until I pick them up later. Now, do we need to go back to Bath first?"

Abi shook her head. "Not if I can borrow your clothes," she said with a small smile. "I've got my money and stuff like that." She paused and frowned. "What d'you mean, coming back to yours for the weekend? It's only Wednesday."

"Weekend starts early this week," said Judy with a laugh. "Got to go to a couple of lectures tomorrow, but taking Friday off. I'll explain all as we go. Are you ready?"

Abi nodded and stood up, gathering up her bag and coat. "I need to let Jess know where I've gone," she said, stopping suddenly. "She'll be worried."

"Does she have a mobile?"

"Yeah, I think I've got her number." Abi delved into her bag, eventually pulling out a small diary. "Yeah, it's in here."

Judy held out her phone to Abi. "Text her. Tell her you'll be back on Sunday."

Abi took the phone tentatively, then looked at Judy with a grimace. "I've never used one before," she said apologetically. "I don't know how to text."

Judy laughed and took the phone back. "Okay, tell

me what to say, and I'll do it."

Abi quickly dictated a message for Jess, and Judy tapped it in and pressed Send. She grinned at Abi. "Right. That's done. You really must get a phone of your own, you know. Now, let's get you to Exeter for a bit of pampering." She caught Abi's arm, and together they stepped out into the now freezing night air.

Abi shivered and pulled her jacket round her tightly. "Judy, you're far too good to me," she said as they hurried as fast as Judy's shoes would allow towards the car park.

"Yeah, probably am," Judy said with chuckle, her breath forming a white cloud in the cold air. "But you're worth it. Now come on. It's far too cold to hang around outside."

****

When Abi awoke the next day, she opened her eyes to see Judy curled up in the chair at the end of the bed, deeply engrossed in a book. She propped herself up on her elbow. "Hi," she said with an apologetic smile. "Is it very late?"

Judy grinned at her. "It's nearly two o'clock," she said, carefully marking her place with a leather bookmark, then laying her book on the bed.

"In the afternoon?" Abi stared at her in horror. "How could I have slept for that long? I'm so sorry..."

Judy laughed and got to her feet. "Don't be daft. You had a lot to sleep off. D'you want a cup of coffee?"

Abi sat up and linked her arms around her knees. "Think I had enough coffee last night," she said with a lopsided grin. "What I'd really like is some orange juice, if you have some."

"Sure, there's some in the fridge. Hang on." Judy disappeared, returning moments later with a tall glass of orange juice. Abi drank it down thirstily, then wiped her mouth on the back of her hand.

"That's better," she gasped. "Beginning to feel more human. Judy, I…"

Judy held up her hand to stop her. "If you're going to apologize again, then don't," she reprimanded. "It's lovely to have you here, and we're gonna have a brilliant weekend." Her eyes glittered with excitement. "I haven't told you what we're doing, yet."

Abi raised her eyebrows and shook her sleep-tangled hair out of her eyes. "What's happening then?" she asked curiously.

"We're going on a road trip," said Judy with a giggle. "To Land's End."

"Land's End?" echoed Abi in surprise. "What…? In Cornwall? Why?"

"'Cause it's brilliant there!" Judy's enthusiasm was sparkling. "I've been three times since I've been in Exeter, and I really love it. You will too. Amazing views you can paint."

Abi smiled at her friend's excitement. "Sounds great," she said. "Where are we staying?"

"In a cottage. They're really cheap at this time of year."

Abi watched Judy closely. "Well, since you had obviously already arranged this trip before you knew I'd be here, I take it some other people are coming too? Will they mind me tagging along?"

"No problem," Judy replied airily. "There's only one other person coming. He won't mind at all."

"He?" Abi asked in surprise. "Just you and a boy?

Is there something I should know?"

Judy's pale, lightly freckled face flushed. "Noo," she said immediately. "We're just friends." She glanced sideways at Abi. "At the moment, anyway."

Abi gasped. "Judy! Tell all. Who is he? What's he like? Do you really want me there?"

Judy giggled. "His name is Robert, and he's studying Environment. He's really, really nice, and of course I want you there!" She sat down on the end of the bed and caught Abi's hand. "In fact, it will make it easier, in a way. I don't want to be too obvious, so if you're there…"

Abi nodded. "And I can disappear if it seems appropriate," she finished. "I can't wait to meet him. How old is he?"

"Twenty-two. He's in his last year."

Abi grinned at Judy. "Oh, I hope it works out for you," she said. "You deserve someone lovely."

Judy slid further onto the bed and curled her legs up under her. "So…" she began, changing the subject. "What are we going to do about you, then?"

Abi shrugged and looked away. "Oh, I'm fine. Last night was just… Well, it was the shock of finding NightHawk were playing…"

Judy gave her a look. "No, Abs, that's not what I mean. You're so unhappy. I know you're drinking, and smoking weed far too much, and I know you haven't got over Gideon in the slightest." She paused and surveyed her friend sympathetically. "I know it's hard, Abi, but it's been four and a half years since he left. You need to move on. It's destroying you."

"I'm not unhappy," Abi protested, her face flushing. "I have great fun at college. I go out every weekend… Yeah, maybe I do drink too much, but that's just…" She rested her head on her knees. "It's to help me forget. Just like the sex is." She raised damp eyes to Judy. "It doesn't work."

"Of course it doesn't work," Judy said briskly. "That's never the answer. You just end up feeling like shit and hating yourself. It's time to sort yourself out, Abi. You can't go on like this."

Abi nodded her head sadly. "I know, but I just don't know how… Jude, I still love him. It's not going away." She paused and looked bleakly up at her friend. "There's something else, too. Something I've never told you. Yesterday brought it all back 'cause of the date."

Judy narrowed her eyes at her. "Something to do with the baby?" she asked tentatively.

"Natasha, her name was Natasha," Abi said immediately. "Yes, to do with Natasha. Judy, you know I told you I held her and said goodbye to her?"

Judy nodded, her face concerned.

"Well, I didn't."

Judy's eyes widened. "What? You never said goodbye? Or you never even held her?"

"Never even held her," Abi whispered. "They wouldn't let me. They said it would make it harder for me. I wanted to—I really, really wanted to—but they wouldn't let me." Her voice had risen and was shaking with emotion. "Then you and your mum assumed I'd said goodbye, and I was too ashamed to admit I hadn't. I haven't been able to tell anyone. Haven't been able to talk about it at all. Oh, Judy, it's been eating away at me all these years!" She burst into tears and buried her face in the pillow.

With a stifled cry, Judy sprang forward and flung

her arms around her. "Oh, Abi, I'm so sorry. I didn't know...of course I didn't know. And you've kept it all to yourself for so long." She gently pulled Abi up into a sitting position and handed her a tissue to wipe her eyes. "But why did you wait so long to tell me?"

Abi sniffed and scrubbed at her eyes with the tissue. "I was too embarrassed," she hiccupped. "I should have been stronger...made them let me hold her. She was my baby, Judy, and they had no right to stop me." She shook her head violently from side to side. "They had no right...just because I was young and scared and upset... They got me to do what they wanted. And I let them. I was just so devastated... I didn't care whether I lived or died. I guess nothing really mattered after that night. I lost everything. Not only Gideon, but also his baby. I had nothing left."

Judy put her arm around Abi's shoulders. "I'm glad you told me now," she said. "I know I can't do anything to make it any better...any of it...but it always helps if you can talk to someone."

Abi looked at her doubtfully, then slowly nodded. "I guess you're right," she admitted eventually. "It does feel as if a bit of weight has been lifted. I so wanted to tell you all along. Sorry."

"Don't be daft," Judy replied briskly. "I wouldn't have told you, either. You were far too upset to think straight at the time, and then afterwards you probably just wanted to forget."

Abi opened her eyes wide. "Judy, I can never forget it...any of it. I know I can't have Natasha again, but to know that Gideon is still out there and having fun...it's too much, Judy. I think about him every day."

Judy gave Abi a squeeze. "I know, I know. But we

need to find something in your life to replace him...
No, don't look at me like that. I don't mean another
boyfriend. I mean a purpose." She paused and surveyed
Abi through narrowed eyes. "Have you given any
thought to what you're going to do after you graduate?
It's only a few months now."

Abi shook her head. "No. I've no idea," she
admitted. "Sometimes I think I'd like to teach, but I
really just want to paint. I don't even know where I'm
going to live."

"Have you contacted your parents at all?" Judy
asked tentatively.

Abi gave her a look. "No," she said briefly, "and
never will."

Judy bit her lip. "Can I make a suggestion?" she
asked.

"You usually do," Abi said with a wry grin. "Of
course you can."

"If you're serious about wanting to teach, you
could come here to do a PGCE course for a year. I've
still got one more year to go, so we could be together.
What d'you think?" Judy looked hopefully at Abi.

Abi flopped back against the pillows and sighed.
"Oh, Jude, I don't know!" she wailed. "That sounds
great, but would it really help me? I still can't forget
him, wherever I am."

"You never will forget him," Judy said with a
shrug. "But you have to be able to function normally
and have a fulfilled life. Give it some thought over the
weekend, yes?"

Abi looked up at her and nodded. "Of course I will.
That does sound like a possibility. It would be lovely to
be with you." She smiled slightly and sat up. "I shall

get up now. When do I get to meet Robert?"

Judy blushed and giggled. "Later. I thought we could go to the student union this evening for a drink...cola for you...and you can meet him then. We're planning to leave first thing tomorrow morning. You must go through my clothes and see what you want to borrow."

****

Abi gazed around her in delight. She was standing on the top of a cliff close to Land's End, staring down at the sea crashing on the rocks below. In her head she had already painted a whole collection of pictures, and for the first time in many years she was genuinely excited. She turned to Judy, her face smarting from the biting wind.

"Judy, it's fantastic!" she cried, above the sound of the sea. "I love it here."

Judy, standing just behind her, grinned with satisfaction. "I knew you would. It's just your sort of place."

"I think I want to live here," Abi continued, catching Judy's hand and spinning her round. "Maybe I should do what you said...take the teaching course next year?"

Judy laughed. "Oh, Abi, yes, that would be great!" She flung her arms around her friend.

"I've seen loads of little schools since we got here," Abi went on enthusiastically. "I'd love to teach at a tiny village school. I think I could be happy here." Her mood darkened slightly. "As much as I could be happy anywhere, anyway."

Judy put her hands on Abi's shoulders and looked her straight in the eye. "You will be happy, Abs," she said firmly. "I know you will." A sound behind them made Judy turn to find Robert hovering a few feet away, an awkward look on his face. "Hi, Rob, come and join us. Abi has just decided she wants to live here!"

Robert, a tall good-looking young man with thick messy light-brown hair and grey eyes, moved towards them and put his arm around Judy's shoulders.

"That's great," he said with a grin. "And is she going to come to Exeter next year, too?"

Abi nodded. "Yeah, I think I will," she said with a smile. "It'll be lovely to be with Judy again. Is that okay with you?"

Robert threw back his head and roared with laughter. "With me?" he said. "Nothing to do with me, but if it makes Judy happy, then I'm happy," and he tightened his arm around her.

Judy rested her head on his shoulder, and grinned at Abi slightly smugly. Things were going well with Robert. They had stayed up really late the night before, Abi having tactfully retired to bed early, and talked for hours, with the result that they were now officially going out together.

"Rob's still going to be at Exeter next year too," Judy said, sliding her arm around his waist. "He's decided to do a Masters. So we can all be together. Now I don't know about you two, but I'm freezing! Let's go and find something warm to do," and the three of them linked arms and headed off towards the car.

Chapter 16

Wednesday 6th May, 2009

"So that was how I came to sort my life out and live in Cornwall," finished Abi, leaning back against the pillows and smiling at Gideon.

"And were you happy?" he asked, his head on one side.

"Ye-es," she said slowly. "I was, I suppose. I got really stuck into my work and getting my cottage in order. Then I made some really good friends, the best one being Chris, of course...and I got the dogs." She paused and bit her lip. "I'd managed to push you to the back of my mind—at least I thought I had—and I was actually living a fairly normal life for a few years. And then my mother died, and you quit the band...and you know the rest." She wriggled across the bed towards him and kissed him on the nose. "I'm much happier now, of course, just for the record."

He put his arms around her and pulled her down onto the bed beside him. "I'm not sure you're very happy just now, though, are you?" he asked. "All this stuff with Nancy leaves a very nasty taste in the mouth."

Abi shrugged. "We'll get past it," she said philosophically, winding her arms around his neck. "We can weather any storm. It was a bit of a shock realising who she was, though. And I really, really hope you're not the father."

Gideon's eyes grew dark. "I'm not," he said firmly. "I'm even more sure now she's so reluctant to let us meet him. I bet he's still not there tomorrow." He paused and looked cautiously at his wife. "Do you want to stay here while I go and see her tomorrow? No point in us both getting upset."

Abi rolled over and hovered above him, her eyes flashing.

"Are you worried I'll lose my temper again?" she asked, fixing him with a baleful stare. "You can trust me."

Gideon gave a short laugh. "Well, I really thought you were going to scratch her eyes out this afternoon," he said. "If I hadn't grabbed you when I did…"

"Well, what d'you expect?" Abi glared down at him. "You know what she did. I was justifiably upset. It brought back all the feelings from that time, and I just lost it. I can still be fiery, you know."

"High maintenance Abi's back, is she?" asked Gideon with a chuckle, cringing as her hands came down on either side of his face, pinning him to the bed.

"Yeah, gonna make something of it?" she asked, her eyes narrowed. "If you honestly think I'm going to let you go and see her on your own tomorrow, you really don't know me! I think you're right to be suspicious of her agenda, though. It's very odd the way she doesn't want us to meet her son."

Gideon frowned, his eyes concerned. "Very odd. The whole thing seems odd to me. There's definitely something not right…there's no way she's telling us the truth…or at least not all of it." He fell silent, a strange look passing over his face.

Abi pulled back from him, and cocked her head on one side. "What have you thought?" she asked.

"I think I might see Simon's hand in this," Gideon muttered, his eyes flashing. "Maybe yet another ruse to try and split us up."

"Really?" Abi sighed. "Don't you think he's given that up? Last time didn't go so well for him. You mean he's put her up to it or something?"

Gideon shrugged. "Maybe... I dunno... Probably not... I'm just a bit paranoid about him after last summer." His hand came up and gently stroked her upper arm.

Abi bent her head and dropped a light kiss on his hand. "Forget Simon," she ordered. "I'm coming with you tomorrow."

With a single movement, Gideon flung her over onto her back on the bed and pinned her down with his leg. "You can come," he conceded. "If I can be sure you'll behave. But now, I'd like you to misbehave. Think you can do that?"

Abi grinned mischievously and wound her arms around his neck, pulling his lips down onto hers. "Oh, that'll be easy," she murmured, shivering as his hands slid over her body, awakening a deep desire.

****

"Last leg." Roger leaned back in his seat and smiled at his wife. "Try and get some sleep, Caroline. It'll be nine in the morning when we arrive at Auckland, and I'm sure you won't be wanting to spend the day in bed."

"Certainly not." Caroline was rifling through her bag. "I plan to spend all day with Penny and the children."

"The children will be at school," Roger pointed out, closing his eyes.

"Oh, yes. Well, with Penny, then, until they finish school. Maybe we could go and pick them up? That would be fun, wouldn't it, Roger? Roger?" She peered over at him and was surprised to see he appeared to have fallen asleep. She narrowed her eyes in suspicion and prodded him on the arm. "Roger, are you really asleep?"

"No, but if I were I wouldn't be now, would I?" Roger answered without opening his eyes. "Now shut up and try to sleep."

Caroline smiled to herself. She was very glad they'd decided to fly out to New Zealand, and even with the nine-hour layover in Tokyo it had been worth it. Just a few more hours and she'd be with the rest of the family. She wriggled into a more comfortable position and closed her eyes. She wondered how Gideon and Abi had got on with that dreadful woman. She definitely hoped the claims weren't true. Although she'd been publicly pooh-poohing the idea, inside she was aware of a tiny niggle of doubt that was eating away at her. She had confidence that, whatever the outcome, Gideon and Abi would overcome any problems, but it wouldn't be very pleasant for them, and she hated the idea that any of her family could be upset. She opened her eyes again and peered out the window to see the lights of Tokyo disappearing far below and behind them, then settled back with a sigh and attempted to get some sleep.

****

"Are you still awake?" Lydia's voice hissed

through the darkness.

"Yeah." Natasha peered across the room at her cousin. "What's up?"

"I've just had a thought. What happens if you get there and Billy the farmhand has gone out?"

Natasha slid out of bed, crept across the room, and climbed onto the end of Lydia's bed. She sat cross-legged and leaned forward. "I thought of that," she whispered, "but he lives on a farm. There's always someone at home on a farm. Anyway, he's very old. He probably doesn't go out much any more."

Lydia propped herself up on her elbow, switched on her torch, and shone it on Natasha's face. "How old is he, then?" she asked. "Grandma and Grandpa still go out."

Natasha put her hand up to shield her eyes from the light. "Oh, he's much older than that," she said with a nod. "He's about seventy-six."

"Grandpa is seventy," Lydia said doubtfully. "I'm sure he'll still go places in six years."

Natasha sighed and wriggled impatiently. "He's different," she said firmly. "Stop worrying, Lydia. It'll be fine."

Lydia lay down on her back and shone her torch on the ceiling, waving it around in circles to make patterns. "Well, I hope so," she said, "'cause this is probably your only chance to do this. Your mum and dad'll be back tomorrow evening. And in a few days your dad has his first concert and you'll be leaving here."

"It'll be fine," repeated Natasha, jumping off the bed again and creeping back across the room. "Now we should get to sleep. we have to get up really early tomorrow, an' it's nearly midnight now."

Lydia flashed the torch on one more circuit of the room, then turned it off and slid back down under her quilt. "Okay, night-night. I'll try and sleep, but I'm really excited!"

"You're not even coming," said Natasha with a chuckle. "Think how I'm feeling! Night-night."

Chapter 17

Thursday 7th May, 2009

"You two are up very early." Penny had stopped in surprise as she entered the kitchen. "It's only six thirty!"

Lydia and Natasha, hard at work making their sandwiches for lunch, turned and smiled at her. "Need to get to school early today," Lydia lied smoothly. "We wanted to do some stuff in the art room, getting ready for the art exhibition. Mr. Lord has discovered Natasha's a really good artist and wants her to do some drawings of animals for the display. We thought we'd get in early and do some today."

Penny looked impressed. "Very industrious of you," she said. "Have you made your own lunches, as well?"

Natasha nodded. "Yep, we're nearly ready to go," she said with a grin.

"Well, remember Grandma and Grandpa will be here when you get home. That'll be nice, won't it? And your mum and dad should be back this evening, Tasha. They rang last night. They have to see someone this morning, but then they're going to try to get a flight this afternoon."

"They're seeing that woman, aren't they?" Natasha wrinkled her nose in distaste. "The sooner they sort that out, the better." She thrust her lunchbox into her bag. "Come on, Lydia, let's get going. Bye, Aunty Penny. See you later," and the two girls swung their bags over their shoulders and headed for the door.

The temperature had dropped noticeably overnight, and Natasha shivered as they sped down the drive and out onto the Beach Road.

"Where's the bus stop?" she puffed as they ran down the nearly deserted street.

"Not far." Lydia pointed vaguely in front of them. and kept running. "When we're on the bus, we can sort out what you're wearing and stuff."

Natasha glanced at her doubtfully. "Have I got to get changed on the bus? You never said that before."

"Don't fuss. It'll be fine." Lydia grinned at her. "Unless you want to go to see Billy the farm hand dressed for school."

Although Natasha didn't have her own uniform for Lydia's school, she was nonetheless dressed in a grey school skirt and plain white polo top, and she had no intention of spending her adventure day like that.

"Here we are." Lydia slowed down and turned a corner. "This is Palm Beach Plaza, where the bus goes from. It's due at ten to seven, so we're in plenty of time." She sank down on a wooden bench at the bus stop and caught her breath. Natasha sat beside her and shrugged her bag off her back. She opened the top and peered inside.

"Can you take home the clothes I don't need?" she asked, pulling out a pair of jeans. "I don't want to carry too much."

Lydia nodded. "'Course I can," she said at once. "That was the plan. Don't get them out now. The bus is just coming."

She stood up and stepped out onto the pavement as the bus came into view. Natasha stuffed everything back into her bag and followed her cousin onto the bus. They made their way to the back seat and slid into the corner. Due to the early hour, the bus was almost empty, and Natasha was able to struggle into her jeans and T-shirt unnoticed. She added a bright red hoody and changed her shoes from smart black school shoes to old blue Converse trainers.

"That's better," she said with a grin, wiggling her feet. "Feel more like me now." Between them the two girls managed to stuff Natasha's discarded clothes into Lydia's bag, leaving Natasha's bag empty apart from her lunch, camera, phone, money, and Joan's diary. She glanced at Lydia. "Thanks for coming on this first bit with me. You didn't have to."

Lydia raised her eyebrows. "I wanted to make sure you got on the right bus in Tauranga," she said with a giggle. "Imagine if you went the wrong way and ended up in Auckland or something! I'll have to leave as soon as we find your bus, though, or I'll be late for school. Are you nervous?"

Natasha hesitated for a moment, loathe to admit how she was feeling, then shrugged and nodded. "Bit," she admitted, "but only 'cause I'm in a strange country. If I was doing this in England, I'd be fine."

Lydia smothered a grin. "Of course you would," she agreed. "Now, have you got plenty of money? We have no idea how much the taxi will cost."

Natasha nodded. "Oh, masses," she said airily. "I brought everything I have. I'll be fine."

The bus journey took just over half an hour, and

when the girls arrived at Wharf Street, they had only five minutes until the connecting bus was due to depart. Lydia led the way along the road and stopped at a busy bus stop a few yards away.

"Here it is," she said, pushing Natasha in front of her. "That's your bus waiting now. Take this. Put it in your bag. Could come in handy." She thrust a small penknife into Natasha's hand. "Now, get on, 'cause it's nearly time for it to leave. Remember where you have to get off, Cambridge, and you've got Billy's address to show the taxi driver." She reached out and gave her cousin a quick hug, then stepped back and watched her board the bus.

Natasha showed her ticket, then made her way to the back of the vehicle and slid into a double seat on the right-hand side. She put her bag on the seat beside her, slipping the penknife into the front pocket, and peered out the window to wave to Lydia. Although she would never have admitted it to anyone, her heart was beating very fast, and her mouth had gone dry. She licked her lips and took a deep breath. Now was not the time to panic. She could do this. She had everything she needed, and she knew where she was going. She would be fine.

****

Abi awoke early to the sound of someone knocking at the door. She lay still for a moment while she got her bearings, then slipped out of bed, pulling a long T-shirt over her head. She cautiously opened the door and peered out.

"Room service," a cheery waitress announced, pushing past Abi with a loaded breakfast trolley.

Abi jumped back and held the door open. "Oh,

thank you," she said, brushing her hair out of her eyes and pulling her T-shirt down. "What time is it, then?"

"Eight thirty." The waitress smiled brightly and left the room. Abi closed the door and leant back against it with her eyes closed. She hated being woken before she was ready, and there was no way she wanted to eat at that time in the morning. What had they been thinking when they'd ordered so much for breakfast? She opened her eyes and walked over to the trolley. It was full of everything anyone could ever think of for breakfast, from cereal and fruit juice to three types of eggs, bacon, sausages, mushrooms, croissants, and a huge cafetière of coffee. She sighed and climbed back onto the bed.

"Gid, wake up." She gently shook Gideon's shoulder. "Breakfast's here. You have a hell of a lot to eat."

Gideon groaned and rolled onto his back. "What?" he muttered, opening one eye. "Did we order breakfast? I don't remember."

"Well we did," Abi said firmly, pulling the covers off him, "and it's arrived. I'll force down some bacon and a cup of coffee, but you're gonna have to eat the rest." She slid off the bed again and disappeared into the bathroom.

Gideon rolled out of bed and ran a hand through his tangled hair. He peered at the breakfast trolley, then poured himself a glass of orange juice. They had talked far into the night, and consequently he was feeling extremely sleep deprived. He poured a coffee and carried it back to bed. He was not looking forward to the morning's confrontation with Nancy, and the very tiny part of him that wondered if he could be the father was tapping loudly at his brain. He was ninety-nine percent sure he wasn't, but although he wasn't going to admit it to Abi, he had to concede that he could be. If he was, he had no idea what would happen. That Nancy had been part of the reason he and Abi had not re-connected sooner would undoubtedly pose a problem, and he had to admit it was doing his head in.

He leaned back against the pillows and sipped his coffee. He was still very suspicious of Nancy's reluctance to let them meet her son, and he had meant what he'd said to Abi the previous evening, that he could sense Simon's involvement. He glanced up as Abi appeared out of the bathroom, a large towel wrapped around her body.

"Oh, Gid, please eat something," she said, picking up a piece of bacon as she passed the trolley. "We can't send it back like this."

"Give me a minute." Gideon frowned at her. "I need a coffee first. The eggs look nice. I'll have some in a minute."

Abi rummaged in her bag and pulled out a bright blue strappy top and black cardigan. She teamed them with her skinny jeans and tied her hair up in a high ponytail. Then she wandered back over to the trolley and poured herself a large milky coffee. The food was beginning to get cold, so she loaded a small plate with bacon and climbed onto the bed next to Gideon.

"Are you nervous?" she asked him between bites.

Gideon looked at her warily. "What d'you mean?" he asked, watching her over the rim of his cup.

"About this morning," she said impatiently. "Meeting her son."

"Why should I be nervous?" Gideon scowled.

"He's not mine. I told you."

Abi surveyed him calmly. "Yes, you did." She narrowed her eyes. "But there's just a teeny tiny bit of you that knows he could be. Doesn't that make you nervous?"

"No," he snapped, finishing his coffee in one gulp before jumping off the bed and going over to the trolley. "He's not mine. I'm not nervous. No need to be." He started piling a large quantity of scrambled eggs and bacon onto his plate. "I don't want to go and see Nancy again—I have big issues with her now—but I have nothing to be nervous about." He climbed back onto the bed again and applied himself to his breakfast with gusto.

Abi watched him silently, sipping her coffee. "Gideon," she said at last, gently laying a hand on his bare leg. "I know you. Of course you're nervous. If it makes you feel any better, I don't think you're the father. She's been far too reluctant to let you meet him. She's up to something."

Gideon glanced at her from under his lashes. "Thanks, Abs. I am a bit nervous, but I didn't want to admit it." He took another bite of bacon. "I do think she's behaving strangely, though. I don't think the boy'll be there this morning, either."

"I thought that too." Abi nodded. "And I've been thinking about what you said about Simon. I hate to think he might be back in our lives, but you're probably right that we haven't heard the last of him." She frowned. "How well did Nancy get on with Simon?"

"She slept with him. He liked anyone who did that." Gideon snorted dismissively. "I seem to remember they dated for a few weeks. He rarely stayed with anyone longer than that." He paused as he tried to remember. "I think she went out with him straight after me, and then when the tour finished she went back to Seattle and stayed there. I never saw her after that, until yesterday. Don't know if Simon did, though."

Abi slid off the bed and walked over to refill her coffee. "Oh, well," she said with a wry grin, "if he turns up, he'll find out just how much he upset us last summer. I could quite enjoy that."

Gideon scowled. "Well he's not going anywhere near you again," he stated firmly, his eyes flashing. "Or Tasha."

"Oh, should we phone Tash this morning?" said Abi suddenly, picking up her phone to see the time. "Or no, they'll have gone to school by now. Never mind. We can call her later."

"Hopefully we'll be back with her later," pointed out Gideon, sliding off the bed and heading for the bathroom. "Can't wait, personally."

****

The bus drew up in the busy street in Cambridge just before nine o'clock, and Natasha breathed a big sigh of relief that the first leg of her journey had been completed successfully. She stepped onto the pavement and looked around her. The town was thronging with morning traffic, with people rushing to work and school, and she felt suddenly overwhelmed. She was in a town she'd never been to before, in a country she was only visiting, and on her way to see someone who would have no idea who she was. She shivered and wrapped her arms around herself. Why did she have such ridiculous ideas? She mentally chastised herself and promised she would stay at home in future. Then

177

she hitched her bag onto her shoulder and went in search of a taxi. She found a line of them outside the Town Hall, and tentatively approached the front one.

"Excuse me…" She bent down, and spoke to the driver. "Could you take me to Kaipaki, please?"

The middle-aged man at the wheel nodded briefly and jerked his head at the back of the car. Natasha got in and carefully did up her seatbelt.

"Where you going, exactly?" the driver asked, half turning his head.

"Um…here." Natasha thrust towards him the crumpled paper with Billy's address written on it.

He took it from her and smoothed it out. "Okay, I know this place." He nodded. "Have you got money?"

Natasha nodded and held out her purse to show him.

He smiled, then pulled out into the stream of traffic flowing along Victoria Street. They crossed the river and headed out of town in the direction of Kaipaki.

Natasha pulled out the map Lydia had printed out for her, and she followed their route carefully. They appeared to be going exactly the way she would have expected, so she began to relax a little. She sat back in her seat and watched as the scenery became more rural and the light rain that had been falling in Cambridge became heavier.

After about twenty minutes, the taxi turned right off Kaipaki Road and onto Mellow Road. Natasha studied her map. They were still going the right way. She leaned forward and peered out the window at the driving rain. The countryside was mainly farmland, mostly populated by large herds of cattle standing dismally in the rain. She took a deep breath as the taxi turned right onto Mystery Creek Road and slowed approaching the entrance to a farm.

"This is it," the driver called over his shoulder. "D'you wanna get out here, or shall I take you up to the house?"

Natasha stared at him. Why wouldn't he take her up to the house? She didn't want to walk in the rain with no coat. She cleared her throat. "To the house...if that's all right, please?" she managed.

As he turned the vehicle onto the dirt track, a large black car that had been on their tail for several miles suddenly accelerated and shot off along the road. The taxi driver shook his head. "Some people are a menace on the roads," he said as drove slowly along the track, attempting to avoid the numerous potholes. "Are these people relatives of yours or something?" he asked, watching Natasha in the mirror.

She swallowed. "Nooo...but they...well, Billy... knew my great-aunt and my grandmother years ago," she explained, shifting uneasily in her seat as they drew closer to the house.

"Right." The driver nodded. "You staying the night, or d'you need a taxi back to Cambridge later?"

"Umm...I'm not staying," Natasha said hesitantly, "but my bus back goes from Hamilton, not Cambridge."

The driver shrugged. "I'll come and get you, if you like," he said. "This is my number. Give me a call when you decide what time you want picking up." He handed her a small business card with a mobile phone number printed on it. She took it and slipped it into the pocket of her jeans.

"Thank you," she said politely, managing a small smile.

The taxi drew up in front of a long, low, white house surrounded by a well kept garden and with a large patio area to one side. Natasha fished out her money and paid her fare, thanked the driver, and stepped out onto the gravel path to stare up at her destination.

Chapter 18

Thursday 7ᵗʰ May, 2009

"Am I prettier than her?" Abi's question came out abruptly as they drove towards Nancy's house.

Gideon glanced at her in surprise. "What?" he asked. "D'you mean Nancy?"

"Yeah. Am I prettier?"

"Of course you are!" Gideon's eyebrows shot up. "Why ever would you ask that?"

Abi rolled her eyes. "You dated her. You must've thought she was pretty. Just checking you think I'm better."

"Good grief, woman," he said, shaking his head. "You're prettier than everyone. I can't believe you asked that." He glanced sideways at her. "And you look younger."

"I am younger!" Abi sounded indignant. "I should hope I do."

Gideon chuckled. "This isn't like you. You usually think you're better than everyone. In every way."

Abi slapped his leg. "No, I don't," she gasped with a grin. "Well...not everyone. Not quite. She just makes me feel...inadequate...and murderous!"

Gideon grinned back. "That's more like you," he approved. "No one is prettier than you in my eyes. Never will be." He shrugged. "Nearly all the girls I went out with had auburn or red hair. I kept looking for people who looked like you. But not too alike...I preferred it if they didn't have blue eyes."

Abi smiled at him. "Yeah, most of mine had longish dark hair and dressed like you," she admitted with an apologetic laugh. "Guess we knew all along we belonged together."

They smiled at each other as Gideon pulled the car up by the white post fence and turned off the engine. "Right," he said, taking a deep breath. "Let's get this over with, shall we?"

Together they walked hand in hand up the dirt path to the front door, and Gideon knocked sharply.

Abi squeezed his hand. "It'll be fine," she said with a small smile. "We can do this."

He looked down at her and winked. "Yeah, we can," he said firmly, then stiffened as the door opened.

Nancy stood aside to let them pass, then closed the door behind them. "Go through," she said, waving in the direction of the living room. "I'll get the coffee."

They walked into the large room and both perched uncomfortably on the sofa while they waited for her.

"She's doing this on purpose," hissed Abi, her face hiding none of her dislike for their hostess. "She's deliberately making us wait. I can't believe you had sex with her."

Gideon opened his mouth to protest, just as Nancy entered the room carrying a tray. She placed it on the coffee table, then sat down on the chair opposite her visitors, nervously licking her lips. She was dressed in cropped jeans and a blue shirt, and she tucked her bare feet underneath her awkwardly.

Gideon raised his eyebrows at her. "Well?" he

asked impatiently. "Where is he? Let's not waste time, Nancy. You know what we're here for."

Nancy shifted uneasily in her chair. "He's not here," she said, then held up her hand to stem their remonstrations. "But he doesn't need to be." She sighed and pulled a photograph out of her pocket. "This is Josh."

"I said no photos, Nancy; we need to see the child." Gideon's eyes flashed dangerously, and Abi moved to the edge of her seat, fixing Nancy with a steely gaze.

Nancy shook her head, and held out the photo. "No, you don't," she said with a sigh. "He's not yours. Look at the picture."

Abi took the photograph and held it where both she and Gideon could see it clearly. She caught her breath. The child in the picture, aged about seven or eight, had blond curly hair and a chubby face. He was standing ankle deep in the sea, beaming at the camera.

"He's Simon's," Abi stated, glancing at Nancy, who nodded. "Why did you say he was Gideon's? Surely you knew we'd find out?"

Nancy got to her feet and walked over to the window. She stared out over the mountains, her fingers drumming nervously on the windowsill. Eventually she spoke without turning round. "It wasn't my idea," she said quietly. "I didn't want to do it, actually. I couldn't see the point. I told him you'd know as soon as you saw Josh, but he had some plan that needed me to do this." She spun round to face them. "I'm not supposed to tell you this," she said, her eyes wide, reflecting her fear. "I was just supposed to make you think he was yours for as long as possible."

Gideon stared at her, his face hard. "What's Simon's plan?" he asked sharply.

"He didn't tell me. I think he needed me to keep you here...but I really don't know why."

"Why are you telling us?" Abi watched her curiously.

"I felt guilty." Nancy shrugged. "You're nice people. I always felt guilty about you, Abi. He offered me money to do this. He hasn't had anything to do with Josh over the years, but he knew about him. I'm finding it hard to manage at the moment, that part was true, and Simon offered me quite a lot of money if I did this for him. I reckoned he owed Josh the money, so I said yes." She paused. "He probably won't pay me now."

Gideon stared at her, a look of incomprehension on his face. "But why does he want you to keep us here? What good would that do him? Is he coming here too?"

Nancy shook her head. "No, he's not here. He's in New Zealand, but I think he's on the North Island. We arranged all this by phone."

Abi caught her breath, and her face paled. "The kids!" she gasped in horror. "He must be after the kids!"

Nancy looked shocked. "Surely not?" she said, her hand flying to her throat. "Why would he do that?"

"Nancy, he tried to kill me and Natasha last summer." Abi spoke tersely. "Gid, we need to phone Penny."

"Way ahead of you." Gideon was holding his phone pressed to his ear, as he paced the room impatiently. "Hello? Penny? It's me...Are the kids all right?...And Tash?...Are you sure she went?...Oh, right. Okay." He paused and took a deep breath. "Listen carefully, Pen. They may be in danger. Obviously if Ollie is with you he'll be fine...I know...And while Tash is at school she's fine, but could you meet them at the gate, perhaps?" He paused again as he walked over to the window. "Really? That would be great. I'll explain later. Just tell Dad it's Simon...What? Oh...almost forgot that. No, it's not my child. Gotta go now." He disconnected the call and spun round to face Nancy. "Right. We need to go. You've wasted far too much of our time already." He walked up close to her and caught her wrist, his eyes boring into her. "And if anything happens to our children, I will hold you personally responsible."

Nancy swallowed and tried to pull her hand away. "I'm sorry, Gid," she stammered. "I had no idea he was planning anything like that. I knew he was a bit selfish, but I never thought he was dangerous. Are you sure...?" She saw the look in his eye.

Abi stepped forward. "Have you any idea whereabouts he was going?" she asked urgently. "Any information might be useful."

Nancy shook her head. "No," she whispered. "He didn't tell me. I think he may have flown to Auckland..." She frowned in her attempt to remember. "Yes, definitely he flew to Auckland, but I don't know where he was going from there. I'm so sorry. If I can do anything to help..."

Abi glanced at Gideon, who still had Nancy's wrist held tightly in his hand.

"That sounds like he's staying somewhere in the north," she said, fear in her voice. "D'you think he's gone to Papamoa?" She took another step towards Nancy. "Did he mention Papamoa? Or Tauranga?" she asked sharply. "Try and remember, please."

Nancy shook her head again. "I don't know. I don't think so. He didn't really tell me anything. He wasn't very nice on the phone, either. I wouldn't have done it if I didn't need the money." She shrugged. "And I probably won't get it now anyway. If he finds out I told you, he won't pay me, and if you find him first, he won't be able to pay me."

Gideon let go of her and caught Abi by the hand. "We're going," he said shortly. "Just one thing—if Simon calls you, find out where he is and let us know. Right?"

Nancy nodded silently, her face pale.

Abi handed her a piece of paper. "These are our numbers," she said. "Please, Nancy, if you think of anything, anything at all, call us." Then, without another word, they headed out the front door and back to the car.

****

Natasha took a deep breath and walked with determination up to the white front door. She failed to locate a bell, so she lifted her hand and knocked timidly on the wood. Nothing happened. She stepped back and looked up at the house. Several of the windows were open, and she could hear the faint sound of talking coming from within the building. She approached the door again and tapped a little louder. This time she heard noises from within and footsteps coming towards her. A moment later the door opened and a short, slim, dark-haired older lady smiled at her.

"Good morning," she said, surprise sounding in her voice. "Well, we don't get many unexpected visitors here! Have you lost your way, dear?"

Natasha shook her head, and swallowed. "Umm...no," she managed. "I've come to see Billy. Billy the farm hand...well, he used to be a farm hand..." She stopped, seeing the look of surprise on the woman's face.

"Billy?" the woman said, a slight smile playing on her lips. "Do you mean my father? How old is this Billy you're looking for?"

"Seventy-six," whispered Natasha, rubbing her left foot up and down her right leg. "He used to know my great-aunt and my grandmother."

"Well, that sounds like it might be my father," the woman said with a smile. "I can hear you're from England. My father came here from England in 1955. Was it before that that he knew them?"

Natasha nodded, not wanting to tell any more of her story to this stranger. She wanted to see Billy. "Please can I see him?" she asked politely. "I'm Natasha Hawk."

The woman stood aside and gestured to Natasha to enter the house. She stepped inside and found herself in a dark hallway, panelled in wood, with a variety of pictures and maps hung on the walls. She stared around her with interest. The woman led the way into a large farmhouse kitchen and pointed to the table.

"Take a seat," she said. "Would you like a drink?"

"Do you have any cola?" Natasha asked, sliding onto a wooden chair and pulling it up to the big pine table.

"Of course. Make yourself comfortable. My name's Joan, by the way."

Natasha caught her breath, and stared at the woman. Billy had named his daughter after his old girlfriend. Her mind reeled as she realised she may have been correct in her assumption that he'd been pining for his lost love all those years. Joan placed a tall glass on the table in front of Natasha and sat down opposite her.

"So, what on earth are you doing here on your own?" she asked, watching her carefully. "You must be a long way from home."

"My aunt lives in Tauranga," Natasha said, taking a long grateful slurp of cola. "We're staying with her for a while before my dad starts his tour. I found out that Billy lived here, and I wanted to see him."

Joan frowned slightly at the mention of the tour and looked more closely at her guest. "Right," she said. "Do your parents know you're here? You look a bit young to be travelling that far alone."

Natasha flushed, and bent her head to let her hair cover her face. "I'm thirteen," she said defensively. "I came by bus and taxi. It was quite safe."

Joan stared at her for a moment, then apparently decided to let it go. "All right. So what made you want to see my father? And how did you find him?"

"My mum and I found a diary that was written by my great-aunt, and it has Billy in it." She looked slightly embarrassed. "She was his girlfriend when he was seventeen."

Joan raised her eyebrows. "Really? Well that is interesting. That was some years before he moved here and met my mother. But how did you find him?" she persisted.

"I wrote to the farm where my great-aunt had stayed back in 1950, and asked them about him. I got a letter back from his sister telling me his address." She looked up at Joan anxiously. "You don't mind, do you?

Will he mind?"

Joan shook her head. "Of course not, pet," she said with a smile. "He'll be surprised, that's for sure, but he won't mind. My mother died a couple of years ago, so he'll probably love to have some unexpected company. I'll go and see if he's awake. He's not been too well recently, and he gets tired so easily."

She got to her feet and disappeared out of the room, leaving Natasha thoughtfully sipping her cola and surveying her surroundings. She was finding it hard to believe she had actually got there. Here she was, sitting in the kitchen at Billy the farmhand's house, drinking cola. In a few minutes she was actually going to meet him. She gave a little shiver of excitement and smiled to herself. This was definitely worth getting into trouble over. She looked up as Joan re-entered the room.

"He'd love to see you, pet. He's a little confused as to why you're here. So am I, to be honest, but he's happy to see you. Come on."

Natasha got to her feet and, taking a deep breath, followed the woman out of the kitchen and down the dark hallway. At the end they turned into a spacious living room, passed right through, and entered a large conservatory overlooking the farmland. An elderly man was sitting in a wicker rocking chair at the far end of the room, his legs covered by a tartan rug and his gnarled bony hands in his lap. He looked up as they entered, and a strange look came over his weatherbeaten face. Joan pushed Natasha in front of her.

"Dad," she said gently, "this is Natasha. She's come to see you to talk about her great-aunt and her grandmother. I'll leave you two together, and I'll bring you some tea in a minute." She patted Natasha on the back and directed her towards a Lloyd Loom chair placed close to the old man. Natasha sat down gingerly on the edge of the chair and smiled at Billy.

"Hello," she said. "I'm Natasha."

"Joan's granddaughter." The old man nodded. "You look just like her."

Natasha swallowed and moistened her lips. She leant forward in her chair, her hands clutched tightly together. "Actually, no," she said. "I'm Pauline's granddaughter. Joan was my great-aunt." She waited for a moment while Billy digested this piece of news, his pale eyes reflecting the confusion he was feeling.

"Pauline?" he said slowly. "But Pauline died. And the baby. Joan wrote to me afterwards." A look of pain passed over his face. "She told me they had to move away and that she wouldn't be able to come and see me again. I hoped that one day…but she didn't come."

Natasha shifted uncomfortably in her chair. "She couldn't come," she said slowly, "because she was the one that was dead. I'll tell you what happened, but please can you promise not to tell anyone else?"

Billy nodded, his eyes fixed firmly on Natasha's face, and his hands clasped in his lap. Slowly and hesitantly at the beginning, she told the tragic tale of Pauline and the baby and how, when Joan accidentally died in Pauline's flat, Pauline had taken her identity. Natasha fished in her bag and pulled out Joan's diary. She handed it to Billy.

"And you'll see from this that she really loved you," she finished. "And if she hadn't died she would definitely have come back to see you." She paused and looked him directly in the eye. "I was worried you thought she didn't love you, or that you'd spent the last fifty-nine years waiting for her. I wanted you to know."

Billy was silent as he gently thumbed through the exercise book filled with the round childish writing. When he finally looked up, his sunken eyes were shining with tears. He reached out and took Natasha's hand in his.

"Thank you," he said simply. "Thank you for caring. I always wondered. I had thought we had something special. I understood when she didn't return. Her sister had died and her father made them move away. She was very young. But I still wondered. I never forgot her. She was my first love."

"You named your daughter after her," Natasha said quietly.

Billy smiled. "Yes. I always felt slightly guilty about that," he said, a twinkle appearing in his eye. "I loved my wife. Very much. But I couldn't forget Joan, and I wanted a permanent reminder of her." He peered more closely at Natasha. "You really do look very like her. Like them. They were identical, of course—in looks, but not in character."

Natasha grinned. "My mother looks the same," she said with a nod. "But I think we're both a bit more like Pauline. My mother had me when she was sixteen." She paused and looked thoughtful for a minute. "That's kind of why I thought it was important for you to know about Joan. My mum and dad were separated before I was born and didn't find each other—or me—again for ten years. It was awful for them, so I thought that might be how it was for you, too."

Billy frowned in concern, and squeezed her hand.

"That story sounds sad," he said. "You're all together now, though?"

Natasha nodded. "Oh, yes, we're fine now." She paused, wondering how much to tell him. "My grandmother, Pauline—she's dead too now—told my mother I was dead when I was born, and took me to a children's home. She'd been so traumatised by the death of her baby and the death of Joan that she was terrified my mum would suffer the same fate, so she took me away." She paused, and her eyes grew dark. "It was very, very wrong of her. But we all found each other in the end."

Billy shook his head in sorrow. "That's a very sad story," he said. "Three generations suffering because of the actions of one young girl. How very sad. But thank you, my dear, for coming to see me. It was very kind of you. I think you're like my Joan in character as well as looks. She was very kind and caring."

Natasha felt her face begin to flame, and she looked away from Billy and out the window. "Please don't tell anyone about Joan and Pauline, will you?" she said anxiously. "We don't want the story to get out. It wouldn't make my grandmother look very good, and she didn't mean any of it to happen. It was all accidents."

Billy patted her hand. "Of course I won't. Don't worry. Now you must stay for lunch before you begin your long journey back. Pop into the kitchen and tell my daughter I've invited you, and then come back and we'll talk some more."

Chapter 19

Thursday 7th May, 2009

Penny put the phone down, a deep frown creasing her face. She didn't like the sound of what Gideon had just told her and hoped he was mistaken. She went into the sun lounge, where her parents were relaxing after their flight.

"Dad..." She sat down opposite him, her eyes worried. "Gideon just phoned. Apparently he's not the father"—she paused as Caroline gave a little grunt of self-satisfied pleasure—"but he seems to think Tasha and Ollie could be in danger. He said he'd explain later but said, 'just tell Dad it's Simon.' "

Roger looked up at her. "Is that all he said?" he asked, leaning forward in his chair.

Penny shook her head. "He was worried about where the children were. I told him Ollie's safe with me and Tasha has gone to school with Lydia, and he said could we meet them at the school gate instead of letting them come home alone. What's this all about, Dad?"

Caroline caught her breath, her face paling. "He's after Tasha again, isn't he," she whispered, staring at Roger in horror. "Do something, Roger. Go and fetch her now!"

"Calm down, Caroline," he replied with a frown. "She can come to no harm at school. Probably safer there than here, actually. You can't get into a school these days, they are so security conscious."

"I told Gideon I thought you and Mum would like to pick up the girls today anyway," Penny continued. "Is that okay?"

Roger nodded. "Good idea," he agreed. "We know they got to school all right, do we?"

Penny nodded. "Yes they must have done. The school always phone if the students aren't there on time. They're quite vigilant. They went in early today to do some art thingy."

Caroline glanced at Roger. "Should we phone to check? Just to be sure."

"Can't do any harm." Roger shrugged. "What d'you think, Penny?"

Penny had already picked up the phone and was rapidly dialling a number. She waited, tapping her foot impatiently. "Hello? Yes, this is Penny MacRae here, Lydia's mother...Yes, that's right. I wonder if you could confirm that she's at school, please?" She waited, anxiously picking at the cuff of her shirt. "Hello? She's there...Okay, thank you. And her cousin too, of course?...Oh, right. Oh, well, that's all right. Thank you, sorry to bother you." She replaced the receiver, and smiled at her parents. "She checked the register and Lydia's there. She couldn't check Tasha because she's not on the register because she's only visiting, but Lydia stays with her all the time, and she'd know if something had happened to her."

Roger nodded. "Right. She's okay for now, then, and your mother and I'll pick them up at—what time do they finish?"

"Three fifteen."

"We'll take the car," he went on. "Then there's no chance of anyone trying to snatch her along the road."

Caroline got to her feet. "We should fetch them now," she said. "I can't bear the thought of that man being around here. Come on, Roger."

Roger shook his head. "No, they're safer at school. If they're here, we'd have to have our eye on them all the time. You know what Tasha's like. She'd be off and up to something in a flash. Much safer for them to stay at school as long as possible. Stop worrying, Caroline. He can't try anything at the school. I'll make a few calls and see if he's been spotted anywhere around here." He got to his feet and left the room, fishing his mobile out of his pocket as he went.

****

"Gid, can't you drive faster?" Abi was sitting forward, her hands gripping the seat. "Oh, god, I knew I shouldn't have come. If he's got Tasha, I shall kill him, Gid, I honestly will."

Gideon kept his eyes on the road as he drove quickly back towards Christchurch. He flicked his hair back impatiently and scowled at the large vehicle hogging the road just in front of them.

"You won't get a chance," he said through gritted teeth. "I'll already have done it." He glanced sideways at her. "Don't worry, babe. Both kids are safe at the moment, and Mum and Dad are there now. They'll make sure nothing happens before we get back. I just hope we can get an early flight." He sped up and shot around the lorry, pulling in front of it just in time to avoid the oncoming traffic. "You wanted me to drive faster," he pointed out, seeing Abi's face.

After returning the hire car to the depot by the

airport, Abi and Gideon hurried into the terminal, and while Gideon attempted to get them booked on a flight as soon as possible, Abi made a quick phone call to Penny.

"Penny? Is everything all right?" She had to shout above the noise of the airport, and stuck her finger in her other ear. "What? Oh, good…Yes, we're at the airport now. Gid's trying to get us on an earlier flight. I'll keep you posted…okay, just make sure she stays put once you get her home. You know what she's like. Thanks, Pen. Bye." She stuck her phone back in her bag and looked around for any sign of Gideon. She finally saw his dark head deep in conversation with a girl at a desk. She hurried over to join him just as he was paying for some tickets.

"When is it?" she asked, stopping beside him.

He grimaced. "Not till one fifty. Best I could get. It gets to Tauranga at four forty-five, with a fifty-minute layover in Wellington."

Abi glanced at her phone. "That's nearly two hours!" she complained. "Was there nothing earlier at all?"

He caught her arm and steered her away from the busy desk. "No. We were lucky to get on that one. Let's go and get some lunch and talk about this. I want to phone Dad, too, in case he can find anything out."

They headed for the nearest café and installed themselves at a window table. Gideon fetched two large cappuccinos and slid into the chair opposite Abi.

She screwed her nose up. "Not sure I can even drink that, but I certainly can't eat. Gid, this is terrible. Why's he doing this?"

Gideon leaned back in his chair and stretched his

long legs out under the table. "He clearly didn't get the result he wanted last summer," he said with a frown. "Although I can't imagine he'd actually try to kill you again. He must have been in hiding since August. Maybe he's fed up with it and thinks he can somehow get his life back by attacking us again."

"That really doesn't make sense," Abi objected, taking a tentative sip of her coffee. "Surely if he wanted us to forgive him he'd approach us nicely—wouldn't he?"

Gideon raised an eyebrow. "This is Simon."

****

Natasha smiled across the table at Joan. "Thank you so much for inviting me to lunch," she said, popping a grape into her mouth. "It's very kind of you."

"No problem." Joan smiled. "My father has really enjoyed talking to you; I think you've done him good." She glanced across the table at Billy, who was tucking into his lunch with gusto. "I haven't seen him eat this well for weeks."

Natasha wiped her mouth on her napkin, and took a long drink of cola. "I have to catch a bus from Hamilton at three fifteen," she said. "I must call the taxi to come and pick me up. The one who brought me here gave me his number."

"Don't do that, love," Joan said at once. "I'll take you to Hamilton. I could do with a shopping trip. Save you a bit of money."

Natasha opened her mouth to protest, but Billy looked up and frowned at her. "Yes, you let Joan take you," he said firmly. "Safer than getting a taxi. And don't you talk to any strangers on the bus."

Joan nodded in agreement. "Quite right. I'm not

convinced your parents know you've come here," she said perceptively. "The least we can do is make sure you get to your bus safely."

Natasha's face flushed, and she bent her head, pretending to be examining her nails. "Okay, thank you." she said. "That's very kind of you."

Joan stood up and began to gather up the dishes. "It only takes about twenty-five minutes to get to Hamilton, so we'll leave around half past two to be on the safe side. You take my father back into the conservatory and have another chat until then."

Natasha got to her feet. "I must help with the dishes," she said, collecting up some glasses and following Joan into the kitchen.

"No, you're doing more good talking to him," Joan replied, giving her a gentle shove towards the door. "Go on. You've got about an hour. You're very good for him."

By half past two, Natasha had told Billy her life story and the two of them had become firm friends. When Joan came to say it was time to leave, Natasha stood up and looked down at Billy. "Thank you for listening to me," she said seriously. "I'm so glad I was able to tell you about Joan and Pauline. Are you glad too?"

Billy reached up and took her hand in his. "Very glad, Tasha," he said, his eyes glistening. "It's been wonderful to meet you. You're a lovely girl. You can tell your mother that. I hope we can meet again one day."

On a sudden impulse, Natasha bent down and placed a kiss on the old man's leathery cheek. "Me too," she said, blushing slightly, then turned and followed Joan out of the room towards the front door.

As she strapped herself into the front seat of Joan's car, she felt the older woman's eyes on her. She glanced up and found her watching her curiously.

"Were Joan and Pauline your grandmother and great-aunt?" she asked, as she started the engine.

Natasha nodded, wondering how much she should tell her. "Yes."

"Was Joan my father's girlfriend?"

Natasha looked awkward, and clasped her hands together on her lap. "Yes."

"It's all right, you don't need to be embarrassed." Joan smiled as she negotiated the potholes in the track. "He called me after his first love. That's rather romantic, don't you think?"

Natasha nodded, smiling slightly.

"What happened to her?"

"She died." Natasha glanced at her. "She loved him, but she died when she was sixteen."

Joan grimaced. "How sad," she said, pulling out onto the road. "I'm glad you were able to tell him about her, though." She smiled at Natasha.

As they accelerated along Mystery Creek Road, neither of them noticed the large black car that pulled out behind them and followed at a discreet distance.

****

As their plane touched down in Wellington, Abi shifted impatiently in her seat. "I can't stand this, Gideon," she stated, pushing her hair back and glaring at him. "I can't stand the fact that we can do nothing. The fate of our children lies in other people's hands, and I can't bear it."

Gideon reached over and squeezed her hand. "I

know. I feel the same. I'll phone Dad as soon as we land, see if he knows anything more. The girls'll still be at school, and I'm sure Penny won't have let Ollie out of her sight."

"I don't think he'd touch Ollie," said Abi thoughtfully. "I think he sees Tasha as being connected to our life before, when we were apart... She's part of all the stuff he sees as a threat." She paused and stared at him. "D'you know what I mean?"

"Yeah, you may be right," Gideon conceded. "But I'm not taking any chances." He got to his feet, pulled his bag out of the overhead locker, and caught her hand to pull her up. "Come on, let's go. We've got about fifty minutes here. Time to make some calls."

Chapter 20

Thursday 7th May, 2009

"I'll be fine now, thank you." Natasha stood in the entrance to Hamilton Bus Station and smiled at Joan. "Honestly, the bus goes in about fifteen minutes. You don't need to wait till then. I'll go straight home, and I'll text my cousin when I'm on the bus."

Joan narrowed her eyes at her doubtfully. "Well, let me just check your bus is running," she said, leading the way into the bus station and up to the ticket desk.

The bus proved to be running on time and was expected to arrive within ten minutes, so Joan bade Natasha a fond goodbye and left her to wait in the café, having extracted a promise to call her when she arrived home.

Natasha watched her leave, then squeezed behind a small table in the window of the café, from where she could command a good view of the approaching buses. She had just settled back in her chair and taken a slurp from her can of cola when she heard her name being called over the tannoy.

"Could Natasha Hawk please come to the ticket office. Natasha Hawk. Thank you."

Her heart plummeting to her boots, Natasha wriggled out of her seat and slowly made her way to the desk. If she was being called by name, then it was clear her adventure had been rumbled by those back in Tauranga, and she was about to get into trouble. She approached the lady behind the counter cautiously.

"I'm Natasha Hawk," she said licking her lips nervously. "You called my name?"

The woman looked up and smiled brightly at her. "Yeah, that's right. Your aunt has sent a car to pick you up," she said, indicating a tall man in chauffeur's uniform, leaning against the counter a few feet away. "She wants you to go with him instead of catching the bus."

"My aunt sent him?" Natasha stared at the man in surprise. "When…I mean how did…"

"Yes, your aunt…" The woman looked down at her notepad. "Penny MacRae. He's to take you straight back to Tauranga. Penny MacRae is your aunt?" she checked, watching Natasha closely.

"Yes," Natasha said in a small voice. "Yes, she's my aunt. She must have found out where I was."

"Well, there you are, then," the woman said briskly. "Off you go. Better not keep her waiting."

With a sigh, Natasha slung her bag over her shoulder and walked over to the waiting chauffeur. "You're to take me back?" she asked bleakly, taking in his grey suit, white shirt, chauffeur's cap, and aviator sunglasses. He nodded, and gestured to her to follow him.

The long black car was parked out the front of the bus station, and the man opened the back door for Natasha to get in. She slid across to the far corner of the seat and put her bag next to her. She was beginning to feel very lonely, and a little scared. When she was in control of her day, she had managed to cope, but now it had been taken out of her hands, she realised the enormity of what she'd done, and just how much trouble she was going to get into. Sending a chauffeur to pick her up must have cost her aunt a fortune, and she suddenly felt very guilty.

She stared at the back of the driver's head and wondered whether to speak to him or not. She almost wished she were sitting in the front with him; maybe then she wouldn't feel so alone. She curled her legs up under her on the seat and leant her head against the window. At least it wouldn't take so long to get back to Tauranga. If she'd caught the bus, she was going to have to change at Rotorua. By car there was a much more direct route.

As they wove their way out of the centre of the town, Natasha pulled her map out of her pocket. She should be able to follow the route quite easily on that. Then she could be sure they were taking the quickest one. She settled back in her seat, the map on her knee, and decided to make the best of things. At least she had got to see Billy.

****

"Grandma! Grandpa! What are you doing here?" Lydia's voice held a note of panic as she found her grandparents waiting at the school gate for her. "I...we're going to a friend's house. I was about to call Mum." She paused, and swallowed. "Oh, but it's nice to see you."

Caroline gave her a quick hug, and looked around expectantly. "Hello, darling. Lovely to see you, too. Where's Natasha?"

Lydia was silent for a moment, her mind turning somersaults as she attempted to make up a convincing story. "Umm…she's already gone to the friend's house," she said hopefully, watching Caroline under her lashes.

Caroline looked over her head and exchanged glances with Roger. "Really, Lydia?" she asked, her voice wavering slightly. "Where is she? You must tell us. Has someone taken her?"

Lydia stared at her in surprise. "Taken her?" she repeated, her brown eyes wide. "What on earth do you mean? Why would someone take her? Take her where?"

Roger stepped forward, and put an arm around her shoulders. "Lydia, you must tell us. Where is she? Wasn't she at school with you today?" he asked urgently.

Lydia stared at them both, her mouth going dry and her mind completely blank. She could think of nothing to say. It suddenly seemed really important for her to tell them where Natasha was. She realised that whatever happened they were going to find out eventually, so she took a deep breath, and slowly shook her head.

Caroline gasped, and her hand flew up to her mouth. "Oh, Roger," she breathed almost silently, her eyes displaying their terror.

Roger squeezed her arm, then steered Lydia towards the waiting car. Lydia slid into the back seat, and Caroline got in beside her.

"Tell us everything, Lydia," Roger ordered, as he climbed in the front and started the engine. "We'll talk as we drive."

Lydia swallowed nervously. "Are we in loads of trouble?" she whispered, her face pale.

Caroline shook her head. "No, darling," she said, "but you must tell us where she is."

"It was such a good plan." Lydia sighed. "I really thought it would work. Tasha wanted to go and see Billy the farmhand, you see, and we worked out how she could get there on the bus, an' we decided to do it when her mum and dad were away. The only problem was that the bus coming back doesn't get in till six thirty, and she has to change in Rotorua. That's why we came up with the plan of going to a friend's house after school." She paused, glancing at Caroline. "We didn't know you'd be picking us up."

Caroline was staring at her in amazement. "Billy the farmhand?" she said faintly. "Who on earth is Billy the farmhand? Is he a pop star or something?"

Lydia's face creased into a huge grin, and she began to giggle. "Oh, Grandma! Of course not. He's the person— Oh! maybe you don't know. It's kind of a secret...to do with Tasha's *other* grandma." She frowned. "I don't think I can tell you."

Roger spoke over his shoulder. "When did she go?"

"She caught the bus to Cambridge at seven twenty-five this morning," Lydia said immediately. "I watched her get on it, so she was okay. What's this about? Why did you ask if someone took her?"

Caroline glanced at the back of Roger's head for a moment, then nodded to herself, and took one of Lydia's hands in hers. "Do you remember what happened to Natasha and her mother last summer when they got attacked by—"

"By Simon, the mad drummer?" Lydia chipped in. "Yeah, she told me all about it."

"Well, we have reason to believe that Simon is here in New Zealand," Caroline continued, "and that he may be trying to hurt Tasha and Abi again. We thought Tasha was at school with you all day, and so would be safe, but…" Her voice broke, and she clenched her hands together.

Lydia stared at her, her mouth going dry. "You mean she may be in danger?" she whispered. "And she's out there all on her own? Oh, no! D'you think someone could have followed her?"

"Possibly." Roger spoke as he turned the car into Penny's driveway. "Have you heard from her at all during the day?"

"She texted when she got to Cambridge," Lydia said with a nod. "Shall I text her now to see if she got the bus in Hamilton okay? She should be on it by now."

Caroline nodded. "Good idea," she said, stepping out of the car and heading for the house. "I'll just go and tell your mother what's happened."

Quickly Lydia wrote a message to Natasha. *"Everyone knows. Sorry. Couldn't help it. Explain later. Are you all right? Are you on bus?"* She pressed Send, then followed her grandparents into the house, ready to receive the wrath of her mother. As she stepped into the kitchen, her phone bleeped, and everyone turned and looked at her expectantly. She fished it out of her pocket and peered at it. She looked slightly taken aback and glanced up at the waiting faces.

"That's weird," she said. "I told her you all know what she did. Listen to what she says… *I know they know. I'm in the car your mum sent. Don't worry, be home sooner now.*" Lydia looked up and frowned.

"You sent a car to fetch her, Mum? How could you know where she was? I only just told Grandma and Grandpa."

Penny stared at her, confusion on her face. "I didn't send a car," she said, shaking her head. "I thought she was at school until just now. What car?"

****

Natasha leaned back in her seat and tried to relax. She knew she would be in a lot of trouble when she got back, and if she was fair she realised she deserved it. She just hoped Lydia didn't suffer too much. After all, it had been her idea, and Lydia had just been helping her organise it. She glanced out of the window and noted they had just passed through Cambridge. She checked her map—yes that was correct. In a short while, if she had been on the bus, it would have continued straight on towards Rotorua, whereas the quicker and more direct route to Tauranga would involve a left turn. Natasha kept her eyes on the road to make sure the driver went the quickest way. He hadn't spoken to her at all, and she was actually hoping he didn't bother. She felt very nervous about facing the rest of the family, and a conversation with a stranger wouldn't really help her mood.

She watched as the countryside flew by, noting the mountainous regions to their right. She had looked up Rotorua on the computer before she left Lydia's house and discovered it was situated in a very beautiful and wild part of the country. In a way she was sorry not to be going that way. She would have got to see more of New Zealand, and it would have made it even more of an adventure.

The car slowed as it approached a large

roundabout. Natasha consulted her map, and decided this was where they would turn off towards Tauranga. She strained her neck to see out the front window, locating the correct exit. As the car started round the roundabout, she became aware that the driver was not heading for the exit she had supposed but seemed to be taking the route the bus had been going to take.

She frowned and looked more closely at her map. It was definitely further that way. Tentatively she tapped on the glass panel that separated her from the driver. After a moment he flicked a switch, and his voice echoed into the back, through a speaker, "Yes?"

Natasha moistened her lips. "Umm…I'm sure you know what you're doing," she began, "but wouldn't it have been quicker to go left at that roundabout? This is the way to Rotorua. My bus was going to go this way, but I don't think it's the quickest."

"Got to drop something off in Rotorua," the driver replied immediately, his eyes, hidden behind their dark glasses, never leaving the road. "Still have you back before the bus."

Natasha sat back in her seat, a slight frown creasing her brow. It seemed odd to her that her aunt would book a driver who was unable to take her straight back. She fished her phone out of her pocket, and rapidly texted a message to Lydia, then turned off the sound and pressed Send. She watched the screen impatiently for the message to go, then realised she had no signal. She thought back to Lydia's previous message. It suggested she had only just told her mother about Natasha's whereabouts, whereas in order for the car to have been waiting for her at the bus station, Penny would need to have known for quite some time.

Surely if that was the case, she would have phoned or texted her? Natasha's heart began to beat a little faster, and she stared at the back of the driver's head. Suppose Aunt Penny hadn't sent the car? Suppose she'd been kidnapped and was being taken away to be murdered? She curled her feet up under her again, and pressed herself into the corner of the seat, at the same time cancelling the message that hadn't sent, and writing a new one. If it was true they had to deliver something to Rotorua, then maybe she could make a break for it then, and lose herself in the town. Then she could phone Lydia and find out what was going on. She sat back and waited, the map clutched tightly in her hand. She would bide her time and not let on she was worried.

****

"It keeps going straight to voice mail." Lydia scowled at her mobile and tried again.

Since receiving the worrying news that Natasha was travelling in a car she believed had been sent by her aunt, the house had become a hive of activity. Lydia had tried constantly to call and text Natasha, Roger had been closeted with the landline in James' study, and Penny and Caroline had been calling all the car hire companies to see if anyone had ordered a chauffeur-driven car to pick up a girl in Hamilton.

"I wish we could contact Gideon," Caroline moaned, running her finger down the list of car hire firms in the phone book. "I can't bear to think this is all happening and they don't know anything about it."

"Probably better that way," Penny said with a shrug. "If you could call them, they wouldn't be able to do anything until they land, and it would just worry them unbearably. Hopefully by the time the plane gets in we'll have some better news." She dialled another number on her mobile.

Suddenly Lydia squeaked and held her phone out. "I've had a text!" she cried. "She must have been out of signal range. It says, *'Didn't Aunt Penny send a car? Have I been kidnapped? Heading for Rotorua.'* She's still okay! Mum, what do we do now?"

Penny ran towards the office. "Dad, Dad, Lydia's had a text. Tasha's realised things aren't right." She paused as her father appeared in the doorway. "She says they're heading for Rotorua. What shall we do?"

"Text her back, ask what the car is like, and where they are now," Roger ordered. "Hopefully she'll have put the phone on silent so we can text without being found out." He picked up his jacket from the back of a chair. "Caroline and I will drive to Rotorua. At least we'll be going in the right direction. Call me as soon as you get any more information." He glanced at Lydia. "She'll probably keep losing the signal—they must be near the mountains. Keep trying. I've alerted the police, but they can't do much with the information we have at present. Penny, keep calling car hire firms. Keep us posted." He jerked his head at Caroline to indicate they were leaving. With a desperate look at Penny and Lydia, Caroline grabbed her bag and hurried after him.

"Mum, what shall I say?" Lydia's voice was trembling, her eyes scared.

"Just what Grandpa said." Penny smiled at her. "Ask her where they are now, and what sort of car it is. Don't worry. We'll find her." She dialled another number and held the phone to her ear. "Keep strong, Lydia. It's not your fault."

Lydia swallowed and looked down at her phone.

"Where are you now? What is car like? G'pa and G'ma driving to Rotorua to look for you." She pressed Send and stared at the screen long after the message had gone. She thought for a moment, then sent another message. *"G'pa thinks it's Simon."*

She thought Natasha ought to know what she was up against. She looked over to where her mother was speaking on the phone, and walked over to join her. Penny disconnected the call and immediately started dialling again.

"What's up, Mum? Did you find something out?" Lydia looked up at her hopefully.

Penny nodded. "Yeah. I may have found something." She started pacing the room impatiently. "Come on, Mum, answer the phone!"

Lydia pulled at her arm. "What did they tell you?" she asked anxiously. "Did they tell you what sort of car is it?"

Penny screwed up her nose. "Yes, eventually. They didn't really want to tell me anything, but I told them it might be a matter of life and death, and they told me what they could. A car was booked yesterday afternoon by a Mr. Martin, and apparently just the car was booked, but not the driver, which is rather unusual. The person who ordered it said they had their own driver. It was booked out for two days, and it was a black BMW. It may not be anything to do with this, but it's all I can find so far." She glanced down at her daughter. "I really need to tell Mum and Dad this, but they're not picking up." She disconnected the call, and looked at the clock. "Still nearly an hour until Gideon and Abi land. I really hope we have something more positive to tell them by then." She looked down at Lydia again and gave her a little smile. "Don't worry, pet. Everything'll turn out all right. It's not really a matter or life or death. I just said that to get them to talk to me." She put her arm around her daughter and gave her a squeeze. "I shall call your father in a minute. We need him to pick up Gideon and Abi from the airport. I don't want to drag all the little ones with us, and anyway I should stay here in case anything happens."

Chapter 21

Thursday 7th May, 2009

Abi leant back in her seat and tried to get comfortable. They had taken off from Wellington at three thirty-five and were due to land at Tauranga at four forty-five. The fact they had not been able to have any communication with Natasha before then was tearing her apart. She just wanted to know the child was safe at home with Penny, and then she could relax a little. She glanced at Gideon and could tell from his demeanour he was feeling the same. She reached out and squeezed his hand. He smiled wearily at her.

"I've had enough of travelling," he stated, lifting her hand to his mouth and kissing it gently. "I shan't relax at all until we're back with the children. I just wish we could call Penny to check everything's all right."

"I'm feeling just the same," Abi agreed with a sigh. "But if she was at school all day, then she'll be fine, surely? And your parents were going to pick them up. By now they should be safe back at Penny's."

Gideon narrowed his eyes at her. "So why do you sound so unsure?" he asked. "Don't you believe that?"

"I don't know." Abi shrugged. "I just have a horrible feeling in my stomach that something's wrong." She grinned wryly at him. "It's probably just because we know Simon's involved. He always leaves a nasty taste…" She stared out the window at the blanket of clouds beneath them. "When will we be free of him, Gid? We really should have made sure the police looked for him harder last summer. They seemed too quick to assume he'd drowned."

Gideon nodded. "Well, I did try to tell them," he murmured. "But this time he won't get away with anything. Hopefully he'll have nothing to get away with, apart from wasting our time these last two days. Now try and relax. We've got nearly an hour till we land." He slid his arm around her shoulders, pulled her closer, and kissed her hair.

****

"We're probably looking for a large black BMW," Caroline reported to Roger as she put her phone down on the dashboard. "It was hired by a Mr. Martin, from Drayton's Executive Car Hire yesterday afternoon, and was booked out for two days. The only reason Penny thinks it might be the right one is because only the car was booked, not the driver. Lydia got another text from Natasha, who says she's just passed Tirau." She peered at the road map she had open on her knee. "That's over there…between Cambridge and Rotorua. Oh, dear, she's much closer to Rotorua than we are. Lydia must have got that message at least five or ten minutes ago."

Roger spoke without taking his eyes off the road. "Send a text to Tasha. Ask her to let us know when they get to Rotorua. See if she can let us know whereabouts in the town they are."

Caroline speedily complied, then sat back in her seat with a sigh. "Roger, this is dreadful. Why can't people leave the family alone? Tasha must be so scared.

If this really is Simon, then he must pay this time."

"Yes." Roger's voice was curt. "He must."

They drove in silence for a while. Then Caroline frowned and glanced at him. "Roger?" she ventured. "What exactly are we going to do if we find her? The person who has her may be armed. You're not planning to tackle him, are you?"

Roger shook his head and pulled out to pass a huge juggernaut. "No, more's the pity," he said. "We'll try and see where they go, and then contact the police again. I have a direct number to the man I spoke to earlier." He pulled in front of the lorry and put his foot down. "I'm not holding out much hope of finding them, actually," he admitted. "But I couldn't have stayed at Penny's and just done nothing. Imagine how Gideon and Abi would feel if they got back and no one was out looking for her?"

Caroline's face paled. "Gideon will go beserk," she murmured. "It would be good if we could find her before they get back."

Roger grunted. "It would, but I doubt if we will. Haven't you had a reply from her yet?"

Caroline shook her head. "Not yet. I would have mentioned it, Roger. She must be out of signal range. Oh, poor child! I do hope she's being treated well."

****

Natasha peered surreptitiously at her map and then looked out the window again. It seemed they were approaching the outskirts of Rotorua, and she needed to keep her eyes peeled for any landmarks she could report back to Caroline. She had had the message, but had decided not to respond until she had something useful to tell them. She was very scared, but also rather excited by the fact that her grandparents were coming to rescue her. She had no idea how they would do it, but if her plan worked and she managed to get out of the car in the town, then she'd be able to phone them.

She peered out of the window again and noted they were driving along Fairy Springs Road. The town was fairly busy, and she considered the possibility of attracting someone's attention to her plight. She glanced at the back of the driver's head and wondered if she could wave at someone without being noticed. As the thought flitted through her mind, he glanced in the mirror and his eyes, still hidden behind the sunglasses, appeared to look directly at her. Natasha looked away and stared out the window again. She couldn't risk it. She would have to wait until they stopped. She studied the map again, and registered that they had just passed a turning to Kuirau Park on their left. Beyond that she could see the shimmering water of Lake Rotorua. The driver was showing no sign of turning off the main road, and Natasha began to feel more agitated. Maybe they weren't going to stop in the town after all. She saw from her map that they'd be leaving the built-up area in about another mile, and unless they turned off before that, they would be travelling even further away from Tauranga and in completely the wrong direction. She shifted in her seat and pulled her bag closer to her, hooking her arm through the strap, ready for a quick getaway. Cautiously she wrote a quick text to Caroline.

"Nearly through Rotorua and haven't stopped yet." She pressed Send, then sat back and swallowed nervously. The habitation was beginning to thin, and ahead of them Natasha could see huge expanses of forest and to the left, in the distance, the mountains. As

they finally left the last of the houses behind them, she glanced at her phone and saw to her dismay that she had no signal, and her text to Caroline had not gone. She sat forward in her seat, and tapped on the glass again. The driver flicked the intercom switch.

"What?"

"You said we were stopping in Rotorua," Natasha said accusingly. "And we're not on the road to Tauranga, either."

The driver flicked the switch off again, and didn't answer her.

She tapped on the glass again. "Don't ignore me!" she shouted. "I get that you've kidnapped me—the least you can do is tell me why, and where we're going!"

The driver's voice came again. "You don't need to know. It's not my job to tell you anything. Just to deliver you."

"Where to?" she shouted again, feeling her face beginning to get hot, and tears pricking behind her eyes.

"You'll find out." He turned off the intercom again, and picked up speed. She slumped back in her seat and bit down hard on her lip in an attempt to stop the tears from coming. She had to find a way to get him to stop, so maybe she could make a break for it. She was a good runner, and from the look of him, she could almost certainly outrun him. She looked at her map again and began to plan, her tummy turning over when she realised it would be getting dark in less than an hour.

****

As the plane touched down at Tauranga, Abi felt her stomach churning, and her throat began to constrict. She caught Gideon's wrist as he reached for his flight bag. "Gid, something's really wrong," she said, her eyes wide. "I can feel it. Tasha's in danger."

Gideon narrowed his eyes at her. "Abi, stop it," he said firmly. "You're just worrying because of Simon. That's perfectly understandable, but Tash has been at school all day, and then Mum and Dad were going to pick her up at the gate. We just need to get back and make sure she stays there. I notice you're not worrying about Ollie," he added with a crooked smile.

Abi tossed her head in frustration. "Ollie's fine. He's never been out of Penny's sight," she said. "It's Tasha I've got the feeling about. A mother knows."

Gideon's face creased into a small frown, and he hoisted his bag onto his shoulder and caught her hand. "Come on, then, let's get back to them, and we'll put an end to Simon's shenanigans once and for all."

As they crossed the tarmac towards the terminal, Abi shivered and pulled her cardigan more tightly around her.

Gideon looked down at her. "Cold?" he asked, taking her hand in his and giving it a squeeze.

"Not really. Just scared." She curled her fingers around his as if seeking safety from her thoughts.

The flight had been full, and by the time they'd passed through arrivals and collected their luggage, it was just after five o'clock.

Gideon looked around impatiently. "I thought Penny would've been here to fetch us by now," he muttered, heading for the exit, Abi's hand still firmly clutched in his own. He dodged past a couple of inquisitive travellers who had recognised him, and pulled Abi through the huge glass doors, out into the drizzly afternoon. The light was beginning to fade as he peered around at the various waiting vehicles outside the terminal.

"Gideon! Over here!" James's voice floated over to them from their left, and they both turned to see Penny's husband waving to them from beside a large estate car. They hurried over, and Abi scrambled into the back while Gideon took the passenger seat next to James. They shot off immediately before there could be any more chance of Gideon being recognised, and within seconds James had joined the slow-moving stream of rush hour traffic heading for Papamoa. He glanced at Gideon, his face serious. "I'm afraid there's a bit of a problem."

Abi caught her breath, and leaned forward between the front seats.

"What d'you mean?" she gasped, her face paling. "What's happened?"

"It seems that Natasha didn't go to school today." James paused as Abi's hand came over the back of the seat and grabbed Gideon's shoulder. "She and Lydia had cooked up some plan for her to go and see someone called Billy." Abi gave a little moan, and rested her forehead on the back of the seat. "Anyway, the idea was she would go while she should have been at school, and get back this evening. Lydia had some plan that she would go to a friend's house after school, and they'd arrive home together—"

"But where is she now?" Gideon's voice was charged with emotion as he interrupted James's flow.

"That's the problem." James glanced sideways at them. "Apparently she got there all right and was supposed to catch a bus back from Hamilton about three thirty. However, Lydia had a text to say she didn't catch the bus but was coming home in the car Penny sent for her."

Abi's head shot up, a look of relief on her face. "Penny sent a car?" she asked faintly.

James shook his head. "That's where the problem is. No. She didn't even know Tasha had gone until Roger and Caroline went to pick them up from school."

Gideon squeezed Abi's hand tightly. "D'you know where she is now?" he asked tersely, his eyes flashing. "Has she been in touch?"

James nodded. "She's managed to text Lydia. We let her know Penny didn't send the car, and she's trying to keep us posted as to where she is. Unfortunately they seem to be in an area where the signal isn't very good, so the texts aren't very frequent. Your mum and dad"— he glanced at Gideon—"have gone off to where she seemed to think they were heading, to see if they can find the car. Bit of a long shot, I'm afraid, but Roger wanted to be doing something."

"Have the police been told?" Abi's voice wavered as she leaned even further forward over the seat.

"Yes, but they can't do anything until we know some more. We couldn't even say for sure she'd been kidnapped. Apparently she said the driver had told her they were stopping in Rotorua for something. That's where Roger and Caroline have gone. We think we're looking for a black BMW." James shifted slightly in his seat. "Penny's really worried you're going to be mad at her, but she honestly thought Natasha was at school. She even phoned the school to check the girls were there. They said Lydia was, but Tasha wasn't on the register because she's not enrolled there. If someone had taken Tasha, Lydia would have known and told us, but Penny never considered that Tasha might have gone off somewhere on her own and that Lydia knew but wasn't saying."

"It's not Penny's fault," Abi assured him, feeling tears threatening behind her eyes. "Gid, what can we do now? Do we go to Rotorua too? Has anyone heard from Roger?"

"They had a text from Tasha saying where she was at the time, but that's a while ago now. Nothing since. She's probably out of signal range."

Gideon glanced round at Abi. "We'll sort it," he said. "She'll be back with us tonight."

"Oh, Gid, she'll be terrified." Abi pulled her hand out of his and sat back in her seat. "D'you think it's Simon driving the car?"

"Of course not!" Gideon almost laughed. "She wouldn't have got in it, would she? No, I expect the driver has been paid to deliver her somewhere."

Abi stared out of the window at the passing scenery. "It'll be dark in about half an hour. That's going to make it even harder to find her!"

"But possibly easier for her to escape," muttered Gideon. "Does her phone have a torch on it?"

Abi nodded. "Yes, quite a good one, actually. D'you think she'll try to escape?"

"Well, *you* would, wouldn't you?" he replied with a shrug. "She's pretty much the same."

"I should have guessed she'd try to see Billy," Abi said with a sigh. "She seemed to agree with me that she shouldn't, but I should have realised she didn't mean it. She's been obsessed with telling him about Joan ever since last summer. Being here was too good a chance to miss."

James turned the car into the drive, and Abi was out almost before he'd come to a stop. She raced into the house and nearly cannoned into Penny, who was running out to meet them.

"Have you heard anything?" Abi gasped, catching the other woman's arm. "Has she texted again?"

Penny shook her head, her sharp features pale and lined with worry. "No, nothing more. Abi...I'm so sorry—"

Abi cut her off. "Not your fault, Penny. You had no reason to know she'd go off like that. And it's not Lydia's fault, either," she added, seeing the child hovering uncertainly behind her mother. "In fact, she was probably much safer, if things had gone according to plan, because she'd had your help."

Gideon and James appeared in the doorway, Gideon with his phone pressed to his ear. "Mum? Any news? Has she contacted you again?" He listened, a frown deepening on his face. "Okay, where are you now?...No, I don't think you can, really...I'm going to call the police again...Oh, did he? Okay, then, Abi and I will head down that way too. I'll keep in touch."

He disconnected the call and slipped his phone into his pocket. "They haven't heard anything else, but Mum says the signal round there is dreadful, and of course Tash will have to be careful not to be seen texting. Dad called the police again, and they're on the lookout for the car, and he's going to keep them updated. I suggest Abi and I head down to Rotorua and take it from there. Can I take your car, Penny?"

Penny nodded, picked up her keys from the table, and threw them to him. "It's got a full tank of petrol," she said. "Should get you well past Rotorua. Keep us in touch, won't you? What d'you want me to do here?"

"Just stay by the phone." Gideon was already on his way out to the car. "We'll call if we find anything." He climbed into the driver's seat of Penny's car and started the engine.

Abi hesitated with her hand on the doorknob. "Wait! Penny, what are your parents driving?" she called.

"It's a hire car, a red Fiat of some sort," Penny called, sliding her arm around Lydia's shoulders as the two of them waved the others off. "Please call as soon as you find anything."

As the car rolled down the drive and out onto the road, Gideon's phone bleeped, heralding the arrival of a text. Abi snatched it up, and her fingers fumbled to operate the keys.

"Oh, my god! It's from Simon!" She peered closely, and read out the words. "*'Don't call the police. I'll be in touch. Simon.'* That's all it says. Gid, does that mean he's got her? Oh, god, what shall we do?" Her voice rose with panic.

Gideon pulled out onto the main road and picked up speed, his face dark with fury. "We'll find them," he said tersely, expertly overtaking a slower vehicle. "How the fuck did he get my number? This is new since I last saw him."

"But Gid, your dad's already spoken to the police!" Abi's voice shook, and she stared wild-eyed at him. "What should we do? If he finds out we called them, he may hurt her...Gid? Shall I call your dad? Shall I try and call Simon?" With shaking hands she picked up her phone, feeling she was spiralling down a never-ending tunnel into the unknown. "I can't cope with this." She held the phone uncertainly to her ear, for once unsure of what to do.

Gideon glanced at her out of the corner of his eye. "Keep calm, Abs," he ordered firmly. "He's not going to hurt her. I reckon he's trying to use her as a bargaining tool. Use her to get us together with him. Try to call him. You never know. Then call Dad and tell him not to speak to the police again until we get there."

Her fingers damp with sweat, Abi rapidly dialled Simon's number and pressed the phone hard against her ear. She waited nervously for him to answer, biting down hard on her lip. After a long time she turned to Gideon. "There's no reply," she said bleakly. "Not even an answer phone message. He knows it's us, and he's not picking up. I'll try your dad now." She dialled again and pressed the phone to her ear once more. "Hello? Roger? It's me...Yes, we're on our way to join you. Listen, don't speak to the police again...Yes, I know, but we've had a message from Simon...I don't know, but he says don't call the police." She paused and listened, impatiently running a damp hand through her hair. "Yes, please, Roger, we must do as he says. We can't take any risks...Okay, just wait until we get to you." She disconnected the call and stared at Gideon. "How long to Rotorua?"

Gideon scowled at the road in front of him. "Not long, if I'm driving," he muttered between clenched teeth.

Chapter 22

Thursday 7th May, 2009

Natasha shifted in her seat again and peered out the window into the gathering dusk. She had decided to wait until it was getting dark before she made a move. There was a very powerful torch on her phone, and she was fairly sure she would be able to lose the driver quite easily in the dark. Then she would head for the nearest house and seek help. They had turned off State Highway 5 a mile or so back and were now running alongside a huge lake. Natasha had identified it from her map as Lake Rerewhakaaitu. Habitation had become much sparser, but there still seemed to be farms at intervals along the road. She leaned forward and tapped on the glass again. There was no reaction. She tapped again much louder. Still the driver ignored her. She scowled fiercely and slammed her fist against the pane.

"I need to talk to you!" she yelled. This time the driver flicked on the intercom.

"What now?"

"I need to go to the toilet," Natasha stated firmly. "Now."

"Well, you can't. You'll have to wait till we get there."

"How long's that?" she demanded. "Where are we

going?"

"Not long." He turned off the intercom and put his foot down.

Natasha sat back with a frustrated sigh. Her plan depended on getting him to stop long enough for her to go to the loo. She stared out of the window and watched as they veered away from the lake and headed towards an area of forest. She hadn't seen a farm for a couple of miles and realised she had to implement her plan very soon. She leaned forward again, and knocked sharply on the glass.

"I really, really need the toilet," she shouted loudly. "If you don't want a puddle in your posh car, you'd better let me out."

The driver glanced briefly over his shoulder at her and sighed. He flicked the switch. "Wait a minute." He slowed down as they approached a T junction, then turned right onto a road Natasha saw was identified as Ash Pit Road. She carefully folded her map and slipped it into the pocket of her jeans. She popped her phone into the same pocket, then slid her hand carefully into her bag and brought out the small penknife Lydia had given her. She concealed the knife in her hand and slid it into the pouch at the front of her hoody.

After a few minutes, the driver slowed down, turned left, and pulled off the road onto an area of bare ground. He turned off the engine, then climbed out and walked round to open the back door. "Right. You can do your stuff behind the car. I need to be able to see you all the time."

Natasha climbed out and stood looking up at him. "You can't watch me pee," she said firmly. "I shall go to the other side of the car and squat down. You can stay here. I won't run off, 'cause you'd see me anyway."

The driver sighed and gave a brief nod, moving to the back of the car and indicating that Natasha should go round the side. The sun had set, the surroundings were gloomy and monochromatic, and Natasha stepped carefully around the car until she was alongside the back door. She squatted down onto the gravelly ground and called loudly, "You're not watching me, are you?"

"No. Now hurry up," came the terse reply.

With a swift movement, Natasha slid the penknife out and opened the slim blade. She carefully placed the tip against the back tyre and pressed hard. At first nothing happened. Then slowly the metal began to pierce the thick rubber. She pressed harder, until the blade went into the tyre up to its hilt. She wiggled it around, then pulled it slowly back out.

"Are you done yet?" the driver sounded impatient.

"Nearly." She folded the knife up again and slid it back into the pouch, then got to her feet and made a show of fiddling with her belt. She walked round the back of the car and stopped in front of him. "Okay. That's better." She got into the car and slid along the seat. The driver slammed her door shut, walked round, got back into the front seat, and started the engine. Natasha cautiously slipped the penknife down inside her sock before hooking her arm through the strap of her bag. She slid across to the other side of the car, behind the passenger seat, and pulled her seatbelt around her. The driver detected her movement and glanced at her in the mirror.

He flicked the intercom. "What are you doing?"

"Just moving seats. Getting bored on that side. The

view's better over here," Natasha replied smoothly, staring out the window towards the dark forest looming on their left.

She moistened her lips and took a deep breath. With any luck, the tyre would have started to go down and would force them to stop soon. The road they were following seemed to be heading up into the mountains and was running alongside a stretch of forest. It was very narrow and full of potholes, which she was sure would get blamed for the puncture. She was just beginning to wonder if her knife had perhaps not done enough damage when she felt the car begin to wobble and a nasty sound came from the back. The driver pulled over to the edge of the narrow road and got out without turning the engine off. He walked to the back of the car and bent down. Natasha heard him utter an oath and watched him carefully through the window. He straightened up, came back, and turned the engine off, and then went and opened the boot. Cautiously she hitched her bag onto her back, opened her door silently, and slid out, squatting down on the cold dusty ground. The driver was heaving the spare wheel out of the boot, and swearing under his breath.

"Stay in the car," he suddenly shouted, not checking to see that she did.

"Okay," Natasha called back, then slid on her bottom down a steep slope at the side of the road. This deposited her in a deep ditch close to the edge of the forest. She lay down flat and waited for a moment to see if her absence had been noticed. She strained her ears, but the only sounds she could hear came from the wheel-changing apparatus. So far he didn't seem to have noticed her actions. She wriggled along on her stomach until she reached the edge of the trees. Once there, she got up onto her knees and pulled her phone out of her pocket, switched on the torch, and shone it along the ground into the forest. As she began to creep further into the wooded area, she heard a shout behind her. The driver had discovered she was missing. She got to her feet and ran as fast as she could, deeper into the forest, the light from her phone bobbing up and down in front of her.

****

"For fuck's sake! What d'you mean you've lost her?" Simon bellowed down the phone, his chubby face suffused red with anger. "You had her in the car. How the fuck could you lose her?" He listened impatiently, his fingers drumming on the windowsill. "And you didn't think to lock the doors? Oh, this is just peachy. So where is she now, d'you think? She can't have got far in the dark. Doesn't make it any easier for us to find her, though…Yeah, well, I guess you could. She probably will make for the road again." He sucked in his breath sharply. "Oh, yeah, and if you don't find her you don't get paid." He slammed the phone down on the table and swore loudly.

Running a sweaty hand through his untidy curls, he began pacing the room in agitation. The plan had been going so well. Nancy had done her bit and kept Gideon out of the way, the kid had fallen for the car business, and all the sodding driver had had to do was deliver her to him in one piece. And now he'd lost her, less than a mile from their destination. He slammed his fist into the back of the sofa and tried to think clearly. He could go out and look for her, but it seemed more sensible for him to remain at the house in case there was any news.

He needed to have everything ready for when the child was finally delivered to him. Grimly he marched into the kitchen and cracked open a can of lager. He took a long swig and wiped his mouth on the back of his hand. Best just to bide his time and wait.

****

"There they are!" Abi pointed to the left, and Gideon swerved the car into the side of the road where his parents were standing waving at them. She was out of the car before it had stopped moving, and ran over to Caroline and Roger. "Have you heard anything?" she asked urgently, catching Caroline's arm.

The older woman patted her hand. "I had a text to say they didn't seem to be stopping in Rotorua after all," she said with a frown, "but nothing since then. What's all this about you hearing from Simon?"

"We had a text from him saying don't call the police, and that he'd be in touch," Abi started to explain, all the time glancing around her as if expecting to see Natasha materialise in front of them. "That's all it said. Now I'm really worried he'll hurt her if he finds out we contacted the police already." Her voice wobbled with emotion.

Caroline leaned forward and gave her a hug. "I'm sure he won't hurt her," she reassured her. "And there's not really any way he could know we spoke to the police. They weren't very helpful, actually, so they probably haven't even done anything yet. I'm so sorry this has happened, Abi. You must be terrified. I really find it hard to believe Simon would try something like this again."

As she spoke, Gideon joined them on the pavement. "Me to," he muttered darkly, glancing over to where his father was looking something up on his phone. "I think we probably need to call the police off. Tell them it was a false alarm or something."

Abi stared at him in terror. "Oh, god, you *are* worried he'll hurt her!" she gasped, her face paling and tears welling up in her eyes.

Gideon put his hands on her shoulders and shook her gently. "No, I don't think he will," he said. "But it's better not to take any chances, and if he knew the police were out looking, it might scare him off. I think he has a plan that will involve us having a confrontation with him, and Tasha is the bait to get us there. What we don't want is him running scared and taking her off somewhere else."

Roger had strolled over and joined them. "I agree." He nodded. "I've already called them and told them it was a false alarm. Any idea where he's taken her? Did he give a clue?"

Gideon shook his head. "Nothing else. Just said don't call the police, and he'd be in touch."

"Of course, we don't know for sure they didn't stop here," Caroline observed. "The last text said they hadn't stopped, but the signal is so bad here she could have tried to contact us again and not been able to."

Abi nodded, wiping her eyes with a tissue and attempting to keep calm. "That's true. Maybe we should do a thorough search of the town and surroundings before we try anywhere else," she suggested. "After all, where else do we look? If they're not here, they could be anywhere."

Gideon raised his eyebrows at his father. "Sounds like a plan," he said, glancing around. "Shall we split up? You and mum take one side of the town, and Abi and I will take the other? We can arrange to meet in an hour, say, and see how we're doing." He paused and squeezed Abi's hand. "Maybe by then we'll have heard from Simon again."

Abi took a deep breath and straightened her shoulders. "Yeah, come on, let's do this. Tasha must be terrified. We need to find her fast. Everyone keep trying to text or call her, too."

"Text is better," Roger put in. "If she's being watched, it's easier for her to respond to a text than a call."

"Right. Let's go, then." Gideon caught Abi by the hand. "Meet back here at"—he glanced at his phone—"eight o'clock? We'll take the south and west of the town, you take the north and east. Keep in touch if you can," and he turned and headed back to the car, Abi stumbling behind him, her heart pounding painfully in her chest. She climbed into the passenger seat and turned on the SATNAV.

"We need to get a map of the town in front of us," she said, her fingers flying over the screen. "And I'll keep trying to text her whenever I get a signal. We will find her, won't we, Gid?" she added, not looking at him.

Gideon started the engine and shifted his position. "Of course we will," he said grimly. "Maybe not here, but we'll find her, and she'll be fine."

Chapter 23

Thursday 7th May, 2009

Natasha squatted on the ground beside a large tree and tried to get her bearings. Although it was only a couple of days from the full moon, the extensive cloud cover meant it was quite dark, and without her torch she would have been completely lost. She stood up again and turned around slowly. If her calculations were correct, the road they'd parked on was away to her left, and she should be heading back the way they'd come. If she could somehow reach the road that led back to Lake Rerewhakaaitu, then she should be able to find a farm where she could take shelter. With a deep breath, she turned her torch back on and set off in what she thought was the right direction.

The undergrowth was thick and dense, and walking was proving a slow and risky business. Several times she caught her ankle in some creepers and fell flat on her face, and she was covered with scratches from the brambles. She tried to pick up a bit of speed, but her feet continued to get trapped in the strangling tendrils. She sighed and swung her torch around her, searching for anything that looked less overgrown and more like a path. In the distance to her left she could just make out what appeared to be a clearing amongst the trees. In the hope it might lead to a path, Natasha leapt over the thick undergrowth and headed towards it, the light from her torch bobbing up and down as she ran.

The night sounds of the forest were all around her, and her heart was pounding in her ribcage. She had to admit she'd never been so terrified in her life. Even the previous summer on Worm's Head had not felt like this. At least then she'd not been on her own. Now she was totally alone, in a foreign country, lost in the forest, with the knowledge she was being pursued by people who apparently meant her harm. As she ran, her breath coming in loud pants, a tear trickled down her cheek. Angrily she brushed it away as she emerged into the small clearing. It certainly wasn't going to help her case if she started blubbing. She fished a tissue out of her pocket and blew her nose, then stepped cautiously into the centre of the clearing and swung her torch around her.

The small area was surrounded by high trees and dense foliage, but Natasha detected a break in the undergrowth to the right. She moved cautiously towards it, and to her delight it proved to be a narrow track running through the trees. She took her bearings again and decided it was leading in roughly the direction she'd been going in, so she took a deep breath, shone her torch in front of her, and began to trot along the path.

It was very narrow, pitted with small holes and rocks, and had a slight incline, but it was much better than having to wade through brambles, and Natasha began to feel slightly more confident of eventually reaching her destination in one piece. She tried her hardest to ignore the unknown noises that filled the dark forest, concentrating on following the path in the hope it would lead back to the road. She was getting very tired and extremely hungry, and her legs were beginning to ache as if she'd run a marathon. She swallowed hard as tears threatened to well up again, and scowled at the deep dark forest ahead of her. She wasn't about to let it beat her.

She quickly peered at her phone—still no signal. Hardly surprising, considering the density of the woodland and the fact that she had barely had one even when they were in the car. If she could only phone her parents, everything would be all right. The sooner she emerged from the forest, the better. Hopefully any house she came across would have a landline anyway, and she would be able to phone whoever she wanted. She peered at the phone again and saw it was half past seven. She had been in the woods for nearly two hours. Surely she should have come to a road or some habitation by now. She stopped running again and stared around her. Maybe she'd got her bearings completely wrong and was heading deeper and deeper into the forest. A feeling of panic rose in her throat, and the tears began to prick behind her eyes again.

Suppose she never found her way out? Suppose no one found her? She would starve to death, and her decomposing body, found in months to come by some intrepid adventurer, would be crawling in maggots, her eyes eaten and her entrails strewn out across the path. She stopped and mentally slapped herself across the face. Of course that wouldn't happen. Her parents would find her. In fact, in the daylight she would probably be able to find her way out easily. She just needed to keep calm.

Taking another deep, shuddery breath, Natasha set

off again along the narrow path, sweeping her light in front of her, looking for any way back to the road. She could hear no sounds other than the occasional call of something that could have been an owl, in the forest, although she recollected that on their journey out here they had passed very few other vehicles, so she wasn't really expecting to hear anything else.

After trotting determinedly on for about another twenty minutes, she stopped suddenly. Peering into the distance, she shone her torch in front of her. There was something ahead of her. Something deep within the trees. She stepped forward slowly, her light illuminating the way ahead. There was definitely something there, something that wasn't a tree. She trotted forward a few more steps, straining her eyes in the dark. It looked like a building. Her heart beginning to pound with anticipation, she picked up speed and ran towards it. As she drew closer, she could make out it was a single-storey building set in a large clearing. A couple of wooden outbuildings were to one side, and just in front of it she could make out the shape of a small car. Confident it wasn't the car she'd escaped from, Natasha jogged towards the house, peering ahead of her to see how it was accessed from the road. If there was a car, then the road couldn't be far away.

She grinned in the darkness—obviously her sense of direction must have been correct. She must have arrived at one of the small farmsteads they had passed on the way there. Her steps slowed as she approached the house, noting with relief that there was a light burning at the front window. She could now see the car was a small pale-coloured one, nothing like the large black car she'd been kidnapped in. A long gravel path led away from the house to the right, presumably heading towards the road. Natasha frowned for a moment. Surely the road should be to her left? She hesitated momentarily, then shrugged and trotted on towards the house. Maybe the path bent round. The light from the window flooded out onto the parking area in front of the building, illuminating the small unkempt garden.

As her feet crunched on the gravel, she slowed to a cautious walk up to the white-painted front door. There was no bell, so she lifted her fist, knocked loudly, then stepped back and waited, her heart pounding uncomfortably in her chest. She glanced up to see if there was a telephone line to the house, but she could not locate one. Well, at the very least she could have something to eat. Footsteps were approaching the door from the other side, and Natasha composed her features into a tense smile ready to greet her potential rescuer.

The door swung open, and a voice snapped out, "Well, you'd better have bloody found her, or..." The man stopped and stared at Natasha is amazement. She stared back, momentarily confused. She took in his dishevelled appearance, the untidy curly brown hair, the curious moustache, the overweight body. She frowned; he looked familiar, but she wasn't sure why. She took a step backwards, and he smiled unpleasantly at her. "So the fly has come to the spider, has she?" He reached out and grasped her wrist before she could move any further away. "That's saved me some time. Don't you recognise me, kid?" He ran a hand through his thick hair. "Amazing what a bit of hair dye can do, isn't it?"

Natasha tried to pull her arm away, a look of horror spreading over her face. "Simon," she whispered, her mouth going dry. "You're Simon." She took a long shuddering breath. "You tried to kill my mother! Let me go!"

Simon gave a short laugh and pulled her through the door and into a narrow hallway.

"Pity I failed," he muttered, slamming the door behind her and locking it. "But I'm not trying to kill anyone this time. That was a mistake. I can see that now." He paused and glanced down at her. "I have other plans now, and you're going to help me."

Natasha wriggled violently and tried to pull her arm away. "Let me go!" she yelled, kicking out with her foot, trying to hit his shins. "My dad'll kill you!"

Simon's hand whipped round and caught her other wrist, pinning her arms to her sides. He dragged her into a small living room and kicked the door shut.

"Shut up and calm down," he hissed, holding her tightly against him. "I'm not going to hurt you. I want your dad to be my friend again, so why would I hurt you?"

Natasha twisted her head round to look at him. "Are you mad?" she gasped. "Why on earth would he be your friend? You shot my mother, and now you've kidnapped me! Friends don't do that!" She started struggling again. "Now let me go, and you won't get into any more trouble."

Simon flung her down onto the sofa and stood looking down at her. "And where would you go?" he demanded. "By my reckoning, you've been out wandering in the forest for hours. You must be very tired, and very hungry. We're right up near the top of the volcano here. There are no other houses for miles. You're better off here with me."

Natasha stared at him in confusion. "The top of the volcano?" she echoed. "What volcano? I thought I'd gone back the way we came. There was no volcano there."

"Mount Tarawera," Simon supplied, folding his arms. "I think you got your bearings wrong. You've actually continued on the way you were travelling in the car." He paused and raised an eyebrow at her. "Clever escape, by the way, but I think I'll take that knife now, if you don't mind," and he held out his hand.

Natasha scowled at him, and folded her arms across her chest defiantly. "Well, you can't have it," she said sullenly. "I lost it in the forest."

"Nice try." He scooped her bag up from the sofa beside her, fumbled in the pockets, and came out empty-handed.

Natasha smirked at him. "Told you," she said. "I lost it. Now give me my bag back," and she held out her hand imperiously.

Simon tossed the backpack onto the sofa, then held out his hand again. "Maybe," he said cautiously, "but I will take your phone."

Natasha sighed, and held it out to him. "There's no signal here anyway," she said with a shrug. "I couldn't phone anyone." She looked up at him with a scowl. "I'm hungry."

Simon slipped the phone into his pocket and nodded. "I thought you would be. I've got some soup. Stay there."

He turned and walked through a door into what Natasha surmised was the kitchen. He left the door wide open, and she could hear him clattering around, presumably preparing her food. She glanced around her, considering escape, but she was so tired and so hungry she decided to wait until she'd eaten, so she leant back on the sofa and considered her surroundings. The room was almost square, and quite sparsely furnished. Apart from the small sofa she was currently sitting on, the only other things in the room were a rocking chair, a small coffee table and a tall bookcase half full of very dusty paperbacks. The floor was covered with a rather worn fawn carpet, in the centre of which was a multicoloured circular rug. There were long blue curtains at the window, pulled tightly across to shut out the night.

Natasha wriggled into a more comfortable position and considered her plight. She thought she believed Simon when he said he wasn't going to hurt her—the fact that he had gone to get her some food surely proved that—but she was still very unsure of him. She knew from her encounter with him the previous summer that he was unhinged, and she wasn't about to let her guard down. If he truly still wanted to be friends with her father, he had a very funny way of going about it. A sound from the kitchen caught her attention, and she looked up just as Simon re-entered the room carrying a tray. He placed it on her knees, then threw himself down into the rocking chair, watching her.

"Eat it," he ordered, waving a hand at the steaming bowl of soup on the tray. Natasha hungrily complied, shovelling the hot broth into her mouth, accompanied by the chunks of white bread he had provided with it.

She looked up, her mouth full. "Can I have a drink?" she said indistinctly. "Milk."

He hesitated a moment, then got to his feet and disappeared into the kitchen again, returning a moment later with a tall glass of milk, which he placed on the tray. She nodded her thanks and continued to eat rapidly, not stopping until the soup bowl was wiped clean and all the bread was gone. She thirstily gulped down the milk, then sat back, wiping her mouth on her sleeve.

"Thank you," she said reluctantly. "Can I go to the toilet now?"

Simon rolled his eyes but stood up and jerked his head at her to follow him. He went back out into the narrow entrance hall and pointed to a door in front of them.

"In there. There's no window, so don't think about trying to escape."

Natasha went into the tiny bathroom and closed the door. She saw to her chagrin that there was no lock, and called out, "There's no lock. Don't come in."

Her ablutions finished, she opened the door and found Simon leaning against the wall waiting for her. He caught her wrist and pulled her back into the living room.

"Sit down," he said brusquely, pushing her back onto the sofa. "Did you manage to tell anyone anything about your journey?"

She shrugged. "Not much, just that we were gonna stop in Rotorua. But then we didn't." She scowled at him. "They'll find me."

"I'm banking on it!" Simon gave a short laugh. "What good is a bargaining tool if you have no one to bargain with?"

Natasha looked at him uncomprehendingly, her brow furrowed. "What d'you mean?" she asked suspiciously. "You want my mum and dad to find me here?"

Simon nodded. "Of course. When I'm ready for them." He stared at her. "I have no life. Since your father ran off to be with your mother, I've lost my life. I am no one. I want my life back. That was what last summer was about." He paused and stared over her head at the expanse of blue curtain. "But I was wrong then. This is much better. This will work."

"What will work?" Natasha was mystified. "How is kidnapping me going to help you get your life back? My parents'll be furious. They won't want to be friends with you."

Simon sat forward in his chair. "But don't you see? I'll show them I don't mean you any harm, and if I can persuade them to drop the charges from last summer, then I can get my life back. This was the only way I could get to talk to them."

Natasha shook her head. "But they can't drop the charges. You shot my mum," she said slowly. "She actually didn't want to press charges, but the police insisted. I think they were right, and so do Grandma and Grandpa. Mum seemed to think you wouldn't do anything again, and that you weren't yourself, and she wanted to give you a second chance." She scowled again. "She's much too nice. If you'd shot me, I'd have made sure you ended up in prison. The police think you drowned, so I don't think they've been looking for you very hard."

"Abi didn't want to bring charges?" Simon echoed in disbelief, his bloodshot eyes narrowed. "I shot her, and she wanted to give me a second chance?" He rolled his eyes. "Wonder what she's thinking now?"

Natasha stared. "Well, I doubt she's very pleased

right now. She will have realised she was wrong and the police were right. Kidnapping me was a very bad idea, by the way, 'cause this time I guess they'll catch you. You're not getting away with it again. They'll know you're still alive, by now. Mum an' Dad will have called the police."

Simon smirked unpleasantly at her. "Not if they know what's good for you," he sneered. "I texted them and told them not to call the police." He glanced round to find Natasha staring at him. "They're probably too terrified to tell anyone now."

"And you think this will make them be your friends again?" Natasha said, her eyes sparking. "What you did last summer was dreadful, and now you'll *really* be in trouble. You won't get away with this. Dad'll *never* be your friend again now."

With a muffled oath, Simon lurched forward and pulled her up from the sofa. He put his face close to hers, his beery breath making her recoil. "Oh, he will," he snarled at her. "He'll have to be, if he wants to see his precious little girl again."

Natasha tried to pull away from him, her eyes reflecting her fear. "But you said you wouldn't hurt me..." She stumbled over the words. "You said I was just the bait."

"Things change," he snapped, pulling her towards the kitchen door. "You're beginning to annoy me. I need time to think."

Pulling her behind him, he strode through the small kitchen and out the half-glazed back door. Natasha stared around her in panic, wondering if she could make a break for it while they were outside. Behind the house were the two small wooden outbuildings she'd noticed as she approached from the forest, and Simon seemed to be making for the nearest one. She attempted to pull her arm out of his grip, but he tightened his fingers until they bit into her skin as he jerked her roughly towards the door of the shed.

"What are you doing?" she asked nervously. He unbolted the door. "I'm not going in there."

"Yes, you are," Simon said tersely, pulling her in front of him and pushing her into the dark space. "A few hours in there should keep you out of my hair while I think what to do next. A few cobwebs never hurt anyone." He slammed the door shut, and Natasha heard the click of a padlock.

She stood in the middle of the tiny room, and stared around her in horror. The little shed was virtually square, about four feet each side, and almost completely dark. A small amount of weak light was filtering between a couple of badly fitting planks on the back wall, but otherwise the room was dark, dank, and very, very cobwebby. Natasha felt the webs catch in her hair as she moved urgently around attempting to find a way out. She put her hand up and brushed them away, shuddering, the slight hint of a memory catching at her mind as she did so.

She stared around her, her eyes beginning to adjust to the dark, and saw the shed was completely empty, apart from a tin bucket in the corner. With a gasp of horror she realised it had probably been provided for her to pee into. She shrank back against the rough wooden wall and slowly sank to the hard, cold, bumpy ground, her eyes fixed firmly on the darkest, most cobwebby corner of the shed. She pulled her knees up to her chest and rested her head on them. As she did, the old, hitherto forgotten memories came flooding back, and tears began to pour unheeded down her cold cheeks.

Chapter 24

Late March, 2000—The Birtwhistle Children's Home, Kent

"Come on, Tasha, come and meet Mr. and Mrs. Crawley. They're very nice." Cathy Masters tried to coax the little girl out of her room. "You met them before, do you remember?" She crawled into the corner of the room where Natasha was crouching, clutching her little grey rabbit tightly in her hand. "Come on, pet. They'd like to meet you again."

Natasha glowered at her, her blue eyes hostile. "Why?" she demanded, curling her feet further underneath her and pressing herself back against the wall. "I don' want to see them again."

Cathy sat back on her heels and sighed. The Crawleys had been trying to get to know Natasha for several weeks, with the intention of fostering the little girl. Unfortunately, Natasha was being less than amenable, but Cathy felt it was her duty to encourage the relationship. She sat down cross-legged, facing the little girl and smiled gently at her.

"Tasha, they're very nice people. Give them a chance. They have two children who'd like to meet you, too. Please come down and see them. They've brought you a present."

Natasha's head came up. "What is it?" she asked

suspiciously. "What have they brought me?"

"You'll have to come downstairs and see," Cathy replied, getting to her feet and holding her hand out to Natasha. Reluctantly the little girl took it and jumped up. She ran over to her bed and gently tucked her little rabbit in under the covers, then walked over to Cathy and took her hand.

She looked up at her. "All wight then," she agreed solemnly. "I'll come, but if I don' like the pwesent I'm coming back up here."

Cathy looked down at her and nodded. "Deal," she said with a conspiratorial smile, and squeezed the little girl's hand. "Come on."

As Cathy led Natasha into the small living room, a tall blonde lady sitting by the fireplace got to her feet. She smiled broadly and held out her hand. "Hello again, Natasha," she said kindly. "It's nice to see you."

Natasha stopped a few feet away and stared at her solemnly. "What have you brought me?" she asked.

Mrs. Crawley smiled slightly and bent to pull something out of her bag. "This," she said, holding out a large stuffed pink elephant. Natasha's eyes widened, and she tentatively reached forward and took the toy in her arms. She studied it carefully for a moment, then cuddled it close to her chest.

She stared up at Mrs. Crawley. "It's nice," she said with a nod. "Thank you."

"Good girl." Cathy patted her on the head, then leant down and spoke gently to her. "You stay in here and have a chat to Mr. and Mrs. Crawley, Tasha," she said, looking the child in the eyes. Natasha paused for a moment, then nodded her head and sat down cross-legged on the floor. Cathy raised her eyebrows at the

Crawleys. "I'll be in the next room if you need me," she said with a smile before she tactfully withdrew.

Tony Crawley joined his wife in front of the fire and squatted down.

"Glad you like the elephant, Tasha," he said with a smile. "We thought you might. You like cuddly toys, don't you?"

Natasha looked up at him over the head of the elephant and nodded silently. Jackie Crawley glanced at her husband, then moved closer to Natasha. She reached out and stroked the elephant's soft fur.

"It's very cuddly, isn't it? What are you going to call it?" she asked with a smile.

Natasha put her head on one side and frowned. "Windy," she said at last, and rubbed her nose in the pink fur.

Jackie smiled. "Windy?" she repeated. "That's nice. Tasha, would you like to come and stay at our house for a little while?" Natasha looked at her blankly. "Just for a bit. Come and meet our children. You'd like them."

The child lowered the elephant and stared at her seriously. "Why?" she asked.

"Well..." Jackie hesitated and looked at her husband for support. "We like you, and we'd like to get to know you better. And our children would like to meet you, too." She watched Natasha warily. "Just for a little bit. You can come back here whenever you want."

Natasha crawled closer to the fire and stared into it. "Have you got a fire?" she asked suddenly.

"Yes. We have two."

"Can I have my own bedroom?"

"Yes, if you want. Or you could share with our

daughter, Kayleigh."

"My own room." Natasha looked round at them. "Just for a bit."

"Just for a bit. As long as you want," Jackie assured her. "And you can call us Aunty and Uncle if you like. It's easier than Mr. and Mrs. Crawley, isn't it?"

Natasha shrugged. "I can say that. Mr. and Mrs. Crawley. See, it's not hard."

Jackie smothered a smile. "Of course you can, darling, but Aunty and Uncle is more friendly, isn't it?"

Natasha shrugged again. "S'pose," she said. "Okay, then. Shall we go now?" She started to stand.

Jackie laughed. "Well, not right now," she said, smiling at the child. "You'll need to pack some clothes, and we need to get your bed ready. How about tomorrow? We'll come back for you tomorrow afternoon."

Natasha hugged the elephant to her and nodded slowly. "All wight." She skipped out of the room and ran back up to her bedroom.

****

Natasha had been at the Crawleys' house for just over a week, and she was beginning to understand it. At first she'd felt very intimidated and small, but Aunty and Uncle were being very kind, and she was starting to feel more secure. She was still a little unsure about the other children, but they hadn't been really mean to her, so she was prepared to stay a bit longer. They were both at school during the day, which was nice, but Aunty had said they broke up for Easter today. Natasha wasn't sure what that meant, but she was afraid it might mean they would be at home all the time. The girl wasn't too bad. She was called Kayleigh, and Natasha thought she was eight. The boy was more of a problem. He was called Ryan and was six. Because he was used to being the baby of the family, he was inclined to resent the intrusion of a younger child. Although she didn't understand why, Natasha had picked up on the fact that he wasn't keen on her being there, and she tried to give him a wide berth.

She was sitting in the sand pit in the garden when they arrived home, happily digging a hole and then filling it up again. Kayleigh went straight over to join her and sat down beside her. Natasha carried on digging. Kayleigh picked up a spade and started her own hole.

"We broke up from school today," she announced, tossing the sand over her shoulder as she dug. "D'you know what that means, Tash?"

Natasha nodded, not wanting to reveal her doubt.

"'Course she doesn't know," came a scornful voice from behind her. "She's only a baby. Babies don't know nothin'."

Kayleigh frowned at her brother. "Don't be so mean, Ryan," she chided. "It means we don't have to go to school till after Easter," she explained kindly to Natasha. "That means we can play with you."

"I won't," Ryan said petulantly. "I don't want her here."

Kayleigh jumped to her feet. "Mum!" she yelled at the top of her voice. "Mum, Ryan's being mean to Tasha."

The tall figure of Jackie Crawley appeared at the back door. She looked slightly harassed and frowned at her son. "Ryan, be nice. Tasha is our visitor," she said mildly. "Kayleigh, bring her in for tea now, will you?" She turned and disappeared back into the house.

Kayleigh looked slightly put out but grabbed Natasha by the hand and pulled her to her feet. "C'mon, then. Tea time," and she hurried the little girl into the house.

Jackie was standing at the stove, rapidly shaking a large frying pan, and Natasha sniffed appreciatively. She might not be too sure about the other children, but she was enjoying the food. She slid into her seat at the long pine table and carefully tucked her napkin into the neck of her T-shirt.

Ryan watched her and laughed unpleasantly. "See, she's a baby. She needs a bib."

Kayleigh kicked her brother under the table, but her eyes slid over to Natasha, and she smothered a grin. Natasha felt her face begin to flame, and she ducked her head down so they couldn't look at her. Her short curls bobbed down over her eyes, and she curled her feet tightly around the legs of the chair.

"There you go, Natasha." Jackie placed a plate of sausage and mash in front of the little girl, set one on the table for each of the other children, as well, and then walked over to the kettle to make herself a cup of tea.

"Thank you," whispered Natasha, picking up her over-large knife and fork and attempting to cut up her sausage. She stuck her fork into it and pressed down hard with the knife. Nothing happened. She frowned at it, then took the fork out and tried again with just the knife. This time the knife slid across the greasy surface of the sausage, which shot off the plate like a bullet, flying across the room and landing on the floor at

Jackie's feet. Ryan, who had watched the whole procedure, burst out laughing, and Kayleigh began to titter. Jackie stared at the sausage in surprise, then bent and picked it up.

"Whose is this?" she demanded icily. "Who's throwing their food around?"

"It's Tasha's!" yelled Ryan in delight. "She's a baby! She can't even eat properly."

Jackie looked at Natasha. "Is this yours?" she asked, wiping the sausage on a piece of paper towel. "How did it get on the floor?"

Natasha stared at her in silence. She knew it had been an accident, but she was fairly sure no one would believe her. She ducked her head down again and clasped her hands together in her lap.

"She was trying to cut it." Kayleigh came to her rescue. "It just slid off the plate. It was funny."

Jackie sighed, popped the sausage back onto Natasha's plate, and cut it into three pieces. "There you go. Now be more careful," she said with a frown.

Natasha slowly picked up her fork again and managed to force the sausage and mashed potato down, aware all the time of Ryan watching her every move. As soon as she'd finished, she laid her knife and fork tidily on her plate and sat with her hands in her lap. Meal times, although tasty, were always a trial. Ryan watched her all the time, and if he was near enough he took food off her plate. Kayleigh usually saw him do it but never said anything. Natasha was quite surprised she had come to her rescue over the sausage. She looked up and smiled at the older girl. Kayleigh gave a little smile back, and Ryan, with a quick glance to make sure his mother wasn't watching, stuck his tongue out at her. Natasha stuck hers out back at him, then swung her feet under the table in the hope she would manage to kick him. She missed, and the toe of her sandal caught the table leg. The table shook violently and her glass of milk, which had been balanced precariously on the edge of the table mat, fell over with a crash, spraying its contents all over the table. With a muttered oath, Jackie shot over to the table with a cloth and began to mop it up.

"It was Tasha," Ryan was quick to say, surreptitiously sticking out his tongue again. "Mum, it was Tasha."

"Don't tell tales, Ryan," his mother said absently, wringing her cloth out into the sink. "I'm sure it was an accident. She's only four. You can leave the table if you've finished, Tasha," she added to the little girl.

In a flash Natasha slid off her chair, scampered out of the room, and up the stairs to her bedroom. It was a tiny box room overlooking the garden, furnished with a single bed, a chest of drawers, and a small bookcase. She jumped on the bed and scooped up her little grey rabbit, Thunder, and cuddled him tightly to her chest. Her tongue flicked out and pulled his ear into her mouth, and she began to suck. She shuffled backwards on the bed until she was tucked into the corner, her back pressed hard against the wall and her legs curled up underneath her. She kept very quiet, silently hoping Ryan didn't come looking for her. She had no way of keeping him out of the room, and he had a very nasty habit of touching her toys. Her eyes hardened as she thought of him picking up her teddies. If he did that again, she would get very cross, and then Aunty would be cross with her. It was far better if he didn't come in the room. As she huddled in the corner, a voice drifted up to her through the open window, and she got onto her knees and peered outside. Aunty was standing in the garden talking to Uncle. They were both holding glasses of wine—Kayleigh had told Natasha what the red liquid was—and Aunty was looking very tired.

"It's getting very difficult, Tony," she was saying as she took a long sip of her drink. "Ryan doesn't like her, and she's not making things easy." There was a muffled reply from Uncle that Natasha failed to catch, and then Aunty continued. "Well I don't know what to do, I just know it's difficult."

Natasha fell back onto her heels and stared at the wall in front of her. What was difficult? Were they talking about her? What did they mean? Ryan was the one who was causing trouble. She wriggled back into her favourite position and pulled Thunder's ear into her mouth again. She held him tightly—so long as she had him, she would be all right.

****

"Coming, ready or not!" Kayleigh's voice rang out around the garden, and Natasha crouched lower behind the dustbin in her attempt to hide. The older children had been home from school now for over a week, and Natasha was finding it very stressful. Ryan constantly taunted her and tried to get her into trouble, and Kayleigh, although not actually mean to her, did nothing to stop her brother's antics. As she waited to be found, Natasha's heart sank as she realised that as usual she would be the first to be discovered. Then she would have to be the seeker, and the other children would go and hide in places she would never be able to find them. She felt tears begin to prick behind her eyes, and she sniffed. She was really missing Aunty Cathy and the children's home. For a couple of days now she'd been trying to pluck up the courage to ask if she could go home, but each time she'd tried, Aunty had been too busy to listen. She shifted her position and knocked the dustbin with her shoulder. The metal lid fell to the ground with a loud clatter that brought Kayleigh running round the side of the house in an instant.

"Found you!" she sang out, grabbing Natasha by the hand and pulling her out of her hiding place. "Come and help me find Ryan."

After ten minutes of fruitless searching, Kayleigh jumped into the sand pit and sat down. "I give up," she grumbled, picking up a handful of sand and throwing it at Natasha. "You find him."

Natasha sat down opposite her. "I don't want to," she said firmly. "I hope he stays hidden."

Kayleigh stared at her in surprise. "You can't say that!" she gasped with a giggle. "He's more important than you. He *lives* here. You're just visiting."

Natasha surveyed her silently. She was glad she was just visiting. She didn't want to live there. When she got her own parents, they wouldn't be like Aunty and Uncle. They would have time for her. She thought for a moment. It really was time she had her own parents. She would have to do something about that when she got back home. Aunty Cathy was lovely, but she wasn't her mummy. And Aunty and Uncle—well, they really wouldn't do at all. She pushed her hands deep into the warm sand and wiggled her fingers. It felt nice. She looked up and found Kayleigh watching her. The older girl threw another handful of sand at her.

"Go on, you find him," she ordered. "You have to

do as I say."

Natasha shook her curly head. "No, I don't," she said and carried on playing with the sand.

Kayleigh scowled at her. Reaching over and pulling one of Natasha's hands out of the sand, she shouted, "Yes, you do! Go and find my brother."

"I'm here." Ryan's voice came from over by the garden shed. Natasha looked up at him. He was standing in front of the door of the tiny building, something small and grey in his hand. He grinned evilly at her. "Look what I've got," he taunted her, holding up her little rabbit and waving it at her. "Look what I found on your bed."

With a cry of pure anger, Natasha scrambled to her feet and flew at him, arms flailing. "Give me my bunny!" she yelled, her little face red with rage. "You can't touch my bunny! You can't touch my things." She flung herself at him, her hands grasping at the toy, but he laughed and held it high above her head where she couldn't reach it. Suddenly he pushed her away with one hand, pulled open the door of the shed with the other, and flung the rabbit into the dark space.

"Go and get it, then, if you want it!" he laughed, holding the door open. Natasha ran forward, straight through the door into the tiny shed, snatching up Thunder as soon as she reached him. She clutched him tightly to her and turned around just as Ryan slammed the door shut and turned the key. Natasha stood perfectly still in the dark and held her breath. He had locked her in. She stared around her nervously. The shed was very tiny, and empty apart from a few gardening tools stacked in the corner. A tiny window in the back wall was too high for the little girl to see through, and all the dark corners seemed to be full of cobwebs. She took a step backwards, and a long trailing cobweb caught in her hair. She squealed, brushed it away with her hands, and ran to the door. She pushed it, hard. Nothing happened, so she pushed harder. It didn't move at all. Clutching Thunder tightly in one hand, she hammered on the door with her other fist.

"Let me out! Let me out!" A laugh from the other side of the door told her that her tormenter was still there. She pressed her face against the rough wood and called again, "Let me out now!" She heard footsteps running away across the garden, and then there was silence.

Choking back tears, Natasha slowly turned around and forced herself to stare into the darkest corner of the shed. If she looked at it, the monster that was hiding in the dark couldn't hurt her. However big and scary, it couldn't hurt her if she kept watching it. Could it? She stared harder, daring it to show itself. But she needed to get out. She needed to pee badly. Suddenly the realisation hit her that she really couldn't get out until Ryan decided to let her. The tears she'd been managing to hold in check burst out and began to run unheeded down her cheeks. She took a deep breath and yelled as loud as she could, at the same time banging on the door with her fists.

"Help! Let me out!" She carried on shouting the same words over and over again, all the time keeping her eyes firmly fixed on the darkest corner. Suddenly she became aware of a shadowy movement deep amongst the cobwebs, and she opened her mouth and screamed louder than she'd ever screamed before. She was still rooted to the spot, her mouth wide open, when the door was flung open, flooding the little room with sunlight. Natasha stopped screaming, blinked, and rubbed her hand across her eyes.

"What on earth is going on?" Jackie was standing in front of her, her hands on her hips. "Natasha, what are you doing in here? It's not safe for children; there are tools in here," and she peered around the child to check everything was still in place. "Tell me, why are you in here and making such a noise?" and she pulled her out onto the grass.

"Ryan locked me in," Natasha whispered, her heart sinking as she realised she wasn't going to be believed.

"Ryan?" His mother turned to look at him. "Did you lock Natasha in the shed?"

Ryan shook his head vigorously. "No," he said at once, his eyes studiously avoiding Natasha's. "'Course not. She hid her stupid rabbit in there, and when she went in to get it, the door slammed shut and got stuck."

"Natasha, I'm sure I told you not to go in the shed on your own." Jackie sighed heavily. "Why did you hide your rabbit in there anyway? And why did you try to blame Ryan?"

Natasha stared up at her, her heart heavy, realising it wasn't even worth trying to get her to believe her. "Can I go home now, please?" she asked in a whisper.

Chapter 25

Thursday 7th May, 2009

"Right. We're no further with this. We need to rethink." Gideon pushed Abi down into a chair at the coffee shop where they'd arranged to meet his parents and placed a large mug in front of her.

"I can't drink that, Gid," she objected, pushing it away. "I'm far too worried."

Gideon slid into the seat next to her and moved the mug back towards her. "Drink it," he ordered sharply. "We may be up all night. You need to stay awake."

"Our daughter is out there somewhere, in the clutches of your lunatic friend, and you want me to sit here calmly drinking coffee?" Abi exploded at him, attempting to get to her feet. "We don't have time for this. She's in danger!"

Gideon caught her arm and pulled her back down into the chair. "Abi, you'll be no use to anyone, least of all Tasha, if you get in a state. We need to remain calm and level-headed, and wide awake," he said patiently. "Drink it and get a grip. I'm just as worried as you, but wandering aimlessly around a town she's probably not even in isn't really helping. We need to talk to Mum and Dad and see if we can come up with a better plan." He fished his phone out of his pocket and laid it on the table. "I'm sure we'll hear from Simon again soon anyway."

"I can't wait for that!" Abi grumbled and shifted uneasily in her seat. "I want to be out looking. Gid, she must be terrified!"

The door to the café opened, and Abi glanced up to see Roger and Caroline making their way across to their table. Caroline sat down opposite Abi and shrugged apologetically. "I'm sorry. We haven't had any luck, I'm afraid," she said, reaching out and patting Abi's hand. "Although, to be honest, I'm not sure we were really expecting to. It's like looking for a needle in a haystack."

Abi felt panic beginning to rise in her throat, and she snatched up her cup of coffee and took a long slurp. Gideon was right. She would be no use to anyone if she couldn't keep it together. She mentally slapped her own face and summoned up a smile for Caroline. "I know. We had no luck either," she managed. "Gid thinks we'll hear from Simon soon."

As she spoke, her own mobile bleeped, heralding the arrival of a text. She whipped it out of her pocket in the hope it was from Natasha, and stared at the screen.

"Oh!" She looked momentarily flummoxed. "It's from Nancy. She just says, *'He mentioned Tarawera.* That's all." She glanced at the others. "What's Tarawera? Is it a place?"

Roger nodded. "Yes. It's a volcano—not too far from here. In the mountains."

"A volcano?" Abi echoed, her mind whirling. "He's taken her to a volcano? Why would he do that?" She felt her voice rising again and clasped her hands tightly together in an attempt to stop them from shaking.

Gideon looked up from his phone. "There's a Lake Tarawera, too," he said. "I guess he could be anywhere in the vicinity. I suggest we head up in that direction and see what happens. It looks like it's fairly wooded around there. Maybe he has some hideout in the forest. I wonder why Nancy texted you and not me?" he added to Abi.

She scowled at him. "Because she values her life," she snapped, then drained her cup and got to her feet. "Now, come on. Let's at least get into the right area."

"Have you tried Simon again?" Roger asked as they made their way back to the cars.

Gideon nodded. "Loads of times," he said shortly. "No luck. I think we should just all head off towards Tarawera. According to my phone, it's about an hour away." He glanced back at the screen. "It's nearly eight thirty now. Gonna be late by the time we get there. Maybe some of this cloud cover will have cleared. We could do with the moonlight tonight. Anyone got a torch?"

They each had one built into their phones, and they set off in tandem in the direction of Mount Tarawera, Abi still struggling to keep her feelings in check. She found her heart rate had increased dramatically, and she was finding it hard to get her breath. She leaned back in her seat and closed her eyes, trying to take long, slow breaths to calm herself down. Part of her was really annoyed with herself for her reaction. She was normally fairly level-headed and could cope with a crisis very well. She could only assume it was a hangover from her encounter with Simon the previous summer. Maybe it had affected her more than she'd realised. She suddenly became aware that Gideon was watching her anxiously.

"Abs? Are you all right? You've gone really pale, and you're breathing way too fast. Shall I stop the car?"

Abi shook her head and took a deep shuddering breath. "No," she managed. "I'm all right. Just a bit panicky. Sorry, not like me." She grimaced at him apologetically.

Gideon frowned at her. "Don't be stupid. You don't need to apologise. Of course you're feeling like that. Our daughter is missing, and it's bringing back all the terror you went through last summer. If you didn't feel panicky, I'd be worried." He increased his speed as they left the town behind them. "Don't worry. We'll find her."

Abi nodded silently and sat back with her hands in her lap, taking slow, calming breaths. Of course they'd find her. The text from Simon indicated he would be telling them where she was at some point. She couldn't bear to wait for that and hoped desperately they managed to get some lead on her whereabouts before he called them. It was always possible she'd managed to escape from the car and was trying to make her way back to the nearest house, but Abi realised that was a long shot. Even if she was, the chance of them finding her in the dark was quite unlikely. She took another deep breath and reminded herself just how resourceful her daughter was. If she had managed to escape, she would be able to keep herself safe until morning.

Half an hour later, they were driving along the side of Lake Rerewhakkaaitu, and Abi was peering nervously out into the dark landscape. She could see the large expanse of forest looming ahead of them, and her heart turned over as she imagined her baby alone there, although she had to admit to herself that was probably preferable to her being Simon's prisoner. After they veered away from the lake and started to climb into the mountains, they turned off onto a smaller road.

Gideon glanced in the mirror. "We seem to have left Mum and Dad behind," he remarked. "I'm going to pull in, in a minute, and wait for them. We're very close to the Tarawera area now, and we need to have a plan."

They continued driving slowly for a few more minutes, and then he pulled off the road onto a gravelly patch of land. He turned the engine off and took Abi's hand in his.

"Are you okay?" he asked, staring intently at her.

She shook her head. "No. Are you? But I'll survive."

He reached forward and pulled her towards him, kissing the top of her head. "We'll find her," he murmured into her hair. "Simon's not going to hurt her."

Abi buried her face in his shoulder. "He won't, will he?" she said, her voice muffled by his shirt. "He just wants to talk, doesn't he?" She raised a tearstained face to his.

Gideon pushed her hair behind her ears and gently kissed her on the lips. "I'm sure that's what he wants," he said with more confidence than he was feeling. "I'm fairly sure we'll get a text or a call from him soon." As he spoke, his parents drew up beside them in their hire car.

Caroline rolled down her window. "Is there a problem?" she called.

Gideon disentangled himself from Abi and shook his head. "No, just thought we'd wait for you to catch up. I think we should stick together for now."

Caroline nodded. "All right. Which way are we going?" She glanced back at the road that forked just behind them. "This one seems to lead up into the mountains through the forest, but from the map they both seem to end up at the top of Mount Tarawera."

"This one." Abi suddenly leaned round Gideon, wiping her eyes with her sleeve. "I think they went this way."

Gideon glanced at her, then turned back to his parents and shrugged. "Mother's intuition," he said. "May as well go with it. We have nothing else to go on." And he closed the window and started the engine again.

They had been driving slowly up the narrow road, bordered on both sides by dense dark forest, for about ten minutes, when Gideon's phone suddenly bleeped. He slammed the brakes on and snatched it up before Abi could reach it.

"It's him," he said tersely, reading the short message. He glanced at Abi. "He says, *'She's safe. We need to talk. Text me your location.'*"

Abi gasped. "That's it?" she said, incredulity sounding in her voice. "That's all he says? We need to speak to him. Call him back, Gid."

Gideon narrowed his eyes. "I'll text first," he said slowly, suiting the action to the word. "You tell Mum and Dad why we've stopped."

Abi opened her mouth to speak, then thought better of it. She jumped out of the car and ran back to relate the latest developments to Gideon's parents, then came and climbed into her seat again.

"Well?" she asked. "What did you say?"

"Told him where we are," Gideon said, frowning at

the screen on his phone. "Asked him to call us."

Abi sat forward in her seat and peered out into the gloom. It was still very cloudy, and the moon hadn't managed to break through and supply them with any light. She couldn't help a tiny feeling of relief that Natasha wasn't roaming around in the woods on her own. Simon had said she was safe, so presumably that meant she was with him. They both jumped as Gideon's phone suddenly began to ring. Abi reached out to pick it up, but Gideon's hand was there before hers.

"Sorry, Abs. We want to get her back. This needs to be done with some diplomacy," he told her, as he lifted the phone to his ear. "Simon. Where is she?" He listened, his face like thunder. "Yes...Yes, we're on that road now...All right, we'll be there in five minutes." He disconnected the call and put his phone down on the dashboard.

Abi stared at him. "Well?" she demanded impatiently. "What's happening? Where are they?"

Gideon started the car and set off along the road at a dangerous speed. "They're in a cottage in the woods about a mile or so further on. He says it's easy to find if we stay on this road."

"But what about Tasha?" Abi persisted, sitting forward and touching him lightly on the arm.

Gideon spoke without taking his eyes off the road. "Didn't ask. He didn't mention her."

"What? Why didn't you ask?" she demanded.

"Mustn't antagonise him. He already said she's safe. We're nearly there, Abs. Be patient. You know how volatile he is."

"So am I," Abi muttered, sitting back and crossing her arms across her chest.

Gideon reached over and squeezed her leg. "Nearly there, Abs. Keep it together and leave the talking to me."

She shot him a dangerous look, then glanced over her shoulder at the following car. "What about them?" she asked, jerking her head backwards. "Does he know they're with us?"

Gideon shook his head and glanced in the mirror. "No. Good point. We can use them as emergency backup. Hang on." He pulled up at the side of the road and screeched to a halt.

Roger pulled in behind him and immediately got out and walked quickly up to them. "What's going on?" he asked bending down at the window.

"Simon called. They're at a cottage just up here. We're to go there now. I think it would be best if you and Mum hang back in case we need backup. Follow us until you see us turn off, then park somewhere unobtrusive until we call you."

Roger nodded his assent and hurried back to his car, following as soon as Gideon took off again.

Five minutes later, they were driving slowly up a narrow track that appeared to lead directly into the forest. Abi sat forward in her seat, peering intently out of the window.

"Look." She pointed ahead. "There's a light. We must be nearly there."

Gideon increased his speed and pulled up in front of the little house with a squeal of brakes. In a single bound he was out of the car and hammering on the door.

Abi followed him and caught his arm. "Be diplomatic," she reminded him. "Otherwise I take over!"

The door swung open, and a slightly sweaty Simon stood before them. His pale blue shirt was stained at the armpits, and his dyed hair was curling more tightly than usual. Abi's eyes widened at the sight of his moustache and hair, and she braced herself, ready to enter the house, attempting to put the previous summer's encounter to the back of her mind.

Simon remained in the doorway and stared at them through narrowed eyes. "We need to talk," he said. "Your child is safe, but we need to talk first, before you see her. Unless you agree to those terms, you can't come in." His demeanour was defensive, and his knuckles were gleaming white on the doorframe.

Gideon took a step forward, his hands balled into fists by his side. "Fuck talking..." he began, but Abi caught his arm and pulled him back.

"We agree," she said firmly, staring Simon in the eyes.

He hesitated for a moment, then stood back and gestured for them to enter the house. Keeping a tight hold of Gideon's hand, Abi stepped over the threshold and forced herself to walk past Simon into the dark hallway. Simon slammed the door behind them and ushered them into the small living room.

"Sit down," he said shortly, waiting by the door until they complied.

"Where's Natasha?" Abi's voice was tightly controlled, her eyes never leaving his face.

"She's safe." Simon leaned against the wall opposite them and lit a cigarette with slightly shaky hands. "You can see her soon. So long as you do as I ask." He paused and looked closely at them both. "I have someone watching her, and if you try anything, all I have to do is press this button on my phone and he'll drive off with her. Understand?"

Gideon sucked in his breath and gripped Abi's hand tightly. "Get on with it," he hissed through clenched teeth.

Simon surveyed them carefully. "When Natasha turned up here, she played right into my hands. She'd managed to escape from the useless driver I employed, but her dreadful sense of direction brought her right to my door." He smirked at them. "My plan had been to get you here and then persuade you to call the police off so I could get my life back. I wanted to apologise for last summer and see if we could make friends." He paused again and considered. "Your kid told me the police think I drowned and so have probably not been looking for me very hard. I guess that's why my rather meagre disguise has worked so well. Anyway, I guess I still want us to be friends again. I figured you'd never agree to speak with me, so I decided the only way to get your attention was to use your kid. Guess that worked." He stared at Abi. "She also told me you didn't want to press charges but the police insisted. Are you crazy? If someone shot me, I'd want them locked up."

Abi took a deep breath and tried to keep her voice calm. "I didn't want to press charges because I thought, maybe erroneously as it turns out, that you were acting out of character. That the monster we confronted at Worm's Head wasn't the real you. I wanted you to have a second chance." She paused and glanced at Gideon before continuing. "He wanted to throw the book at you, and to be perfectly honest, I now realise he was right. How could you possibly think that by kidnapping our daughter you would get us to agree to be your friends again? Simon, you are seriously deranged if you honestly thought that. Now, where is she? This has gone on long enough."

Simon picked up his phone. "One press and she disappears again," he threatened. "You agree to what I want, and you can see her straight away. Take her away with you. She's a fucking liability anyway."

Abi glanced at Gideon again, biting back the words she really wanted to speak.

Gideon squeezed her hand. "What do you want then, Simon?" he asked quietly, his demeanour deceptively calm. "You haven't actually said yet."

"Yes, I did." Simon frowned at him. "I want my life back. I want to be free of all this. No police, nothing hanging over me. Free to go about my business."

"So not only do you want forgiveness for last summer," Gideon began, "but now, having compounded your crime by kidnapping my daughter, you expect us to forgive everything and let you walk free? Is that it? Or do you want to join the band again, too? Be my best friend again? Is that what you want, Simon?"

Simon swallowed audibly and took a step towards them. "I want my life back," he repeated. "I know you'll never have me back in the band. I haven't hurt the kid. I just used her as a means to get you here. I admit last summer was wrong. I never really wanted to kill them. I'm sorry for that." He paused and moistened his lips. "Forget about this, and try and get the police to drop charges for last year, and I'll leave you alone for ever. Maybe one day we can be friends again."

Gideon stared at him in amazement. "Seriously? You seriously think we could ever be friends again? Jesus, Simon, you really do have problems." He paused and took a very deep breath. "However I"—he emphasised the pronoun—"do agree to your other terms in order to get our daughter back. You can walk free from here just as soon as she's back in our car. Until that time, you stay right with us." He squeezed Abi's hand tightly and pulled her to her feet. "Now take us to her, and then you can go where the fuck you want and never come near us again."

Simon looked at him doubtfully for a moment. "And you'll call the police off?" he asked. Gideon inclined his head, and Simon nodded briefly and indicated they should follow him. He led the way through the small kitchen and opened the half-glazed back door that led to the back yard.

Abi frowned. "Where are we going?" she asked suspiciously. "I thought she was here with you. Why are we going outside?"

Simon turned. "She's in the shed." He pointed to a small wooden building a few yards from the back door. "She was being a right pest, and I needed to keep her locked up. She's quite safe."

Abi gasped. "So there was no one guarding her at all?" she said, her voice icy.

Simon shrugged. "Needed some way to make sure you did as I wanted. Don't worry. She's fine. She's only been in there a couple of hours."

"A couple of hours!" Abi's voice rose in horror. "Tasha hates being locked in small spaces. Why isn't she screaming? What have you done to her?" She ran over to the shed door and began to tug at it. "Tash!

Tash! Are you all right? We're here to get you."

Simon pushed her aside and inserted a key in the padlock. "I haven't done anything to her," he muttered as he eased the metal post out of the hook. "Look, she's fine." And he swung the door open.

Abi rushed straight into the dark building, while Gideon stayed in the doorway, one eye fixed firmly on Simon.

"Gid?" Abi's voice shook with fear. "Gid, she's not here! Where is she? He's tricked us." Tears began to trickle down her cheeks as she peered desperately around the obviously empty shed.

In a single movement, Gideon had Simon pinned up against the rough wooden wall, his hand clasped around the other man's neck. "Where the fuck is she?" he snapped, his eyes flashing dangerously. "Tell me now, or I'll kill you right here, right now, just like I should have done last summer. Where is she?"

Simon's face suffused with colour, and he tried to shake his head.

"She was in there, Gid—really, she was in there. I locked her in myself." His voice croaked as Gideon's hand squeezed tighter. "Honestly, man, I didn't hurt her! She really was in there!"

"Gid!" Abi appeared in the doorway, her eyes shining with tears. "I think she's escaped. There's a broken plank in the back wall. I think there's room for her to get through. There's certainly evidence someone has been moving around in here. The ground is all messed up."

Gideon let go of Simon's throat, and the other man fell to the ground, gasping for air. "Get up," he snapped at him. "You're not going anywhere." He strode into the shed and stared at the back wall where Abi was on her knees, peering through the narrow hole.

"Yes, I'm sure she could have got through here," she said, getting to her feet with a nod. "I'm going to get her. She must be in the forest. She can't have got far. You give Simon to your parents to deal with, and then come and find me." In a flash she ran past them both and disappeared off into the forest behind the shed without another word.

Gideon stared after her, his arm shooting out to catch her. "Abs, wait! I'll come too."

"Catch me up…" Her voice floated back to him as she bounded away into the woods. "Can't waste any more time."

Gideon swung back round to face Simon. He brought his face up close and snarled at him. "You're coming with me. No escape this time."

"But you said I could go if…" Simon started to whine, sweat dripping down his face and soaking his collar.

Gideon turned on him. "I said if you gave us our daughter back *I* would agree to your terms." Once again he emphasised the pronoun. "I never said Abi would agree to them. And anyway, you reneged on the deal. No daughter, no deal. Come on." He pushed Simon roughly in front of him, back through the house.

Chapter 26

Thursday 7ᵗʰ May, 2009

Natasha sat slumped against the rough wooden wall of the shed, her eyes firmly fixed on the darkest cobwebby corner. The memories that her incarceration had triggered had left her feeling bereft and insecure, and she pulled her knees up to her chin to hug them tightly. She had completely buried the events of her fostering experience, and to have them suddenly dragged to the surface was traumatic. She had never told anyone about it, preferring, even at the tender age of four, to bury it deep in her subconscious. Now it had fought its way out, and her head was pounding with the memories.

She closed her eyes tightly, willing the pictures in her head to disappear—to vanish back into the deep recesses of her mind. Maybe if she concentrated on her present predicament that would help. Opening her eyes again and resting her chin on her knees, she considered her position. She was fairly sure Simon meant her no actual harm and was probably just keeping her out of the way until her parents arrived.

However, she had no proof of that, and if there was any way she could manage to escape, then that was definitely what she should do. She peered around the room cautiously, carefully avoiding the very dark corner, and assessed the situation. She remembered that when she'd first entered the shed she had noticed a small amount of light filtering between some badly fitting planks.

Her eyes quickly flitted around the shed searching for them again. It had got noticeably darker, and no light was appearing from anywhere. Natasha recalled that originally the light had seemed to come from the back wall, so she dropped to her knees on the cold hard ground and began to feel her way along the rough wood. Eventually her fingers encountered slight movement in one of the planks, and with her heart beating almost audibly in her chest, she attempted to insert a finger underneath it. The gap was too small, and she muttered an oath under her breath, then sat back on her heels and thought for a moment.

A small smile appeared on her lips, and she slipped her hand down inside her Converse and pulled out the tiny penknife Lydia had given her. She had no idea what had prompted her to hide it there, but when Simon had searched her bag she had been glad of her deception.

She grinned in the dark and inserted the blade of the little knife under the plank. It began to move towards her, and after a few moments the gap was large enough for her to get three fingers in. She hooked them securely around the wood and pulled hard. The plank began to creak, but then she lost her grip, fell back on her bottom, and the wood sprang back into place. She crawled forward again, and this time she was able to get her fingers underneath it again straight away. She manoeuvred it so she could get three fingers from each hand underneath, and with an almighty tug she managed to crack the plank. She took a deep breath and, with both hands gripping firmly, tugged and twisted as hard as she could until the broken piece came away in her hands. Then she sat back and surveyed her work.

The hole she'd created was approximately two feet high but only about four or five inches across. There was no way she could fit through that. She crawled over to it again and caught hold of the next plank, firmly, with both hands. She pulled at it, and to her delight it began to move slightly. She gently began to wiggle it backwards and forwards until it began to come away from the rest of the wall. Hooking her foot underneath it and using that and both hands, she finally managed to break it off at a similar height to the first one.

She grinned in the darkness. The hole was now about two feet high and ten inches wide, and Natasha reckoned that with a bit of wriggling she could fit through. She took off her hoody so as to make it easier, tossed it through in front of her, then lay down on her side and stuck her head through the hole. She wriggled forward, kicking with her feet, until she got one hand out and followed it by levering the rest of her body out to lie panting on the cold ground behind the shed. She quickly pulled her hoody back over her head, then cautiously got to her feet. Keeping bent low, she crept around the shed and headed into the forest, back the way she had originally come.

After about five minutes, Natasha's steps slowed, and she bent forward with her hands on her knees to catch her breath. She reckoned she was far enough away from the cottage to be able to take stock of her situation and her position. She was well aware that on her earlier trip through the forest she had got her bearings wrong, so she now knew that the road was to her left, and not to her right as she had first thought.

She stood upright and stared around her. This trip wasn't going to be so easy. This time she had no torch, and the moon was still obscured by clouds. She leant against a tree and waited for her eyes to become better accustomed to the dark, all the time keeping her ears open for any sounds of pursuit. She felt fairly confident Simon wouldn't yet have discovered her absence, and she also felt that if he had he wouldn't be very much use in a dark forest. She was also confident of her ability to elude him were he to pursue her. Now all she needed to do was to make her way back to the road and hopefully either intercept her parents when they came to rescue her or make her way to the next house or farm and ask for help. She took a deep breath and squinted ahead of herself into the dark forest.

It was still almost impossible to see anything. So long as she followed the path she had started out on, she would be all right, but in order to get back to the road she was going to need to veer off to her left at some point. That was when her difficulties would start. She held her breath and listened intently, just in case she could hear any sounds that might indicate the road wasn't too far away. There was nothing. Natasha sighed. She was beginning to get hungry again, and she badly needed to pee. She managed to deal with the second problem fairly easily, but realised she would just have to put up with the hunger. She didn't even have a piece of chewing gum in her pocket.

Slowly she started to carry on along the path, taking great care not to trip on the dense undergrowth, all the while keeping her eyes peeled for any paths that led off to the left, to possibly take her to the road. She could still hear no sounds other than those of the wildlife in the woods, and as she hurried along she began to feel very lost and alone again.

The memories that had surfaced while she was incarcerated in the shed had affected her deeply, and she badly needed to talk to someone about them, preferably her mother. A solitary tear trickled down her cheek as she once more relived the feelings she had experienced as a small child, and she brushed it away impatiently. Now was not the time to start getting emotional. She really needed to keep her wits about her if she was going to find her way out of the forest and back to her parents.

Her steps slowed as she approached the clearing she had found earlier in the evening, and she came to a halt in the centre of it. Her legs were aching, and she realised just how tired she was. She had been up and on the go since six o'clock that morning, and by her calculations it must now be after ten in the evening. She walked over to a large tree in the centre of the clearing and sat down in front of it. She leant back against its rough trunk and closed her eyes. No harm in having a tiny rest—just for a few minutes to get her strength back.

****

When Abi set off into the woods in pursuit of Natasha, she had no real plan in mind. All she knew was that she had to find her daughter and would die trying if she had to. She shone her torch in front of her as she ran, making wide sweeps with the beam in order to take in as much of the woods as possible.

She had heard Gideon calling for her to wait, but she knew that the longer Natasha was alone in the woods, the harder it would be to find her and the more terrified the child would get. They had no way of knowing when she'd escaped from the shed, and she could have been out there for as much as an hour already. Abi realised Natasha wouldn't have her torch with her, because Simon had told them he'd taken her phone from her when she arrived.

Her pace slowed to a fast walk, and she felt her heart thundering in her chest. Her breath was coming in ragged bursts, and if she hadn't been fuelled by adrenaline, she would probably have collapsed sobbing in a heap on the forest floor. She swung her torch around in front of her, illuminating the rough path that ran through the woods. If Natasha had no light, she would probably have kept to the path where possible, so Abi set off again, jogging slowly, her eyes alternating between the way ahead and the uneven ground beneath her feet.

The dense undergrowth to either side encroached onto the path, and Abi grimaced with pain as long trailing brambles whipped around her ankles and tried to impede her progress. She pulled her feet free and continued on her way, leaping over obstacles where necessary, her eyes always on the lookout for clues to her daughter's whereabouts.

Suddenly something small and white got caught in the beam of her torch, and she stopped abruptly. She bent down and shone her light directly on the item. It was a screwed up tissue. She gently prodded it with her toe. It was dry, and still relatively clean. Since arriving in New Zealand, Natasha had had a lot of problems with hay fever, and consequently she always had a good number of tissues stuffed up her sleeves and in her pockets. This one had clearly only been on the forest floor a very short time, and Abi stood up and stared around her, her heart pounding in her chest in anticipation. She put her hands up to her mouth and shouted as loudly as she could, "Tasha! Tasha, are you there?"

When she got no reply, she set off again at a fast trot, all the time keeping her eyes peeled for any more clues. She guessed Natasha would have been trying to get back to the road for a better chance of getting help, and she kept a close eye on the undergrowth to her left for any signs of it being trampled underfoot. There had been no paths leading off in either direction since she left the cottage, and she kept her fingers crossed that Natasha had stayed on the path and not attempted to force her way through the dense undergrowth.

No more clues presented themselves, so Abi continued in the same direction, making careful sweeps with her torch as she did. The forest was eerily silent, and her heart clenched as she thought how terrified her daughter would be if she was in there alone. As she raised her eyes to do another sweep with her light, she failed to notice a large root sticking out of the path in front of her, and fell heavily, rolling onto a branch and causing a loud crack that echoed around her.

The sound caused a number of birds to take off from the trees, while Abi lay on the ground catching her breath. She struggled to her feet, brushed herself down, and once more shone her light all around her. This time she noticed she was coming close to a large clearing. In the hope that this might have a path leading towards the road, Abi picked up her speed and headed towards it.

****

Natasha awoke with a start to the sound of birds squawking and taking off from the trees. She sat for a moment disoriented, her heart pounding uncomfortably in her chest. Then she pushed herself away from the tree and up onto her knees. Something must have startled the birds.

She got cautiously to her feet and strained her eyes in the dark. How could she have allowed herself to fall asleep? She scowled in the dark. Just when she really needed to keep her wits about her, and she fell asleep. A slight sound from the direction of Simon's cottage caught her attention, and her head snapped round. She screwed up her eyes and peered at where the path ran through the forest.

After a moment she saw a tiny light flickering in the trees. She caught her breath and stepped back against the large tree, her hands feeling behind her for something secure. She edged her way behind its huge trunk, all the while keeping her eyes fixed on the bobbing light. She was sure it was Simon, coming to find her and take her back. He would have discovered she'd escaped, and he'd be even more angry than he had been before.

Natasha glanced around her desperately. The tree didn't provide nearly enough cover; she needed something she could really hide behind. The light was getting ever closer, and she dropped to her knees in an attempt to avoid its searching beam. Scrambling across the forest floor, she made her way to the cover of some large bushes next to the path. From there she would be able to see whoever was following her yet remain hidden from view.

She held her breath and pressed back against the prickly foliage. She could hear the footsteps coming closer, and her sharp ears could just detect heavy breathing from her pursuer. She shrank back even further into the bush and resisted the temptation to screw her eyes tightly shut. She wanted to see who it was, just in case it wasn't Simon, and she peered intently through the leaves.

Suddenly a figure came into view, slowing as they approached the clearing, then coming to a halt just in front of Natasha's hiding place. She strained to see through the leaves, then couldn't contain the squeak of surprise that escaped her lips. In a flash the leaves of the bush parted, and Abi stood staring down at her.

Natasha looked up at her, her eyes huge, a memory suddenly triggered, and as one they gasped, "It was you! In the museum..."

They stared at each other, and Abi dropped to her knees in front of her daughter. "Tasha," she croaked, her voice full of emotion. "You're all right." She flung her arms around her, and the two of them clung together, tears of relief beginning to roll down their cheeks. "It was you—in the museum," Abi repeated obscurely, her lips pressed into Natasha's hair. "You were hiding in the corner. Do you remember too?" She pulled back and stared down at her daughter's tear-streaked face.

Natasha nodded slowly. "Yes," she whispered. "I remember. I remember it very well."

Chapter 27

Late July, 2001—Bath

Natasha was bored. Very bored. They had left the children's home very early that morning, and it seemed to her they'd been in the minibus for about a month. She sighed and pressed her nose against the cold glass of the window. The countryside flying by was alien to her, and she wriggled in annoyance at having been torn from her nice comfy bed so early in the day. It was the summer holidays, and they were usually allowed to stay in bed a little bit later.

According to Aunty Cathy, they were going on a very exciting day out to Bath. Natasha was annoyed about that, too; she had had a bath the night before and didn't think she needed another one just yet. As she watched out the window, the minibus began to slow and make its way into a busy town. She curled her legs up under her on the seat and sighed again. She was the youngest child on the bus, and she was fairly sure that wasn't a good thing.

The girl sitting next to her smiled at her. "You all right, Tasha?" she asked kindly. "We're nearly there. Are you bored?"

Natasha nodded silently, her blue eyes serious. "Yes," she said dismally. "And I don't need another bath, either."

The girl looked startled, then began to giggle. "Oh, Tasha, you don't have to *have* a bath. We are going to a place *called* Bath!" She patted the younger girl on the shoulder. "Silly little thing. We are going to have a brill day. We're gonna see loads of in'sting things."

"What sort of things?" Natasha looked suspicious.

"Oh, museums and stuff." The girl waved her hand vaguely. "An' we're gonna have a picnic lunch. It'll be fun."

Natasha was unconvinced. She had no idea what a museum was, and was very concerned about the "and stuff." That could be anything. She was fairly sure she was going to be spending the day walking around things she didn't understand. She looked up at her companion.

"Will you stay with me, Jenny?" she asked in a small voice.

"'Course I will." Jenny grinned at her, her freckled face lighting up. "I'll make sure you don't get lost. An' I can 'splain all the stuff to you," she added confidently from the vantage point of a very wise eleven years.

Natasha smiled at her, then settled back in her seat feeling a little happier. She was very fond of the older girl, and if she could spend the day in her company it would probably be all right.

A couple of hours later she was not so sure. Their first visit had been to something that was called the Roman Baths. It looked like a dirty swimming pool to Natasha, and she made sure she kept in the background in case anyone suggested she take a dip. Then they'd visited a large house that seemed to be decorated in a very old-fashioned way, and everyone except Natasha had appeared to enjoy it. She stuck close to Jenny and made sure she kept up with the others, but she didn't really understand what all the fuss was about. When they finally walked back out of the house into the huge crescent-shaped road, Natasha was beginning to feel very hungry and thirsty. She squeezed Jenny's hand as they hurried along the pavement after the rest of the group.

Jenny squeezed back. "Are you okay?" she asked the little girl kindly.

"I'm thirsty an' hungry," Natasha replied sadly, dragging her feet on the hot pavement. "Can we have lunch soon?"

"I'm hungry too. Let's go an' ask Aunty Cathy, shall we?" Jenny replied with a smile, and pulling Natasha behind her, she trotted to the front of the line and fell into step beside Cathy Masters. "Aunty Cathy, me an' Tasha are hungry. Are we having lunch soon?" she asked with a winning smile.

Cathy smiled at the two girls and nodded. "Very soon, girls. We're going to have our lunch in Royal Victoria Park, just over there." She pointed ahead of them. "It's a lovely place for a picnic, and you can all have a run around on the grass. I've brought some balls with us."

Jenny squeezed Natasha's hand again, with another smile. "There you go, nearly time for food. That sounds more fun, doesn't it?"

Natasha nodded her curly head, and Cathy smiled at her. "Getting a bit bored, Tash?" she asked kindly. "I'm afraid it's all a bit old for you. Never mind. This afternoon we're going to the Museum of Costume. You may like that a bit better. Lots of clothes that people wore in the old days. Some of them are really pretty, and some are very strange. Now let's get to the park and have a run around." She led the way across a busy road and through the entrance to the park.

Natasha smiled as they found a nice spot to set up their picnic, and within a couple of seconds she had kicked off her sandals and socks and was running around barefoot on the newly mown grass. Cathy produced a couple of balls, and the children had a happy half an hour playing in the sun before settling down and partaking of a very tasty picnic.

By the time Cathy called for the children to get their shoes back on and help to pack up the picnic, Natasha was feeling much happier. She had a full tummy and had had a lovely time rolling about on the grass. The front of her blue and white summer dress was covered in green stains, and her chubby face was covered in chocolate.

Cathy laughed at her. "Come here, Tasha," she said, pulling the child towards her. "Let's get the worst of that off your face, shall we?" and she rubbed at Natasha's cheeks with a damp tissue. Natasha screwed up her face and tried to wriggle free, but Cathy was persistent and refused to let her go until her face was acceptable. "There you go. Now you can be seen in public again!" she said with a laugh, ruffling the little girl's curls. "Now stay with Jenny while we walk to the museum."

They set off through the town again in the direction of the Assembly Rooms, where the Museum of Costume was located. Natasha skipped along beside Jenny feeling much more refreshed and ready to face the museum, whatever it turned out to be. She wondered why there needed to be a museum to put old clothes in—surely it was better to send them to a charity shop. Still, she was prepared to have a look at it. Aunty Cathy seemed to think she would enjoy it. She really wished they could have gone to the zoo, or even to an art gallery where she could have seen some pictures of animals. Next time they were planning a trip, she would have to ask to do that.

It took them about fifteen minutes to walk across the town to the museum, and by the time they got there all the children were thirsty again. Cathy quickly whipped out water bottles for them all, then did a head count and ushered them into the museum.

With a quick word to the older children to keep an eye on the little ones, Cathy gave them permission to wander around and view the exhibits on their own, promising to meet back at the entrance in an hour.

Jenny caught Natasha by the hand, and they hurried after the others in the direction of the special display located on the lower ground floor of the museum. They ran down the stairs and emerged in the huge exhibition room at the bottom of the building.

Natasha stared around her in awe. The room was dark, the only light coming from within the huge glass display cases that housed the clothes. She let go of Jenny's hand and wandered towards a display of eighteenth-century French dresses. She stared up at them in amazement. They were a very funny shape. She put her head on one side and tried to decide how they worked.

The top part of the dress was all right—fairly tight, with three-quarter-length sleeves and buttons up the front—but the skirt! Natasha pressed her nose against the glass and wondered what shape people had been in the old days. The skirt of the dress stuck out on both sides like a shelf before billowing out and falling to the floor. Natasha looked down at her body and ran her hands down over her hips. They didn't have shelves that stuck out at the side. People must have been made very differently in those days. She shook her head in wonder and wandered along to the next display cabinet.

She had to admit it was more fun than the Roman Baths or the old house had been, and she soon got quite caught up in the strange and sometimes beautiful clothes that were on display. She decided she would like to try drawing some of them when she got home, and she turned to tell Jenny, only to discover the older girl was no longer with her.

She looked around nervously, suddenly realising she was all alone in the dark room. She stood perfectly still and listened intently to see if she could work out which way the others had gone, but she could hear nothing. She sidled over to one of the cabinets and leant against the glass for a moment.

She could feel tears pricking at the back of her eyes and screwed her hands into fists at her sides. She wasn't going to cry. That was for babies. Jenny would find her if she just stayed where she was. That was the best thing to do. She glanced fearfully over her shoulder at the headless models in the cabinet. Unless the ghosts got her first. She backed away from the display and glanced around her quickly. She needed somewhere safe to hide until Jenny found her.

Noticing a small display cabinet that housed some pairs of jewelled gloves, Natasha squeezed herself behind it and crouched down. She could still see if anyone was coming, but they wouldn't be able to see her, and since she had her back to the wall, no one could creep up on her. Even ghosts. She heard footsteps approaching and held her body tense, waiting to see who it was.

****

Abi had managed to find a parking space fairly close to the centre of Bath, locked her new little car, and set off on what would hopefully be a lovely day. She had finished her teaching course at Exeter University a few weeks before, and in another few weeks she was moving into a little cottage she'd found to rent in the village of Sennen in Cornwall. She had passed her driving test, managed to buy a nice little car with the money she'd made painting portraits of the other students, and she'd finally got a mobile phone.

All in all, she was feeling quite pleased with herself, and happy her life seemed to be going well. She had also got herself a part-time job teaching art at a primary school near her new home, and with the night school class she was planning to run, she thought she would be able to get by quite comfortably.

She was feeling particularly hungry, so she slipped into Marks and Spencer's to pick up a sandwich. As she passed through the clothing department, she caught sight of herself in one of the mirrors and gave a start of surprise. She grinned to herself. As part of the end of term celebrations at Exeter, she and Judy had dyed their hair, and she still had bright blue streaks mixed in with her normal auburn colour.

She shook her head in despair—the things they did without thinking! She hadn't realised just how silly it looked. She made a mental note to wash her hair several times when she got back. She bought a sandwich and carried it out into the hot sunshine, where she found a bench to sit on. She had made the visit to Bath as a nostalgic trip to look up all her favourite places from when she was at Art College. Although she had not been very happy at that time, she still had some lovely memories and had adored the town itself.

Her most favourite haunt had been the Museum of Costume, and she was planning a trip there straight away. A group of giggling children accompanied by two smiling ladies passed her by as she ate her sandwich, and she had a little shiver of excitement when she realised she would be teaching soon and would be able to take her class on trips out. How very grown-up, she thought to herself with a wry grin, then tossed her wrapper into the nearest bin, wiped her hands on her tissue, and made her way towards the museum.

Abi had spent many a happy hour in the museum during her Art School days, sketching the clothes and generally just soaking up the atmosphere, and she was really looking forward to revisiting it. She paid her entrance fee and started down the stairs to the basement. She could hear giggles from a group of children ahead of her, and she couldn't help hoping they'd moved on to the next section before she got there. The thing she liked best was when she could have the place to herself. Then she could wander at will, taking as long as she liked on each exhibit and letting her imagination transport her to an earlier time.

As she reached the large exhibition area she smiled to herself. The room appeared to be empty, so the children must have already passed through and gone on to the next part. She wandered up to a large display case and stared at the beautiful eighteenth-century dresses on show. Although she was a thoroughly modern young lady, Abi could easily imagine herself wearing one of the elaborately ornamented dresses and mixing with the people of the pre-revolutionary French court. She smiled as she imagined trying to manoeuvre the huge skirts through throngs of people. As she turned to look at a smaller display cabinet to her right, a tiny sound caught her attention. She stepped back and peered round the side of the cabinet. A pair of bright blue eyes stared back at her, framed by a mass of dark curls. Abi gave a start of surprise and looked down at the little girl hiding in the shadows, her face serious. She was just about to offer her assistance when the sound of running footsteps heralded the arrival of a lanky girl of about eleven. She stopped when she saw Abi and peered round her to see what she was looking at.

"There you are!" she exclaimed, relief sounding in her voice. "I've been lookin' everywhere for you! Come on, it's time to go now," and she reached in and caught the little girl by the hand, pulling her out of her hiding place and past Abi. For just a second Abi and the little girl stared at each other. Then the children disappeared around the corner, and Abi was left in silence again. She shivered and shook off a morbid thought—Her own little girl would have been about that age by now.

Chapter 28

Thursday 7ᵗʰ May, 2009

"But it *was* me!" Natasha's voice cracked with emotion as she stared in consternation at her mother. "It *was* me. We met all those years ago, and we didn't know each other." The tears were pouring down her cheeks, and she flung her arms around Abi's neck. "We didn't know each other, and we should have done!"

"Of course we didn't," Abi said, gently stroking her daughter's head. "How could we? I thought you were dead, and you had no idea what I looked like. There was no way we could have known who each other was." She paused and stared over Natasha's head into the dark forest. "We might never have found this out if you hadn't hidden behind that bush." She pulled back a little and smiled at her. "You looked just the same, you know. All big eyes, curly hair, and solemn face."

Natasha sniffed and rubbed her nose on her sleeve. "Your hair was weird," she remembered suddenly, frowning. "It didn't look like it does now. If it had, I might have recognised you when we met properly. What was different?"

Abi looked slightly embarrassed. "It had blue streaks," she said apologetically. "Judy and I had dyed our hair to celebrate leaving Uni, and it hadn't all washed out by then. It probably looked really silly."

Natasha gave a watery smile. "Yeah, I guess it did," she said. "I've never forgotten that day. I was really scared in the museum. I thought the dummies were going to come to life and chase me, and I'd lost Jenny, who was looking after me. When you appeared I thought you were a ghost!"

Abi grinned. "A ghost with blue hair," she said with a giggle. "I've never forgotten it either. It was so dark all I could see of you was the big eyes and the curls. You were much older when we finally met, and of course I never thought to connect the two." She looked down at Natasha in concern. "Are you all right? Here we are bothering about something that happened eight years ago, and you've just been kidnapped! He didn't hurt you, did he?"

Natasha shook her head. "No. He gave me food." She paused and bit her lip. "Then he locked me in the shed." She raised huge eyes to her mother. "I didn't like that."

"I'm sure you didn't," Abi agreed, her eyes darkening. "That must have been scary. Listen, I must tell your father you're all right. Hang on a sec..." She fished her phone out of her pocket and quickly dialled his number. "Gid...Yeah, I've found her. She's fine...Yeah, I know, but he didn't hurt her...Okay, if you like, but we can just make our way back to the cottage and meet you there...All right. That does make more sense. Silly, you coming out here. We'll only be a few minutes." She held the phone out to Natasha. "He wants to speak to you—make sure you're all right."

Shakily Natasha took the phone and held it to her ear. "Dad? I'm okay." She listened, her mouth curving into a slight smile. "I know…He didn't hurt me, but if you want to anyway…Okay, love you, Dad, see you in a minute." She disconnected the call and handed the phone back to Abi, a gleam in her eye.

"What did he say?" Abi asked suspiciously, narrowing her eyes.

Natasha grinned. "He says he's gonna beat Simon up. He says he needs to, to make himself feel better." She shrugged. "I said that was all right by me…" She giggled as Abi swore and leapt to her feet.

"Well, it's not all right by me," she said firmly, pulling Natasha to her feet. "I'm not having him end up in prison too. Come on. We'd better get back and sort them out. Grandma and Grandpa are with us, too."

They started jogging slowly back through the forest towards the cottage, Abi holding tight to Natasha's hand. After a few minutes Natasha slowed to a stop.

"Can we walk?" she asked, taking a deep breath. "I'm too tired to jog any more."

"Oh, darling, I'm sorry!" Abi was contrite. "I forgot what a day you've had. Of course we can walk. You can start to tell me what happened to you, if you like, or do you want to wait and tell us all together?"

Natasha shrugged. "S'pose I should tell you all together, really," she said. "Saves doing it twice. But Mum…" She stood still, looking slightly awkward. "What happened about…do I have another brother?"

So much had happened since their meeting with Nancy that just for a second Abi couldn't think what she meant. When she realised, she gave a short laugh. "Oh! No, you don't," she said with a smile. "It was all a setup to get your father and me out of the way so Simon could kidnap you. The child is Simon's."

Natasha gasped. "Really? Wow! Is there anything he hasn't done?" she said in surprise. "Was it horrid, meeting one of Dad's girlfriends?"

"Ex-girlfriends," Abi corrected with a scowl. "Yes, it was dreadful. Especially when I realised I'd met her before…" Natasha gasped, and Abi went on. "It was years ago in Bristol. She knew who I was at the time, but she didn't tell Dad."

Natasha stared at her in horror. "Mum! What did you do? I would have killed her!"

Abi gave a little giggle. "Well, Dad did have to pull me off her," she admitted. "It was a tense few minutes. I'll tell you the whole story later. It seems it's been a time of memories, hasn't it?"

Natasha bit her lip. "Yeah," she said quietly. "I had another one in the shed, too." Abi looked at her questioningly. "It made me remember the time when I was fostered by some people. The boy locked me in the shed." She stopped, and her face took on a closed look. "I've never told anyone about it. I don't want to talk about it now. I'll tell you and Dad later."

Abi took her hand and squeezed it tightly. "Whenever you're ready, pet. Now let's get back and prevent a bloodbath."

When they finally arrived back at Simon's cottage, it was a hive of activity. Roger and Caroline had driven up, and Caroline stood watching the path into the woods anxiously. A police car had pulled up alongside them, and sounds from within the house alerted Abi to the fact that Gideon was inside. Caroline stepped forward as they appeared and opened her arms out to Natasha, who ran into them and buried her face in her grandmother's shoulder.

"Oh, Grandma," she whispered. "It's so good to see you. Sorry I caused such trouble."

Caroline squeezed her tightly and glanced at Abi over her head. Abi gave a little smile and nodded, then disappeared into the house. Two policemen, Simon, Roger, and Gideon were crowded into the tiny living room, and Abi stopped in the doorway, slightly out of breath after her jaunt through the forest.

Gideon glanced round at her. "Abi, is she really all right?" He barked the words out, his hand clutching Simon's arm.

Abi stepped forward and stood beside him. "Yes, she's fine," she said at once, trying to assess the situation. The police were hovering uncertainly to one side, while Gideon and Simon appeared to be in the middle of a row. Both men had red faces, and Gideon's eyes were sparking dangerously. "What's going on, Gideon?" she asked with a frown. "Are the police not here to arrest Simon?"

Gideon scowled at her. "Yeah, Dad called them, but I haven't finished with him yet." He moved forward as if to catch Simon round the throat. The policemen both moved towards them, but Abi jumped between Gideon and Simon and put her hand on Gideon's arm.

"Leave it, Gid," she ordered tersely. "You'll be no use to anyone if you get arrested too. Let the police do their job." She watched him closely as he narrowed his eyes at his former friend, but made no move to stand down. "Gideon, do as I say. You'll achieve nothing if you fight with him. Let them have him."

"I'll achieve personal satisfaction," ground out Gideon through gritted teeth. "Let me have that."

"Dad!" Natasha's voice cut through his words, and

she flew across the room towards him, flinging her arms around his waist. "Dad, I'm so sorry I got kidnapped. I shouldn't have gone to see Billy. I've caused you so much trouble."

Gideon relaxed slightly and stepped back from Simon, putting his arms around his daughter and holding her close. "It's not your fault," he murmured into her hair. "God, Tasha, we were so worried. Are you sure you're okay? He didn't hurt you?" He pulled back from her and stared down into her face.

She shook her head. "No. He gave me soup. He wasn't mean." She paused, and wrinkled her nose a bit. "Until he locked me in the shed. I didn't like that." She turned her head and scowled at Simon. "I hope you go to prison," she said sharply to him. "You really can't go round behaving like that."

Abi stifled a small smile and put her hand on Natasha's shoulder. "I expect he will," she said, her eyes flicking to Simon's scarlet, sweaty face. "He has a lot to answer for." She turned to the two policemen. "I should take him now, if I were you. Nothing else is going to happen here."

The first policeman stepped forward and snapped some handcuffs on Simon's wrists with a muttered caution and ushered him none too gently out the door and into the waiting car.

The second policeman turned to Abi and Gideon. "We'll need you to come to the station and give statements," he said. "And I'm afraid the child will have to come too."

Abi nodded. "That's fine," she said calmly. "We'll follow you. Is it Rotorua you're taking him to?"

"Yes, for now. We can charge him there and then

decide what to do with him." He nodded to them. "Glad your daughter is all right. We'll try not to keep you too long at the station." With that he turned and followed his colleague out to the car.

Gideon looked at Abi. "I really wanted to kill him," he said quietly. "I've only ever felt that angry once before."

Abi put her arm around his waist and leant her head against his shoulder. "I know," she said, reaching out a hand and stroking Natasha's head. "But you do see why I had to stop you, don't you? Imagine if you'd got arrested, just days before your tour starts."

Gideon grinned. "Good publicity," he said with a shrug.

Abi frowned at him. "Publicity, yes," she said firmly, "but not good. Now come on. We'd better follow the police car and get this over with." She ushered them all out of the small house.

****

"They're on their way back." Penny replaced the receiver in its cradle and smiled at James and Lydia.

Lydia burst into tears and slumped down on the sofa. "It was all my fault!" she wailed. "She would never have been kidnapped if I hadn't helped her."

Penny sat down beside her and took her in her arms. "Don't be silly, darling," she said, stroking her shiny hair. "Of course it's not your fault. Simon was going to get hold of her one way or another. That was why he got her parents out of the way. Neither of you had any idea any of this was happening. Okay, maybe it was a bit unwise of Natasha to go and see Billy on her own, but I'm fairly sure your help made her trip much safer anyway. Lydia, look at me..." She put a finger under her daughter's chin and tilted it up to face her. "You are *not* to blame. And anyway, Natasha's fine. They're all fine, and Simon has been arrested. He can't hurt them any more."

Lydia hiccupped and rubbed her hand across her eyes. "Sure?" she whispered. "She's really all right? He didn't hurt her?"

"Apparently he gave her soup, and then locked her in a shed." James grinned as he sat down on the other side of his daughter. "She's fine. They'll be back in about half an hour, and you can see for yourself then."

"I can stay up?" Lydia asked, her eyes beseeching.

Penny laughed. "Of course you can. It would be really cruel if we made you go to bed now. They'll all be really tired, though, and probably won't want to talk much till tomorrow."

Lydia nodded. "Okay. Can Tasha still sleep in my room, though?"

Penny looked puzzled. "Of course," she said. "Why not?"

"Well, her parents might want to keep her with them, after this," she said wisely. "You know, not let her out of their sight?"

"I'm sure she can still sleep in your room," James assured her. "I doubt she'd want to sleep on the floor in their bedroom. Yours is only next door." He looked over her head at his wife and raised his eyebrows. "I suspect a day off school might be called for tomorrow. What do you think, Pen?"

Penny nodded. "Definitely," she said. "You'll both be much too tired and emotionally exhausted to go to school. We'll start the weekend early."

Lydia managed a watery grin. "Cool," she said,

snuggling up between her parents. "That'd be nice."

****

"Can you remember back to being at Nancy's house?" Abi turned to Gideon as they got ready for bed. "It seems like about a week ago."

Gideon glanced up from where he was pulling his jeans off and grimaced wryly. "And we thought *that* was going to be the unpleasant part of the day," he commented. "Little did we know how bad it was going to get."

Abi turned and gazed out the window over the dark sea. "She *is* all right, isn't she, Gid?" she asked quietly. "This isn't going to have too much of an effect on her, is it?"

"She'll be fine." Gideon strolled over to join her. "She's a tough little cookie. She was far more affected last summer when she saw you being hurt. If it's just her, she can cope very well." He chuckled. "I can't wait to get the whole story out of her. I reckon she was causing him grief, if he felt he needed to lock her in the shed. That's my girl."

Abi gasped and looked up at him. "I just remembered what she told me in the woods—after we'd remembered that time in Bath? She said she didn't like the shed because when she was fostered, another child locked her in a shed. She said she'd never told anyone about it, and that she didn't want to talk about it yet."

Gideon's eyes darkened. "And they said she was 'difficult,' d'you remember, when we first met her? She told us we wouldn't want to foster her because she was difficult. My god, that poor little kid!" He put his arm around Abi's shoulders and pulled her close. "All things considered, she's pretty well-balanced, isn't she?"

Abi nodded slowly. "Yeah. She's still got some baggage, though. We must try and get her to talk about the shed incident. It wouldn't surprise me if she tells Lydia first, actually. They get on really well." She smiled in the darkness. "Kinda remind me of me and Judy."

Gideon chuckled. "Well, good," he said. "I reckon Tasha could do with a sensible friend. Pity they live so far apart."

"Oh, it's much easier nowadays." Abi waved her hand vaguely. "You know, Facebook and stuff. We never had that. Much easier for them to talk and keep in touch." She leant her head on his shoulder and stared out across the moonlit sea.

Gideon planted a kiss on her head. "Come to bed," he whispered, gently pulling her across the room.

She followed willingly, and together they climbed into the huge king-size bed and lay down. Abi rested her head on his chest and ran her fingers up and down his stomach. "I hope she *does* talk to us," she said. "I'd hate to think she kept things from us."

Gideon smiled in the dark. "She's thirteen, Abs. She's bound to keep things from us. But I know what you mean. Talk to us about things from years ago. She will. Bit by bit, when she's ready." He rolled over and looked down at her. "Now I need a good night's sleep. I don't know about you, but I know the best way to get one."

Abi grinned at him, and slid her arms around his neck. "Sounds like a plan," she murmured as his lips came down onto hers.

Chapter 29

Saturday 9th May, 2009

"Are we staying here until your first gig, Dad?"
Natasha looked up from the game of Cluedo she and
Lydia were playing with Lydia's younger brother and
sister, which was constantly being disrupted by little
Oliver trying to eat the pieces.

Gideon shrugged. "If Penny'll have us," he said
with a grin at his sister. "I'll probably need to be in
Auckland the day before, but other than that, yes."

"Glad to have you." Penny smiled across at him.
"It's rather fun having such a full house, actually."

Roger looked over his glasses at her. "And you
don't mind us either?" he asked, just as Caroline
appeared from the kitchen carrying a large chocolate
cake.

Penny laughed. "So long as Mum keeps the cakes
coming, you can stay as long as you like," she said,
stretching out in her chair. "Is no one wanting to go
anywhere today? The weather's quite nice. We could
go out and sightsee." She was greeted by total silence,
and glanced round at them all with a grin. "Well, I
guess that answers that. Still need another day to be
cosy at home then?"

Natasha looked up and smiled at her. "Yeah," she
said firmly. "Can't beat cosy if you've been

kidnapped."

Lydia giggled. "You make it sound like it happens all the time," she commented, peering at the Cluedo board.

"Well, when you have a famous father, it's always a worry," Natasha said with a toss of her curls. "I'm pretty lucky it's only happened the once, actually. You don't know how lucky you are, Lydia, with Uncle James just working in a bank."

Lydia frowned at her. "Nothing wrong with working in a bank," she said at once, moving Miss Scarlet into the conservatory.

"Never said there was," said Natasha patiently. "I said you were lucky he did. No one's going to want to kidnap you."

Abi burst out laughing and threw a cushion at her daughter. "Tasha! That sounds very rude," she said. "You make it sound as though you like the threat of being kidnapped."

Natasha grinned at her. "Well, it does make life more exciting," she said with a shrug.

Gideon snorted. "Well, it ain't gonna happen again," he said firmly. "You're not leaving my sight from now on."

Lydia glanced significantly at her mother, and raised her eyebrows at Gideon. "So she's not going to school then?" she asked pertly.

"Well, maybe we can make an exception for that." Abi grinned at her. "But I bet Dad'll want to deliver her each day."

"Too right." Gideon stretched his long legs out in front of him. "Take her, and pick her up."

"Dad! You spoil all my fun!" Natasha scowled at

him and moved Professor Plum into the library. "No one's going to kidnap me again. I've had my moment of glory," and she turned her full attention to the game.

Abi watched them playing, and her heart turned over. Natasha seemed to have got over her ordeal remarkably quickly, but she and Gideon were finding it much harder. The hours they'd spent knowing she was in Simon's clutches and they were unable to get to her had taken their toll on them, and they were both feeling very vulnerable, and, in Abi's case, constantly close to tears. She leant against Gideon and put her head on his shoulder.

He looked down at her. "Love you, Abs," he whispered, gently brushing his lips across the top of her head. "She's fine. We will be eventually."

She looked up at him solemnly. "Will we?" she asked. "I don't think I can ever forget the feelings I went through while we were searching. Gid, I thought we might lose her..." Her eyes strayed back to where her daughter was laughing with her cousins on the floor.

"Now you know how I felt last summer," Gideon said softly into her hair. "It's hard to shake off."

She wriggled closer to him and captured his hand in hers. "It'll all be all right now, though, won't it? Simon's getting locked up, and no one else is after us."

Gideon gave a short laugh. "For now," he said with a grin. "It's no fun being famous, remember? Yeah, hopefully Simon will be out of our hair. Still got to have the trial, though."

Abi looked up at him in horror. "You mean he may get off?" she gasped. "Surely not!"

"Doubt it," Gideon admitted. "But I'm not going to

relax until he's properly constrained." He glanced down at her. "You do realise we'll all have to give evidence at the trial, don't you? Even Tasha."

Abi sighed. "I know," she said. "There's no way round that, really. And of course he'll be done for last summer too, won't he? I guess he shouldn't really get away with that."

Gideon raised his eyebrows at her. "Too bloody right!" he said at once. "Throw the book at him, I say, and I rather expect they will."

"Yeah. I guess he'll get into a lot of trouble for both things," she said slowly. "The trial won't be for months, I suppose."

"Probably not. These things take ages. I think they're going to move him to England to stand trial. That would be easier for us."

"Can we forget it for now?" Abi said suddenly. "You've got your tour starting on Friday, and I don't want this spoiling it." She glanced down at where the game of Cluedo had just finished, and smiled at Natasha. The child smiled back, then crawled across the floor to sit at her parents' feet.

"What're you talking about?" she asked, looking up at them.

"Just stuff." Abi ruffled her hair. "Are you excited about Dad's first gig?"

Natasha nodded enthusiastically. "'Course I am," she said. "Are we all going?"

"Yes, of course, if you all want to." Gideon looked round at them. "I know you're not really very keen, Mum…"

Caroline smiled. "Of course I'll come, darling. It may not be my favourite music, but you are my favourite son, so I must support you."

"He's your only son," Lydia objected with a frown.

"So of course he's her favourite," Penny said with a grin. "Where is it you're going after this?"

"Wellington and Christchurch, and then over to Australia for Sydney, Darwin, Adelaide, and Perth, then to the USA and Canada," Gideon reeled off.

"Are you doing New York?" Natasha asked suddenly. "I've still never been to New York."

"Yeah, we're doing New York, Washington, Los Angeles, and Seattle."

"Can we come to New York too?" Natasha looked imploringly up at her father.

Gideon grinned. "The way I feel at the moment," he said, "I'm not going anywhere without you lot, so yes, you can."

Natasha clapped her hands and bounced up and down. "Wow! I get to see New York! Will we stay in a huge hotel?"

Abi laughed. "Probably," she said. "Maybe the same one your dad was staying in when he decided to leave the band in '05."

"Wow, that would be weird." Natasha paused for a moment, frowning. "Is that the only time you've played in New York?"

Gideon shook his head. "Good god, no. Our very first gig was there in '95, when I was only just nineteen." He felt Abi wriggle beside him and squeezed her hand. "Then again in '97, '99, 2001, and then 2005. The one in 2001 was on September the tenth."

Abi stared at him in surprise. "You were there for 9/11?" she gasped in shock. "You never said!"

"To be honest, I never think about it," Gideon said

with a shrug. "We left really early that morning, on one of the last flights to fly out of New York that day. It had happened by the time we landed in Los Angeles, and we were stranded there for ages. Had to travel everywhere by road after that for a while."

"So you never saw it happen?"

"No, we left before that. Spent the rest of the day watching it on the TV, though. Glad we'd left. Wouldn't have wanted to be there when it actually happened."

Abi stared at him in consternation. "I actually thought of you that day," she said. "I'd managed not to think of you for months, and then I saw it on the telly and couldn't help wondering if you were in America." She paused, looking pensive. "I actually moved into my cottage that day. I'd just got the telly plugged in when it happened. Judy and Rob were helping me move, and we all just sat glued to the telly and ignored all the unpacking." She paused and glanced up at Gideon. "And to think you were nearly caught up in it."

He shrugged. "Yeah, I knew a few people who were there at the time. None of them got hurt, luckily. It was a very strange atmosphere in the States for a long while after that." He glanced at Abi. "But this is a bit morbid. Let's change the subject, shall we?"

Natasha grinned at him. "I guess I *am* glad you're a star," she said. "I wouldn't really like it if you were an accountant. I wouldn't get to go all over the world. I can't wait for your first concert. I've never been to anything like that before."

"Me too." Abi glanced up at Gideon under her lashes. "I've been waiting for this for fourteen years."

Epilogue

Friday 15th May, 2009

Abi stood in the wings of the Vector Arena in Auckland and watched wide-eyed as NightHawk played their first number. She watched transfixed as Gideon leant in to the microphone at the end of the first song and grunted out a short message to the twelve thousand strong audience. Then he nodded to Justin and Charles, stepped slightly back from the microphone, and as the first few notes of "Storm Rising" rang out across the huge arena, he half turned to face Abi, his piercing blue eyes fixing onto hers. Abi held her breath. She was transported back to the first time she'd seen Gideon perform, the first night she met him, at her school dance in '94. He'd performed the whole song directly to her that night, as well. She bit her lip and stared back at him, her hands clasped tightly together behind her back to stop them from shaking. She suddenly felt fifteen again. All the excitement of that night came flooding back, and for the first time she experienced what it would have been like had she been able to go on tour with him back in '95. A tiny smile flickered around her lips, and her eyes filled with tears. This was how it was meant to be. How it should have been all those years ago. She blinked her eyes to rid them of the unshed tears, and smiled broadly at Gideon.

Finally things really were as they had been meant to be. She glanced down to her left. In fact they were even better—and she put her arm around Natasha's shoulders and pulled her close. The child's eyes were shining with excitement, and she was jigging up and down to the music, her eyes never leaving her father's face. Abi grinned in the darkness. Everything was going to be fine.

If you enjoyed *Cobwebs in the Dark*, you'll want to read the next book in the series:

The Girl in the Painting

by

Rachael Richey

The NightHawk Series, Book Four

Here's an excerpt:

Newbury—Friday 23rd July, 2010

Newbury—Friday 23rd July, 2010

"God, Mum! What a load of junk! Do all old people hoard like this?" Natasha raised her head from the tattered cardboard box she was rummaging in and blew ineffectually at a cobweb that had attached itself to her nose.

Abi glanced over at her. "Believe me, Tash, this isn't bad at all. My parents were very organised, and this attic is going to be pretty easy to clear."

"Yeah, maybe it's tidy," Natasha conceded, "but why did they *keep* all this stuff? Look, this is just old phone bills. So boring!" She pushed the box away in disgust and crawled over to a dark corner of the attic to investigate further.

"It was in this attic that I discovered the letters from your dad." Abi smiled whimsically and sat back on her heels. "Not everything in here is boring."

"Maybe we'll find some more old diaries, like Joan and Pauline's." Natasha's voice was muffled as she delved deeper into the corner. "That would be amazing."

Abi laughed. "Don't think so," she said. "I reckon this attic has yielded up all its treasures by now. I doubt we're in for any surprises today."

"The funeral was quite nice, wasn't it?" Natasha reversed out from the corner and sneezed violently. "I mean, as nice as a funeral can be?"

Abi nodded. "Yeah, certainly better than my mother's. He did know we loved him, didn't he, Tash?"

Natasha shrugged. "Guess so. I'd invited him to stay. What more could he want?" She crawled away into another dark corner. "He couldn't expect us to condone his past actions, but he knew we wanted to be friends."

Smiling at her daughter's very adult turn of phrase, Abi continued sorting through boxes, ruthlessly discarding anything that wasn't of value.

"Ooh, Mum!" Natasha's voice echoed from another dark corner. "I think I've found something interesting." She reversed out carefully, pulling a large object behind her.

Abi glanced over. "What is it? Is it a painting? I guess there may be a couple of mine up here that I did when I was at school. Let's see."

Natasha hauled the large canvas out into the middle of the floored loft space and brushed it down with her arm. "There are more. This one was at the front. Is it one of yours?"

Abi peered closely at the portrait of a very young Judy and laughed. "Yes, that's mine! Part of my A level course work. I'd completely forgotten about that. Hmm. I think I've improved, don't you?"

Natasha studied the painting critically. "Yeah, I guess so, although this is actually very good. You can see it's Judy. Let's see what else there is." She disappeared back into the corner to collect another painting.

After a moment Abi heard a sharp intake of breath. "What is it, Tash? What have you found?"

Natasha wriggled back out holding a canvas

pressed against her chest. Her eyes were wide. "Mum? Is this you?" she asked, her tone strangled. Slowly she turned the painting around and presented it to her mother.

Abi crawled forward and stared at the large dark, dusty canvas. She caught her breath. It showed a girl of about seventeen or eighteen, her back turned to the artist. She was looking over her shoulder and her very long auburn hair hung around her otherwise naked body. Her bright blue eyes shone out from the canvas with a bold expression, and a small smile played about her lips.

"Mum," repeated Natasha, "Is it you?"

Abi shook her head violently. "Of course it's not me!" she exclaimed indignantly. "I've never been that fat, and anyway it's quite obviously far too old a painting to be me. Just because she has auburn hair... Honestly, Tash!"

"Oh, right, so you're annoyed I thought it was you because she's too fat, not because she's naked? Really, Mother, I despair of you sometimes." Natasha shook her head. "So, if it's not you, then who is it? She looks a lot like you. You must be related." She peered closer at the painting. "D'you think it's Joan or Pauline?"

Abi shook her head. "No...apart from the fact that I think we pretty much know their story now, this is even older than that. They didn't have red hair, anyway. Let's see... Does it have a date, or a signature anywhere?" She reached forward, gently took the large canvas out of her daughter's hands, and carried it over to the single light bulb suspended from a beam in the centre of the attic. Carefully brushing off the thick layer of dust that covered the painting, Abi searched the lower half of the work for any sign of a signature. She frowned and rubbed gently at the bottom right-hand corner.

"What is it? Have you found something?" Natasha leaned over Abi's shoulder, her eyes sparkling with excitement. "Is it valuable?"

"You really have to stop thinking of things in monetary terms," Abi murmured, "but in this case you may be right." She moved the painting even nearer to the inadequate light and sucked in her breath. She glanced over her shoulder at Natasha. "Look, see here?" She pointed to a barely discernable squiggle in the bottom corner. "That's a signature. And unless I'm very much mistaken, it's the signature of Andrew Deveraux, which means, yes, it certainly is valuable."

Natasha scrambled round and peered closely at the painting. "Wow," she said. "So who's this Andrew… thingywhatsit, then? And why is one of his paintings in your parent's attic? And who's the girl?"

Gently Abi laid the painting down. "Andrew Deveraux was probably the most brilliant portrait artist around in the twentieth century. He was American, but he did his most famous work in Paris. He was part of the artistic community at Montparnasse in the years between the wars." She smiled at Natasha, "He would have known Picasso, and F. Scott Fitzgerald, and…ooh, loads of people you won't even have heard of! It would have been the most exciting time to live in Paris. We learnt all about him in Art College, and to be honest, Andrew Deveraux was my biggest influence."

"An' he must have known one of our relatives…" Natasha was staring at the painting again. "Who is it, Mum? And why is it here?"

Abi shook her head slowly and lifted the painting up to the light again. "I don't know…maybe…" She carefully turned the canvas over and studied the back. A small smile played on her lips. "Ah, there we are. Look, Tash. See that? He's dated it, Paris 1928."

"But that still doesn't tell us who it is," Natasha pushed her hair off her face in annoyance. "Don't artists usually put who it is?"

Abi shrugged. "Sometimes, but think about it, Tasha; this girl is naked. Maybe she didn't want her name on it. In those days there was a stigma attached to modelling for an artist." She paused and glanced at Natasha. "I can take a guess as to who she is, though."

Natasha's head shot round, and she grabbed her mother's arm. "Who? Are we related? Is it Pauline or Joan?"

"Don't be daft. They weren't even born until 1934. No, I think this is their mother. My grandmother, Janet. The date would be right. She was born in 1910, so she would have been about seventeen or eighteen in 1928."

"Janet?" Natasha almost squeaked in surprise. "Boring housewife Janet, who was so horrible to her daughter?"

Abi raised an eyebrow. "All we know about her is what we got from Pauline's diary. Most teenage girls think their mothers are boring"—she paused as Natasha giggled—"but this would have been painted long before she married my grandfather. I doubt the twins would have known anything about it. And she didn't mean to be horrible to Pauline. She was scared of her husband's reaction, and if you remember, she did eventually help."

"Yeah, too late, though." Natasha looked solemn

for a moment, remembering the sad tale they had discovered a couple of years before, to do with Abi's mother. Then she stared at the painting again. "So that means she must have been in Paris. Did you know she went there?"

"I hardly know anything about her," Abi admitted, wrinkling her nose. "My mother never talked about her, and she died about the time I was born, I believe, so I never met her. I've seen a few photographs, and yes, she did look a lot like me. She always looked tired, and a bit sad, actually. Pretty much all I know is her name and date of birth, and that's only because I found her birth certificate with some other stuff one day. Her maiden name was St. Clair. I've always thought that sounded rather romantic."

"Not as good as Hawk," Natasha said firmly, crawling back to the corner of the attic where she had found the painting. "There are some more canvasses back here. Maybe there's another by Andrew whatsit."

Abi watched as her daughter squeezed into the dark corner, her mind whirling. The attic seemed never to fail to produce a surprise, and to find a painting by—to her mind—the greatest artist of the twentieth century was beyond amazing. She bit her lip anxiously as Natasha reversed back out, pulling three more paintings with her. She crawled over to join her and gently took the first one in her hands.

"Not another Deveraux, then," she murmured as she studied the view of Paris, its already muted colours further stifled by the thick layer of dust that covered it. Carefully she wiped her arm across it and caught her breath. "This is amazing. Look at how the artist has captured the light. God, I wish I could paint like this!"

"I thought you preferred doing portraits." Natasha was picking cobwebs out of her hair. "This is just a picture of a city."

"It's a very good picture of a city!" Abi smiled. "I've tried my hand at this sort of thing too, but I've never been able to capture light like that. I wonder who did this?" She carried it to the hanging bulb and gently rubbed her arm across it again. A fairly large, rounded signature in the bottom corner emerged. "Oh...wow. Well, that's a surprise."

Natasha slid across to join her and peered at the painting. "St Clair," she read out slowly. "That was Janet's name! Did she paint this?"

Abi turned the painting over and studied the back. "It's looking that way. Look here... 'Paris at sunrise. Emily St Clair 1929.' "

Natasha looked crestfallen. "Oh. Not Janet then. Who's Emily?"

"I rather think that was Janet's middle name." Abi frowned as she tried to remember. "Yeah, I'm pretty sure it was. Maybe she liked it better. Are those other two pictures hers, too?"

Natasha handed the next painting to her mother and leaned in to look at it. "Oh, look, there's the Eiffel Tower. That's very good, too." She screwed up her eyes and peered at the bottom corner. "Yeah, this says St. Clair too. Quick! Look at the last one!" She snatched it up and thrust it at Abi.

"Careful, Tasha! These need to be treated gently. They shouldn't have been stored up here without being covered. We're very lucky they don't seem to be damaged. Let's see this one... Yep, this is St. Clair, too. This one is of Montmartre. They are really very, very good. I had no idea my grandmother was an artist. Must be where I get it from." She carefully laid the painting down and grinned at Natasha. "Well, we'll have plenty to tell Dad about now, won't we? We'll take these home with us. I need to find out if this is a known painting by Deveraux or not."

Natasha wriggled impatiently. "But I want to know more about Janet…or Emily or whatever she was called. I want to know what happened in Paris and why she ended up boring and living in Luton. Mum, how can we find out?"

"Only one way, I'm afraid." Abi grimaced. "We'll have to go and see Aunt Margaret. She's Janet's daughter too, remember. If anyone knows anything, it has to be her."

"Let's go now." Natasha began to collect things up, ready to leave. "I know you don't like her much, but we must go. Come on!"

Abi laughed. "Calm down. We have to finish up here first. Aunt Margaret will still be there tomorrow. I'll call her when we get back to Judy's and see if we can go over there in the morning." She paused. "But remember, she may not know anything. After all, if her mother posed naked for an artist in Paris, she may not have told her daughters about it. From what I know of my grandfather, I'm fairly sure he wouldn't have approved. Now let's get this done. Then we can go back to Judy's, see Ollie, and tell her all about it."